USA TODAY bestselling, RITA®-nominated and critically acclaimed author **Caitlin Crews** has written more than one hundred books and counting. She has a Master's and a PhD in English Literature, thinks everyone should read more category romance, and is always available to discuss her beloved alpha heroes. Just ask! She lives in the Pacific Northwest with her comic book artist husband, she is always planning her next trip, and she will never, ever, read all the books in her 'to-be-read' pile. Thank goodness.

Millie Adams has always loved books. She considers herself a mix of Anne Shirley— loquacious, but charming, and willing to break a slate over a boy's head if need be—and Charlotte Doyle—a lady at heart, but with the spirit to become a mutineer should the occasion arise. Millie lives in a small house on the edge of the woods, which she finds allows her to escape in the way she loves best: in the pages of a book. She loves intense alpha heroes and the women who dare to go toe-to-toe with them. Or break a slate over their heads…

MISTLETOE SEDUCTIONS

CAITLIN CREWS

MILLIE ADAMS

MILLS & BOON

First published in Great Britain 2024
by Mills & Boon, an imprint of HarperCollins*Publishers* Ltd,
1 London Bridge Street, London, SE1 9GF

www.harpercollins.co.uk

HarperCollins*Publishers*, Macken House, 39/40 Mayor Street Upper, Dublin 1, D01 C9W8, Ireland

ISBN: 978-0-263-32028-2

10/24

This book contains FSC™ certified paper and other controlled sources to ensure responsible forest management.

For more information visit www.harpercollins.co.uk/green.

Printed and Bound in the UK using 100% Renewable Electricity at CPI Group (UK) Ltd, Croydon, CR0 4YY

GREEK'S CHRISTMAS HEIR

CAITLIN CREWS

MILLS & BOON

CHAPTER ONE

ANAX IGNATIOS HAD empires to run, rivals to decimate with his innate superiority, and whole worlds to claim.

His father had given him the great gift of being a useless brute who was terrible at all things paternal, so Anax had been faced with two choices in this life. He could have followed in the footsteps of the rest of the men in his family, all of them drunk, disorderly, and too free with their fists. Or he could do what he'd done instead— and rise.

Anax had risen so high, in fact, that he often thought that he *was* the stratosphere, as a fawning journalist had claimed once in an article.

He had made his first million by teaching himself how to trade his own securities and doing so brilliantly, taking no small amount of pleasure in beating the much-lauded financial wizards of New York, London, and Tokyo at their own games. These days he concentrated more on finding vile, bullying corporations, buying them out, and transforming them entirely.

Your little gift to the world, his sharp-mouthed sister, Vasiliki, had sniffed once. *Not fewer corporations, just nicer ones. You can clearly hear the people sing.*

Another gift to the world, but mostly to you, is that I allow you to work in these awful corporations of mine, he had pointed out. *You are welcome, sister. Your gratitude is overwhelming.*

There were some men in his position who would not tolerate a sister like his, with her innate disrespect that billowed like a flowing cloak behind her and swirled all around her every time she laid eyes on the brother who had literally saved her. From the rough neighborhood in Athens where they'd had to fight every day to stay alive. From the life she would have had there, like so many girls they'd known growing up, all toil and pain and darkness.

A life like the one they'd watched their own mother live.

Anax had not had the chance to rid the world of his overbearing monster of a father, though he had dreamed of little else when he was still too small to do anything about it. The old man had seen to his own end. Paraskevas Ignatios had finally gotten too drunk and too belligerent one night, at the wrong time and in the wrong company. He had started one of the fights he loved to throw himself into, all burly shoulders and that face of his marked with scars from innumerable brawls past.

It was out there in the nasty streets of one of Athens's most dangerous neighborhoods that the old man had gotten his comeuppance. Not from his own son, to Anax's sorrow.

Though on the rare occasions Anax concerned himself with thoughts regarding his soul, he could accept the possibility that this twist of fate had been the saving of his.

But that didn't make him happy about it.

In response to being cruelly denied the one thing the teenage version of him had desired more than anything, Anax had made himself a force for good, if not in the whole world, then at least in his own, personal world. He had set his mother up in a house far from the slums where he had watched her weep, had patched up her injuries, and had fumed over her bruises—and his own helplessness back then. He had seen to his sister's education—not a privilege he had ever enjoyed himself, not that she was appropriately grateful for her opportunities, to his mind. He had made it clear to the remaining reprobates who shared his blood that they should consider the relationship permanently severed unless and until they cleaned themselves up, which none of them had.

He had dedicated himself to changing his life for the better, but had also applied his time, energy, and ever-growing fortune to improve the lives of everyone he loved.

Anax doubted that he was a good man, but he tried to do good things. By any objective measure, surely, that should have mattered in the cosmic scheme of things.

And yet here he was.

In a cornfield. In a grand succession of cornfields, in fact—some shorn low and some weighed down heavily with snow.

In one of those American states that was almost entirely composed of vowels.

Tracking down an act of violation so extreme he wasn't sure he would ever fully comprehend it. All he could do was hope against hope that this was one more lie the treacherous Delphine had told—

But he had to see for himself.

He had to make sure.

And if it was true, well. He knew what he needed to do.

The sins of his own father lived in his bones, his blood. He had never doubted this for a moment. Anax knew *ex-*

actly how much he had wished to kill his own father with his own two hands.

He had never had the slightest intention of passing the Ignatios family legacy along. All those fists. All that pain. All the broken bodies and broken lives.

Yet here I am, he thought, while what little light there was flirted with the low horizon, as if even the sun itself found this part of the world too bitter and cold.

Anax scowled out at the fields that stretched out on either side, on into eternity. This was not the America he knew, all those grandiose coastal cities packed with people and possibility. This was a land of gigantic skies and gentle, undulating hills. There were far-off agricultural structures clustered together, reminding him somehow of medieval villages in places like Tuscany, huddled in on themselves in the cold of this December afternoon. With gleaming lights suggesting that there were yet people here, too.

Reminding him that, despite everything, it was Christmas Eve.

But all he saw was the face of his ex-lover.

An ex-lover he doubted he would recall much at all, had she not made certain that she was unforgettable to him for all the wrong reasons.

The sumptuously theatrical Delphine had not accepted it when he no longer took her calls. First she had tried to access him through his various offices, and had thrown fits when denied—repeatedly—by his security personnel. Then she had changed her approach, claiming to every media outlet she could locate that Anax had treated her appallingly. She had dined out on fabricated tales of his bad behavior for quite a few months.

When he had only enjoyed her company for only a

month or so, and infrequently at that, and had never given her the slightest reason to believe that he saw her as anything but a pleasant diversion.

He was always scrupulously clear on that score. With every woman who ventured near.

Anax had seen too much of what his parents had called *passion*. He had watched it sour and curdle over the years. He had witnessed its slide into a misery almost beyond recounting, but neither his father nor mother had wished to leave because they had married in the church. Because marriage *meant something*, his mother would whisper fiercely. Because they had *taken vows*.

Though he rather thought his father had been more concerned with the more prosaic benefits of having his wife be little more than his servant, at his beck and call. Evgenia had provided the unworthy Paraskevas with food. She had kept the succession of ever seedier flats clean and something like homey. She knew better than to question him about where he went or what he did when he was out. And she'd learned fast not to fight back. Or even look at him funny.

It had not taken young Anax much to conclude that marriage was a curse, passion was a lie, and love was a good, hard, bitter laugh.

His father had never spoken of such things. It was his mother who spoke of love. Evgenia still did and had, in recent years, become more and more dedicated to the church that, to Anax's way of thinking, kept its own foot as firmly on her neck as her husband always had.

He knew that he had not given Delphine any false hope concerning his attentions.

You are not the only person alive with admirers, Anax, she had hissed at him the last time they had come face-to-face with each other. The last time she had engineered such a meeting, that was. *You might be surprised to learn that I have a great many admirers, too.*

He had not doubted it. She was perilously beautiful. Anax would not have noticed her otherwise.

But that particular night he had been trying to be his better self. Not the furious Ignatios male inside of him, who had wanted to snarl at her. Who had wanted to hurl out harsh words, because surely she deserved them after all the lies she'd told—

He hadn't. He'd only inclined his head and murmured the dismissive, *Endaxi.*

Later, he would interrogate the host of that ball and his own security team. Later he would demand to know how she could possibly have found her way into the party when he had made it clear to the entire planet that she could not appear anywhere he was. That she could be neither invited nor welcomed to any event that invited or welcomed him.

This had not been a hard choice for anyone.

Delphine was a little-known hyphenate and had never been very good at any part of the many things she claimed to do. Acting. Modeling. Influencing.

Meanwhile Anax was…himself.

He had been pleased with himself for remaining polite. It had felt like growth.

You might as well end the tabloid games, he had said after a moment, when all she'd done was stare at him as if imparting some kind of subliminal message that way. Anax could have told her that such things did not work on him. Despite a great many attempts. *I revel in a bad reputation. It matters to no one and, if I am honest, makes me sound much more interesting than I am.*

Delphine had bared her teeth at him. *It can always get worse, Anax. Always.*

Anax had shrugged at that. *Unlikely. But by all means, try.*

He hadn't thought much about her since. Nearly eighteen months had passed. There had been no more tabloid stories. Delphine had not made any surprise appearances. If he'd remembered her at all, it was only to assume that some other shiny thing had caught her attention and diverted it from him.

But then, two weeks ago, his head of security had come to him in his gleaming offices in Athens. It was a chilly December, cold for Greece yet bright. Anax had been enjoying a few rounds of intense negotiations that week, something he liked to keep his hand in despite the phalanx of attorneys he had at the ready.

A man had to make his own fun.

You have received a worrying letter, Stavros had told him grimly.

My understanding is that I receive a great number of worrying letters, Anax had replied mildly.

He'd closed his laptop and sat back in his chair. He had not been thinking about letters. He'd been thinking of the fiery actress who had indicated she would like to see more of him, which was a pity, as it meant he needed to extricate himself. He was wondering how worried he should be about Evgenia these days, as his mother's devotion to her church schedule was taking up the bulk of her time when, surely, she should be resting her way through her later years. He was deliberately not responding to his sister's latest spate of accusatory texts that would get anyone else fired.

Negotiations were a charming distraction from these things.

But his head of security continued to stand there before Anax's admittedly extravagant desk, a slab of marble that could rival the Acropolis.

We took pains to authenticate this letter before bringing it to your attention, sir, he had said. *It would have given me great pleasure to be able to dismiss it.*

And then, with great deliberation, Stavros had laid it all out.

Step by violating step.

Anax found his hands in fists, there in the back of the hardy SUV that was whisking him from the airfield they'd landed in to…wherever they were headed. A tiny village, by all accounts. His assistants had showed him endless maps, but he hadn't taken it in.

He still couldn't take it in.

The past two weeks had been a blur, but one part was monstrously, unequivocally clear.

Delphine had disappeared from Anax's view, but not from his life. She had not moved on at all. What she had done instead was enact her vile plot.

What he could not understand was how that shallow woman, who he barely knew and who had certainly never known anything substantive about him aside from his body and net worth, had managed to come up with the one weapon that would actually hurt him.

Maybe he would never understand.

Beside him, his personal assistant—her actual title was *executive assistant*, but Vasiliki preferred to be called his *chief of staff*—shifted in her seat. She tapped his arm and widened her eyes in the direction of his fists.

She didn't have to tell him to unclench his fists. They

had grown up in the same house. They had been subject to the same rages, the same tantrums, the same bursts of shouting and sudden attacks.

Anax threatened to fire her at least three times a week, but he never would. His sister was invaluable. She was an excellent executive assistant. She could take on that role anywhere and would likely take over the company. But here, with him, she also acted as his barometer.

The Paraskevas test, they called it.

And he was failing it.

He let his fingers uncurl.

"We are nearly there," she said, looking out the window, her expression unreadable.

He felt a rage in him he had always sworn would never grow there within him. *Never.* "Good."

But there was nothing good about this. It was a tragedy in real time and once again, he could not stop it. He could not end it. He could only deal with the fallout.

Delphine had gone to America. Anax's men had pieced together her movements after she'd landed in New York and as best they could understand, she had infiltrated the bar at a medical conference outside Manhattan. That she had fully intended to seduce one of the doctors was clear, but in case there had been any doubt, Anax's team had found the old footage the hotel kept for its own security purposes.

The doctor in question was a highly regarded fertility specialist in a clinic in another one of those places that sounded fake to Anax's ears. He was also married. That had likely been another requirement for Delphine, who had showed up at the man's place of business after the very steamy week she'd spent with him.

They had records of that, too.

Her threats to the man could only be imagined.

The rest they'd had to figure out backwards, based on the contents of the letter she'd sent.

I warned you this would get worse, Delphine had written. *Congratulations, Daddy. Too bad the child of the mighty Anax Ignatios will be little more than a grubby little peasant farmer in the middle of nowhere. I can't wait until the tabloids find out.*

When his security team caught up with her earlier this week, Delphine had been living it up in St. Barts. She had been only too happy to spitefully tell them exactly what she'd done—though she'd coyly pretended it was a book she'd read, so as not to overtly implicate herself. A story about a terrible man and a woman who had taught him a lesson by helping herself to the contents of a condom they'd used, preserving it, and then having her married fertility doctor impregnate a nobody with it.

I asked her why she would do such a detestable thing, Stavros had told Anax. *And she said, I am afraid, that she did it because she could. Because that was what you have always done.*

The injustice of that had burned in him. It still did.

When pressed, Stavros had also admitted that Delphine had laughed uproariously and had then toasted Anax in absentia. *Shoe's on the other foot now, isn't it?*

Though she had used more profanity.

It would be difficult to prove what she'd done, his lawyers had told him. It was easier to make sure her married lover never worked again. Anax had started there.

And now there was this.

He was going to meet the woman who was pregnant with child.

A woman he had never met, carrying the child he had never wanted.

He felt *entirely too much* about both of those things. So much that he had worried on the flight here that he might very well decimate the Paraskevas test altogether with the great, driving force of his fury.

Anax would break the whole of America in half if he could.

But that makes you no better than him, he reminded himself curtly.

And he was willing to be many things in this life, but never his father. He had planned to make sure he was never any kind of father at all, but Delphine had destroyed that.

Anax had seen the paperwork with his own eyes. He had read it and reread it. But the DNA matched his.

"Tell me again what I can expect," he said now, making himself lean back in his seat. He could not relax. That was an impossibility. But he could pretend.

And pretending almost felt like action.

That his sister did not snap at him that she had told him these details a hundred times already—and he knew she had—was a clear indication that she was having trouble getting her head around this, too.

"The mother's name is Constance Jones," Vasiliki said, her Greek accent making that very American-sounding name seem almost exotic. "She has always lived in this same village. Her family has been in the area for generations. They were farmers, though her grandfather sold off all the farmland before she was born and she was raised in the town, such as it is. This is all in the paperwork she filled out for the clinic."

The paperwork that Delphine had pored over while

blackmailing her lover, looking for what she thought Anax would consider the mother most below him. A woman who bore no resemblance whatever to the great beauties that he had been seen with all his life. A woman of no status and precious little means.

She likely hoped his child would be raised in squalor.

"Constance Jones is thirty years old," Vasiliki was saying. "She has worked in the parish church since she graduated from high school. Her parents died when she was sixteen, and she lived with her grandparents. Her grandfather died when she was twenty-five, her grandmother died a little over a year ago. She is single. Never been married. Our people dug deep and there is nothing to suggest she has ever had any sort of relationship with a man."

"Marvelous," Anax muttered, and he could not tell if he was being sardonic or not.

"And apparently," Vasiliki continued, "her pregnancy is a bit of a scandal."

Anax tried to imagine what that would look like in a place like this, as the car made its way into the town that nestled on either side of what was likely a creek of some kind in warmer weather. Not that it was much of a town, to his mind. A petrol station nearer the motorway. A few buildings scattered here and there. A water tower was the only thing that created some drama against the horizon.

What was a scandal when there were no tabloids to amplify it all and create narratives from thin air?

Here, too, there were Christmas lights everywhere. He kept forgetting what day it was.

Vasiliki was looking at her mobile. "The other car drove to the woman's house, but it's empty. They think that everyone is at church."

"Wonderful," Anax said bitterly. "As our sainted mother always says, I am likely to bring the place down in flames around me should I dare to enter. Let's find out."

His sister only raised a brow at him. But it didn't matter, because there was only one church in this tiny town, set next to a tidy graveyard that looked old and faintly spooky beneath the bare-limbed trees. They were there in no time.

And this was no time to become whimsical.

Anax got out of the SUV and braced himself against the profound punch of the cold, made worse by the wind. From inside the church, he could hear quite a lot of animated singing. He looked over at his sister as she came to stand beside him, her cheeks already red from the cold, as neither one of them was used to weather like this.

Vasiliki nodded, and together they walked up to the church's double doors, then let themselves inside.

The place was bright and blazingly hot, an instant furnace. The temperature difference was so extreme it took Anax a moment to make sense of what he was seeing.

The little church was packed full. There were a surprising amount of people stuffed into the pews. There were children running in the aisles. There was also, unless he was mistaken or having a quiet stroke, *livestock* near the altar.

"Oh, no!" cried a boy from the front.

Anax squinted at him. He looked no more than ten, though he was swaddled in a voluminous beard and appeared to be wearing a dress.

"There's no *room* in the *inn*!"

The boy turned with great, grand gestures, and Anax's gaze followed him, like a reflex.

Then he froze.

Because he understood then that he was witnessing some kind of living, breathing nativity scene.

The boy was clearly meant to be Joseph. And the Mary in question that Anax could now behold with his own eyes was not only old enough to be the boy's mother, she was *actually* pregnant.

Hugely, heavily, distractingly pregnant.

So pregnant it was almost hard to notice that she was also far lovelier, with a *glow* about her, than he had ever imagined the Virgin Mother to be.

The kind of pregnant a woman would be if she had gotten pregnant on the precise date and time that the clinic's paperwork had said the woman carrying his child had. Or if she had been subjected to the sort of divine intervention the character she was playing had been, but he rather doubted that.

Anax imagined that it was unlikely that there were two such enormously pregnant women wandering around this tiny speck of a town that wasn't on most of the maps he'd looked at.

That meant, first, that it was real. It was happening. Delphine had enacted this revenge in the form of a brand-new human that was soon to be born. Very soon, by all appearances.

And that the woman playing Mary, Mother of God, to a church made over into a stable yard in the wilds of the American Midwest on Christmas Eve, was none other than the very Constance Jones he had come here to meet.

The woman who looked as if she was about to have his child right then and there on a bale of hay, next to a goat.

But Anax could not allow that to happen. Not even in service of a nativity scene on Christmas Eve.

Because he intended to marry her first.

CHAPTER TWO

LEFT TO HER own devices, Constance Jones would never have paraded her hugely pregnant body around at all, much less make a spectacle of herself like this—sticking out in the middle of the church's nativity play like a sore thumb. An enormously pregnant sore thumb.

People were already talking about her enough as it was.

This, obviously, was not her idea.

Until Christmas Break started a few days ago, she'd run the nursery school here at the church. She'd been doing it for years and she was everyone's favorite teacher—the children said so every year, without prompting. This year, as her belly grew bigger and the truth about her pregnancy could no longer be hidden, her kids had decided all on their own that she would make the perfect Mary for the traditional nativity play. They'd lobbied their parents. They'd put it to an adorable vote, in which Constance had squeaked out a narrow victory over Patty Cakes, the nursery school's beloved stuffed elephant. How could she say no?

She hadn't.

Maybe she should have.

But either way, she—an actual virgin worryingly close to her due date, a sentence she liked to repeat to herself because it was so absurd, yet true—was playing the Virgin Mary in full sight of all the people who had been gossiping about her since her grandmother had died and left her that money in her will. The same folks who had amped up that gossip once Constance had made it clear what she planned to do with her inheritance.

She fixed a beatific smile to her face now, trying to exude holiness despite how much more closely the temperature in the church tonight suggested the opposite of holiness. All the children, dressed as shepherds, various innkeeping assistants, and a questionable heavenly host of angels, were sweating. Visibly.

She, a lady playing the Holy Mother herself, could only hope she *glowed*.

But that was difficult to do while locking eyes with the curmudgeonly Brandt Goss in the first row where the Gosses always sat, the better to quietly proclaim their local and regional importance. Brandt openly considered himself the unofficial mayor of their little town of Halburg. Constance had always thought that must be a bone of contention between him and his wife, the long-suffering and stoic Marlene, who was also the actual mayor.

Brandt's official title was proprietor of the little shop in town that functioned as a bit of a grocery—though it stocked a little bit of everything like any good country store. It was a place for essentials, to tide folks over between runs out to the much bigger towns some ways away that had proper stores. It was also a kind of gathering place, especially when there was coffee. It was there that Brandt had gone out of his way to make it clear that *he* did not approve of Constance's plans or choices.

She suspected he'd figured he could shame her, but he had only made her miss her grandmother with an even more powerful ache than usual. Dorothy Jones—never Dot or Dottie, not if you valued your life—had not given one single hoot about anyone's opinion save her own for as long as she'd lived. Constance had spent her own life trying to model this approach.

Especially the last nine months.

And now it was Christmas Eve. There was an intense heaviness inside of her that was expanding, bearing down, and felt like more than the simple carrying of the baby that she'd gotten used to by now. Constance felt as certain as a first-time mother could that her child was planning to make an imminent appearance.

In other words, it was too late to worry about public opinion.

But she was, it seemed. Possibly because she was finding it difficult not to over-relate to the role she was playing tonight.

Constance kept reminding herself that *she*, thank goodness, did not have to bed down in a stable. Fred Stewart's prize goat gave her a reproachful sort of side-eye at that, as if suggesting she was *fancy* for wanting a bed, not a manger. But she didn't care. She was lucky enough to live in the little house she'd grown up in that her father had paid off long ago, and that gift went a lot further than any frankincense or myrrh. She'd lived in tiny, sleepy Halburg her whole life. Most of her family was buried in the graveyard outside this church—though not Grandma Dorothy, who had proclaimed that as she had always preferred her own company in life, she assumed she'd like it in death, too, and had been interred in the old family plot. Everyone in this church tonight knew her history—and Dorothy's preferences and proclamations—almost as well as Constance did. This congregation had watched her grow up, had gone to school with her, had entrusted their kids to her care.

That was a gift, too, though it didn't quite feel like one just at present.

The nativity play kept going. Little Tommy Vanderburg was finding a head of steam as he took a little poetic license with the innkeeper, who was his older brother Amos and therefore happy enough to give it right back.

Constance stopped looking at Brandt Goss, because it didn't matter what he thought.

She knew her grandmother better than he did because she'd known what her grandmother thought *about* him, and it was hardly as complimentary as he seemed to believe. Dorothy Jones had not been one to mince words. Dorothy had known Brandt his whole life and had thought he was a fool, and she had possessed precious little patience where fools were concerned.

It wasn't Constance's fault that Brandt had interpreted that as evidence of a sweeter disposition than Dorothy had ever claimed for herself.

What was his fault, she thought, shifting uncomfortably on her feet and wishing she could sit down to take a bit of the pregnancy load off, was the way he'd taken it upon himself to share his thoughts on Constance's pursuit of motherhood with half the county.

It's shameful, is what it is, he'd told everyone who would listen. And had eventually told Constance to her face. *There are ways to go about having a family, Constance. And it's not going to a clinic in Ohio.*

Constance had wanted to say, *What would you suggest I do? Drive down to Des Moines? Get drunk, hit the bars, hope for the best?*

But she hadn't. And not only because people whispered that a night like that was how Brandt had come by the first of his grandchildren.

One of Constance's great regrets in life was that she had not inherited her grandmother's delightfully sharp tongue. She had only smiled at Brandt. *Not everyone is as lucky as you and Marlene,* she had replied calmly. *With all six of your kids.*

Brandt had not been appeased. Possibly because all six had left town, and the state of Iowa, as quickly as possible after graduating high school.

She had wanted to mention the possibility that his children's geographic choices were commentary on his own parenting, but had graciously refrained.

That had been her guide to this entire pregnancy, and the many appointments and preparations before it. Constance had been given almost a whole year now to come to terms with the fact that she didn't really know the people in her town at all. She would've sworn she had, having lived here her whole life.

But she had never seen what they were like to someone they thought had made a mistake. *She* had never made any mistakes before. Her parents had died in a snowstorm when she was a teenager and she had lived quietly with her grandmother ever since. The town had been treating her like a geriatric old lady for years now.

They did not like the reminder that she wasn't one. She supposed the way they saw her was part of the reason—though she hadn't fully understood it until she'd already started down the path of her pregnancy—why she'd decided that she could not possibly turn thirty without changing her life.

It wasn't that Constance didn't *like* her life. On the contrary, she had always been quite pleased with it. She didn't make much at the nursery school, but then, she didn't need much. Her grandmother had imparted a lot of wisdom over the years. Much of it having to do with how to economize, how to make do, how to get by with a few clever purchases and a little common sense.

She was certain she could live quite contentedly just as she always had.

But after Grandma Dorothy passed, Constance was all alone.

Oh, she had a house full of ghosts. Beautiful ghosts, who she loved deeply. But it didn't matter how many times she talked to the photographs on the walls, or made merry with her own memories. The facts were still the facts. She was the only one of her family left.

Having lived in Halburg since before she was born, she knew every single eligible male in the county. It was all well and good to think that she ought to pick one of them and settle down. The trouble was that she'd never felt the slightest urge to get to know any of them better than she already did.

It wasn't that she was *picky*. Or Constance really didn't think she was. She daydreamed about finding the right person and living happily ever after like anyone else. But she did think that on a basic, fundamental level, a person should only marry someone who they *felt something* for. *Anything*. Polite interest wasn't enough for a *lifetime*.

She felt sure of that, somehow.

Constance knew that Brandt and his cronies found that laughable. They'd all decided that she was putting on airs, slapping the local men in the face by rejecting them all so thoroughly and going the clinic route instead of finding herself a nice husband to do the honors.

She's always been a nice girl, she'd heard Brandt say one day.

She had been in the back of the church while he was holding court in the lobby. He'd had no idea she was there, she was sure. Or she was *nearly* sure.

But it's clear to see that when Dorothy left her that money, it went straight to her head.

It was bad enough that he'd said it. It was worse that everyone around him had agreed.

It wasn't that Constance had expected that they'd throw her a parade. But also it wasn't the nineteen fifties. She hadn't been on a date in her entire life, and not because she was slapping eligible men in the face or because she had such airs about her.

No one had ever asked.

Maybe she would have found one of them more interesting if they had.

But there was no changing what was, only what could be, and Constance wanted a family. Not her sweet ghosts, but a living, flesh and blood family to carry on with.

And so, thanks to Grandma Dorothy, she'd set out to make herself one.

When it had gone much easier than she'd expected it would, she'd taken that to mean that she had Dorothy's approval.

One of her best friends from school was a midwife. Constance knew that if she looked, she would find Alyssa's eyes in the crowd, ready to wade in and get Mother Mary out of the crowd if her time came in the middle of the service. For all the people who gossiped about her and said she was uppity and all the rest, there were also her actual friends. Who supported her. Cared for her. And were nothing but supportive when she told them that she was choosing to have her own baby, with no input from any man.

I wish I'd done the same, declared her friend Kelly, who always talked about her husband Mike as if he was another one of her toddlers. *It's the smarter way to go, in my opinion. And easier in the long run.*

Constance took a breath. She tried to focus on the children, because the nativity play was where the children of Halburg got to shine. Every child who wanted one had a part, and if it wasn't the strictest interpretation of the Bible story, well. It made everyone happy.

That was the point of Christmas, to her mind. And she hoped that one day, her own child would take part in it, too.

"Just not tonight," she murmured beneath her breath, knowing she would be drowned out by little Ally Martingale's piercing rendition of "Silent Night," in her role as the singing sheep.

She and little Tommy made their way behind the trough serving as the manger, where, happily, they could sit on one of the bales of hay that had been set there. Tommy bounced back up again, while Constance had to fight back a sigh of relief.

And once her body felt slightly less…*heavy,* she let the singing make her heart happy the way it usually did, and congratulated herself on being *this close* to the finish line.

She hadn't wavered in her goals along the way, no matter how much commentary her pregnancy had caused. She was going to have this baby. She was going to make a family. People like Brandt were so convinced that she would soon be taught the folly of her ways that she didn't bother to tell them that if she wanted, she might go ahead and have another baby one day—because she'd always wanted a big family. Growing up as an only child who became an orphan in her teens did that to a person.

There had been physical challenges, to be sure. She had watched her body change in expected ways and also wholly unexpected ways, and had tried to tell herself that it was a marvel no matter what. Sometimes that even worked. She had not found herself turning into some kind of beacon of maternal, pregnant energy, that was for sure. She'd met women who claimed they'd never been happier or felt better than when they were pregnant, but she couldn't say the same.

Still, Constance knew that she was doing the right thing. She already loved her baby more than it should be possible to love anything, much less a being she'd not yet met. She thought she was reasonably apprehensive about labor, but mostly, she was just excited to meet her daughter.

Her sweet little daughter, who she would teach all the things that her mother and her grandmother had taught her. Her daughter, who would make her a mother and who would make the two of them a family.

Thinking about her child helped with the beatific smile, and she looked at the rest of the congregation, which was bursting at the seams tonight. It was standing room only. The children's nativity play always drew a crowd, and she could see almost all of her friends and neighbors there before her. That felt like its own gift. A gift for her baby's birthday, which she was beginning to think was going to happen sooner rather than later.

"Welcome to the world, little girl," she murmured beneath her breath. "I can't wait to watch your beautiful life."

And it was then, surprisingly, that she had a pang she

hadn't really had before. The sudden thought of what it would be like if she could share this moment with someone. If she had that husband she'd come to accept she never would. How marvelous it would be to meet his gaze at a time like this, across the shouting children, the proud parents gazing on, the candles and the crowd. To share this notion that there was a pageant being thrown tonight and their soon-to-be-born child had the starring role already.

It's a good omen, she would say.

Our girl will have nothing but good omens, he would reply.

It seemed almost real. She was something like wistful…

Then it was as if she lost access to the ability to think altogether.

Because there was a man standing there at the back of the church. And it was as if everything in her body hummed out a response to the sight of him, a song that sounded a lot like, *There he is!*

But that didn't make any sense.

It seemed to her that he was staring right at her, though she didn't see how that could be true. Her brain spun around, feeling sluggish and a lot like the time her grandmother had overserved them both her favorite Kahlúa coffee. The man had to be someone's out-of-town relative, she told herself sternly. Here in town for the holiday.

Though for the life of her, she couldn't imagine who *he* could possibly be related to.

Old Sally Howard was always talking about her fancy son with his real estate license over in Galena, but Constance somehow doubted that a small-town Illinois real estate broker would command a whole church with a glance like this man. Similarly, she doubted very much that Dirk Brown's long-lost son, the infamous Jared Brown, rumored to have lit out for the big-city splendor somewhere coastal, would come back in shockingly fancy-looking clothes like this.

Constance couldn't have said what it was about what the man was wearing that indicated he was fancy, she only knew that he was. It was that sumptuously dark coat, and more, the way he wore it. Where anyone else would have looked bulky, he looked...sleek.

And that should have been difficult on a man so tall, with shoulders that broad.

His hair was as dark black as his coat. Even from the front of the church, she could see that his eyes were intense, a kind of smoky gray that made that song inside her lift into a sort of crescendo. And there was something about his face. She tried to figure it out. It was *something* about the angles, the planes, the hint of an uncontainable shadow on his jaw. He had cheekbones that should have made him look haughty, but there was that boxer's chin. It might have been belligerent on another face. But instead, this man looked...expensively, hypnotically *dangerous*.

Not something a girl saw every day in rural Iowa.

It took Constance a moment to realize that the new swirl of sensation moving around inside of her had nothing to do with the baby she carried. But with him. With that mouth of his, and the way she could tell that it was *sensual*—a word she liked to read about but had never applied to her real life—despite the way he pressed his lips together as he stared back at her.

She jerked her gaze to the woman who stood next to him, who looked taut and *waiting*, like some kind of swanky serpent. She was tall and thin, though not as tall as the man beside her, and thin in that very specific way that fashionable people were. Constance would have thought this clearly powerful woman was a perfect match for a man like that, but their family resemblance was obvious. That same jet-black hair, though hers was pulled up into something that looked both complicated and effortless on the top of her head. The same harsh features as him, making her not quite pretty, but *arresting*.

Constance might have been able to convince herself that this was someone's prodigal son or daughter, but she would certainly know if someone had *two* such members of the family. Because Halburg was the sort of place you had to *mean* to visit. People didn't happen along here. It wasn't on the way to anything. That was its charm, in Constance's opinion. It was an *intentional* kind of place. It was easier to leave than to find, so a person had to really, truly want to come here if they were going to stay here.

She had roots sunk deep in the soil of Halburg, like it or not.

And she found herself continuing to sneak looks at the two of them as they stood there in the back of the church, wondering not just what had brought them here, but why tonight? Why Christmas Eve? Particularly when it was a cold and blustery one, with snow in the forecast.

But the wise men were wrapping up their endless offerings, which in this year's version stretched to a few musical numbers and a baton routine, and a bunch of adorable toddlers who tipped this way and that like silly little drunks. And soon enough, she was able to reach down into the manger and pull out the doll that lay there, hidden from view, so that finally, the words could be spoken.

"The child is born."

The congregation burst into song. "Joy to the World" was belted out from every mouth.

And Constance was much more interested in having her own baby, all of a sudden. As soon as possible, for that matter. Because she was…uncomfortable. Just deeply uncomfortable, everywhere. As the song carried on around her, she was already planning what to do with her night. Go home, do some squats, bounce up and down on the inflatable ball she had for this purpose, and see if she could hasten the birth along.

But as everyone started milling around, she didn't rush to get to her feet. She told herself it was because she was pregnant and needed to work up to it, but the truth was, she was being nosy. It was one reason she couldn't really, truly take against any of her friends or neighbors when they gossiped about her. She knew that kind of talk was considered neighborly in a place like this. It was how people passed news along—the kind of news that mattered, because it affected everyone around them.

Her grandmother had always said that it was important to know what was happening across the planet, but not if it came at the expense of what was happening next door.

This was how Constance justified the fact that she was watching that man and the woman she was sure was the sister like a hawk, trying to see who they belonged to.

They were already making a stir, as all the rest of the congregants realized that there were strangers in the mix. She was not the only one watching the steady progress they made as they moved against the tide, down the central aisle of the church as if they were approaching the nativity scene itself.

But there was no reason for them to do that, Constance thought. By this point, she was only one sitting there. All the kids had raced off to make sure that their extended families had been paying close attention to their theatrical achievements.

So she held her breath when the pair of them came all the way up to the manger itself and stopped before her. She had the urge to stand. Or something even sillier, like curtsy—though she'd only seen curtsies on television, having never lived the sort of life that required a working knowledge of the form—and thinking something so foolish made her feel flushed and silly.

The woman looked her over with a critical eye, as if cataloging her flaws. Constance was sure there were many, not that a woman this close to giving birth could really be expected to care about such things. She would have said she hadn't, before being caught in that basilisk's glare.

But her attention was really caught by the man.

She could…*feel* him.

It was as if the simple fact of his presence before her was causing a seismic effect.

He seemed to…ripple. Everywhere. All through her body, for one thing, but she was sure that in her peripheral vision, she could see matching ripples of reaction rolling out everywhere.

Shimmering like a whole Christmas season all his own.

He studied her, too, and while his gaze was no less critical than his sister's, there was something else in it, too. Something almost…wondering. Or maybe it was *curious*.

These were not the kind of reactions Constance Jones, nursery school teacher and honorary geriatric, normally inspired in men.

In fact, most men looked at her and clearly saw their grandmothers, frumpy and old-fashioned.

Not this one.

She felt her lips part of their own accord. Then she had no idea if she wanted to say something, or if she was gasping, or if she was simply *undone* by the undeniable force of him.

That was what it was.

There was a *force* all around him, and she could feel it like a touch.

It was extraordinary.

He was extraordinary.

He was even better looking up close, and that didn't help. There was something about a gorgeous man. Not that she'd considered this in any serious way before, but they were just...*too much*, weren't they? It was all too much, all that *rampant masculinity* where most men were just *there*. It was impossible to have any meaningful thoughts about it, or him, because *the force* of it all was everywhere.

And he was absurd, and who had eyes like that, like smoke ringed with those impossibly sooty *lashes*, and—

"You are Constance Jones, are you not?" he asked, though it sounded more like a command than a question.

And that was both a relief and a new bit of trouble. A relief, because it allowed her to stop that cascade of silly thoughts that she was slightly afraid had taken over her whole face, like a broadcast. But the trouble was, his voice was an epic journey all its own.

It was so *gravelly*. He had an *accent*.

And the way he said her name made that shimmering thing stronger. Deeper.

"I am," she said, though she would have said she was her own late grandmother if that was what he'd asked. This was not the sort of man a person denied. She cleared her throat, though it didn't need clearing. "I am Constance Jones."

She wasn't prepared for the way he smiled, though that wasn't the right word. It was not a kind smile. Nor was it a happy one. But it was a curve of his mouth, nonetheless, sensual and stern. It was a flash of those intoxicating eyes, smoke and a kind of fascination that made her bones feel *odd* inside her body.

"Then I am delighted to make your acquaintance," he said then, in a way that made it perfectly clear to Constance that *delight* had nothing to do with this. On his side, anyway. "I am Anax Ignatios. The father of your child."

CHAPTER THREE

THIS WOMAN—THE putative Mother Mary and mother of his child—gazed back at him as if he was an apparition. As if she was not sure he was truly standing before her at all.

"The father...?" she echoed, but it was as if the words only penetrated as she said them. Because it was then that her eyes widened and her lips parted, and for a moment, all she could seem to do was stare.

And it had been a great, encompassing fury that had driven Anax here. A fury that had taken him from his office in Athens, where Stavros had delivered the impossible news, across the planet in search of Delphine, and to that little clinic in a different part of what Americans called their *Mid*west—presumably because there was so much *West* left on either side. He had been focused on nothing else save the same driving need to see for himself. To see if it was true.

To handle this all himself, as if that might solve the problem.

Because, of course, it usually did.

But somehow, in all of this, he hadn't really considered the woman herself.

He knew things about her. His sister had delivered those details to him—repeatedly. He could list off her stats from memory without any effort. He had been told that she was of medium height, medium build. Brown hair, brown eyes.

All that was true.

But none of that described her at all.

Maybe it was because he'd been jetting all over the world in a particular fury this time. That was nothing new to him. But very rarely were his emotions flying the plane, metaphorically speaking.

In point of fact, Anax preferred to behave as if he had never encountered an emotion in his life. Even though he knew the truth that most men seem to miss. Anger was the primary male emotion, and he had that in spades. He had never met a man who didn't.

That didn't mean he acted on his. He wasn't an adolescent any longer.

And maybe it was because they were standing in a church and he had yet to burst into flame. It seemed that despite all the sins his mother had accused him of over the years, he was apparently not too profane to darken God's door after all. He couldn't wait to tell her.

But right now, in this overwarm church teeming with loud children and curious spectators, Anax found himself feeling…caught, somehow.

It didn't make sense.

Then again, this Constance Jones didn't make any sense either. She had pushed back the hood of the cloak she wore, in the typical blue to denote the Virgin Mary. Her hair was brown, yes, but it was a thick, rich dark brown that looked as if it might curl. Given the right encouragement. It was coiled on one side of her neck and braided loosely as it fell down over her shoulder. Her eyes were also brown, but it was a fascinating shade. Deep pools of that rich color, ringed in onyx. Like some kind of smoky quartz.

There he went again. Getting whimsical when he was a man known and feared for his relentless practicality.

He had never paid specific attention one way or another to pregnancy, or pregnant women. Why should he have? But *this* woman was pregnant with *his* child.

It was astonishing what a difference that made. He told himself that had to be the reason he kept...*noticing* her in all these ways.

Anax wanted to put his hands on her. He wanted to trace the shape of that enormous belly with his palms. He had the strangest urge to close the distance between them and press his mouth against the crest of that great mound where he knew his child rested—

But that was both insane and inappropriate.

Obviously.

She might be carrying his child, but she didn't know him. Just as he didn't know her.

The reality of the situation slammed back into him like a kick to the head. He chose to consider it a kind of clarity.

"Perhaps," suggested his sister from beside him in her typically icy way, "there might be a place we could speak privately?"

"Oh," Constance said, sounding scattered. And as shaken as he was. Or would have been, he corrected himself. If he had not known about this pregnancy already. If he had been the one ambushed tonight. He knew this because he remembered precisely how he had reacted two weeks ago. "Yes, of course. I'm sorry, I just..."

"It is a shock," Anax agreed. Vasiliki shot him a look

at that conciliatory tone, it was so unlike him, but he ignored her. "I have had longer to process it."

"I'm not sure what I should be processing," she said, and then laughed.

And it was so unexpected, that laugh.

That was what he told himself. It was a surprise, that was all. The light, dancing from the candles that were lit and flickering in all the windows didn't change. The din in the room didn't still for a moment. There was no choir singing. The service was over.

Her laugh was unexpected, that was all.

It seemed to take a moment for Constance to remember herself. She blinked once, then again. She held a hand to her belly as she moved around from behind the manger and started for the main aisle, walking with a little bit of a waddle to her step. It should have looked cumbersome. He supposed it did.

But Anax seemed to be caught up in some strange, internal loop. All he could think about was her astounding femininity. A woman so ripe with new life was the very pinnacle of womanhood—

As if he had the slightest idea what the pinnacle of anything was. As if he had spent even twelve consecutive seconds in his whole life before this moment considering the ramifications of femininity.

He had always appreciated it, yes. But not like this.

What was happening to him?

The look that his sister was giving him suggested that she didn't know either.

"Are you quite well?" Vasiliki asked, a little sharply. In Greek, on the off chance anyone here recognized them. Or was listening in, as the speculative expressions he saw on the faces they passed suggested might be a possibility. "You are acting unlike yourself."

"I'm not acting like anything," he replied, in the tone he knew full well irritated his sister the most, dismissive and faintly condescending. "This is the situation we are in. It doesn't matter how we act."

His sister did not rise to his bait. She only lifted a brow. "You are handling this so beautifully, Anax, but perhaps you could do something about your jaw. You're clenching it so hard that I rather fear you will break every last one of your teeth in the next five minutes if you do not stop."

"I have no idea what you're talking about."

But he released his jaw. And found himself feeling something like relieved that Vasiliki wasn't commenting on anything else he might have been doing. Like staring a little too hard at this woman who he should never have met. Because she should never have had any access to him. He was the stratosphere and this was a small farm town that people more than a few miles away had never heard of. That was the truth of things.

It wasn't her fault. But it wasn't his, either.

Inside, he felt something click into place at that, like a heavy latch on an iron gate.

At the back of the church, Constance marched through the lobby as if she was unaware it was crowded. Following behind her, Anax found himself faintly amazed that the people simply...parted before her. She didn't have to ask. It almost suggested that he was missing something about this woman. It whispered of the sort of power a wise man always paid attention to at the negotiation table—

But she did not lead them into any kind of boardroom. The room she walked them into was small. Airless. She flicked on the lights, and it immediately became clear that it was some kind of a classroom. A classroom for very small children, if the desks that looked like toys and barely cleared his shins were any indication.

Constance smiled apologetically as she looked around, as if seeing the classroom for the very first time. "We hold nursery school classes in here. I would invite you to sit, but the desks are rather…"

She didn't finish.

Anax could not account for the fact he felt he *needed* to. "Rather."

He got another sharp look from Vasiliki for that. "We understand this is a delicate matter," his sister said briskly, jumping straight in as was her wont. "It is delicate on all sides, as must be obvious."

Then she waited. But Constance did not do the expected thing. She did not stare harder at Anax until the light dawned, and then start issuing effusive apologies. That wasn't to say she wasn't staring at him, but if she recognized him, she was hiding it masterfully.

He allowed as how it was difficult for him to imagine that a nursery school teacher *here* could have even encountered Delphine and her machinations.

"My brother only learned of you two weeks ago," Vasiliki said, in a tone that suggested that while she wasn't issuing accusations *yet*, she could start at any moment.

Constance shook her head, her cheeks still as flushed as they had been in the much hotter main part of the church. And her hands were at her rounded sides, as if holding her belly aloft. "But I'm trying to understand how anyone has heard of me at all. My understanding was that everything was kept private. That's the whole point of going through a clinic, isn't it?"

"The doctor you worked with has lost his medical license," Anax said abruptly. "He allowed a vindictive woman to blackmail him into letting her dispense material that was never donated to that clinic."

He watched Constance take that in. She only blinked, yet he thought he saw a different sort of trembling as she slid her hands up and folded them over the top of her big belly. In this room, the cloak fell back and he could see that she was wearing a very prosaic shirt and trousers beneath. There was nothing supernatural about her. No choirs. No light.

She was not mesmerizing at all, he told himself, and yet he could not look away.

"Are you saying that this woman…*stole* that material?"

That iron deep inside him seemed heavier. Colder. "That is exactly what she did."

"Why would she do that? Why would anyone do that?"

"That is a much longer conversation, and it is an unpleasant one." Anax ran a hand through his hair, then wondered at himself. He was considered one of the greatest poker players of all time, though he did not gamble. Not with cards. But he did not have the tells that other, lesser men did. He did not *fidget*. He dropped his hand. "The fact remains that she did this thing. And it looks as if the result of this is about to be born. Unless I am misreading how far along you are."

Surely, he thought, no woman could be *that* pregnant and have much farther to go.

"No," Constance agreed. "You're not misreading it. In fact I think—" But she shook her head. "Let me make sure I'm following all of this. I'm guessing that you didn't come here to congratulate me on this happy accident."

"I had no intention of ever having children," Anax

said, very distinctly, very solemnly. He held her gaze. He did not look away. "I have never had any interest in it. I do not feel my genetics are well suited to continuing on."

Constance blew out a breath. "Oh, well. Oh, dear. I guess we'll find out, hey?"

And in any other situation, Anax would have assumed that she was being sardonic. Provoking, at the very least. That this was some hayseed act she was putting on.

But this woman looked nothing but wide-eyed and innocent, and more than a little overawed by him. That in itself was nothing out of the ordinary, but the way she looked at him was more like he was some far-off constellation she'd never noticed in the sky before. As if she found him magnificent, but it wasn't *personal*. It was simply a fact, and not an important one.

Frankly, it was distracting. He didn't like it. Or it was more that he didn't quite know what to make of it. He was used to women making fools of themselves for a scrap of his attention. He was not used to women having the full force of his attention and behaving as if they were just waiting for him to…put it somewhere else.

It took him a long, awkward moment to understand that the bizarre sensation inside his person was him feeling…disconcerted.

Anax was not certain he had ever experienced such a thing before.

"You do not seem to have heard of my brother," Vasiliki said then. She was leaning against the door, looking entirely languid. Yet Anax had no doubt that if someone tried to enter, she would deal with them, and swiftly. "Nor do you seem to recognize him."

It shouldn't have been possible, yet Constance's eyes

widened even further as she looked at him. "Should I have?"

They had discussed the possibility that Delphine had not chosen this seemingly random woman out of the ether. That she might very well have chosen some patsy or other. Some grasping sort of girl she knew somehow. It seemed as possible as anything else, and frankly, more likely.

Later, Anax knew that he and Vasiliki would debate this moment, but he felt that same gut feeling of certainty that he often did in business. He knew Constance wasn't putting on an act.

He knew this as well as he knew himself.

She had never heard of him. She had no idea who he was. She had gone to that clinic in good faith, and this was the result.

And somehow, there was relief in that. It brought his fury down several notches immediately, and he preferred that. Indulging his fury was too close to a lack of control, and Anax was scrupulously careful about maintaining control of himself. He wasn't uptight like his sister. He simply had boundaries he maintained, always.

It was another deep relief that he could ratchet back that dark, simmering thing inside him that had driven him here. Constance hadn't done anything to deserve it. That mattered.

"Are you someone I'm supposed to recognize?" she asked, and peered at him as if he was a puzzle that needed immediate solving.

"I am a man of some renown," he told her, ignoring the sound his sister made at that. "Any child of mine will have to be protected. Do you understand?"

"Almost certainly not." And Constance smiled at him

then. It wasn't that smile she'd been beaming around the church earlier. This one was as warm as it was tired, and it made him...want things he didn't know how to name. It was another shade of *disconcerting* and he could not like it. But he also couldn't seem to look away. "It's been a long day. It's actually been a lot of long days and I'm not sleeping well. I'm guessing neither one of you slick-looking folks knows a whole lot about pregnancy, but it's...a lot. People say it's a happy time, and I suppose that's true, but you sleep less and less. Your body isn't your own. Everything is very heavy and sluggish, and then you still have labor to look forward to. So, really, the only thing I understand is that everything you're talking about isn't going to matter to me at all once the contractions hit."

There was not a single situation, in the entirety of his existence, when Anax had ever been treated to a lecture on pregnancy. Much less invited to think about the *contractions* that would soon occur in the woman standing before him.

It occurred to him then that he was not used to women that he was not related to speaking to him in so frank a manner.

He should have found it disagreeable.

Yet he...did not.

"I don't know what they told you at this clinic," he said then, sidestepping the *contractions* discussion. "I assume they signed a great many documents and you did, too, but you see, all of them are based on a false premise. I never gave my permission. And so we find ourselves in a strange situation, you and me." He held up a hand. "I'm not accusing you of anything. You did nothing wrong.

But all the same, you are about to have *my child*. I cannot pretend that that's not happening."

She rubbed her belly in a wide, circular motion. "I understand that."

"I'm sure you already have a plan in place about how you are going to care for the child," he continued, trying to sound as friendly and nonthreatening as possible, to start. "I would like my first offer, on Christmas Eve, to be my assurance that I will, of course, contribute in any way I can. I want to make certain that the child's life is as easy as possible."

"Oh." She blew out a breath, and that seemed to take a minute. She put one hand at the small of her back. "That's very nice of you. But I think I have everything I need."

For a moment, they all stared at each other. Outside the doors, there were the sounds of spontaneous Christmas carols, conversations and laughter, and the pounding feet of running children.

No one moved.

"My brother is not offering you some extra diapers and babysitter," Vasiliki said after a moment, and sharply. "He is astronomically wealthy. He can have a fleet of nannies and an expert medical team at your beck and call with a click of his fingers."

Constance frowned at Anax's fingers. "I have a midwife and friends. So."

Vasiliki made an impatient noise. "You do not seem to grasp your situation. The child you are about to give birth to will be the sole heir to all that my brother has amassed in his lifetime. This child will inherit the entirety of my brother's vast empire."

"That does sound very fancy," Constance said, and then laughed again. "Buck Lewiston calls himself the cow emperor of the county, but mostly folks laugh at that. There's not much call for empires, if you want to know the truth. This is Iowa."

"My brother has homes all over the planet," Vasiliki said matter-of-factly. "Yet real estate is only a small portion of his portfolio. Anax is a billionaire, Ms. Jones. As the lucky woman who is producing the accidental heir to Anax's fortune, this is your lucky day. But you don't seem to grasp that."

"I've always thought Christmas Eve is lucky by default."

Constance still sounded as if she was laughing. Her eyes looked suspiciously bright. Was that laughter, Anax wondered, or sheer hysteria? Was the poor woman overset by her good fortune?

But she was still talking. "You'll forgive me, but *this* Christmas Eve doesn't seem all that lucky. I was the oldest person in the nativity play by roughly twenty years. I was sharing space with a goat and a donkey and a ten-year-old boy, and I'm not sure which was the stinkiest. Happily, they were all pretty cute. But I'm not sure what your presence has to do with any of this."

"As I have been at pains to make clear," Vasiliki began.

Constance shook her head, just slightly, but it was definitive. Another glimpse of that other, more powerful version of her Anax thought he'd glimpsed before.

And shockingly, it actually worked. Vasiliki fell silent.

"I'm not sure what you want me to say," Constance said in a quiet, firm sort of way. "It never occurred to me that I'd ever have occasion to deal with the father of this child. I'm not sure I *want* to deal, if that's all the same to you."

It was not all the same to Anax, as his presence here should have made more than obvious. But when Vasiliki looked as if she might be about to launch into attack mode, he called her off with an almost imperceptible shake of his head.

"It is a lot to take on," he said, almost soothingly, to the woman before him. Who was still rubbing her belly, and was now shifting very slightly, side to side. "I apologize. But there is one pressing thing."

"Somehow," Constance said, she sounded almost dry, though she was smiling all the same, "I'm guessing that your pressing thing and my pressing thing are not the same."

"I don't want my child coming into the world illegitimate."

Anax had intended to deliver this part of what he had to say differently. He'd expected her to be different, if he was honest. But instead she was *Constance*, and he didn't have it in him to follow the expected scripts.

He moved closer to her instead, and watched as her lips parted once more. Following an urge he would not have indulged under any other circumstance, he reached out and put his hand on her belly.

"Forgive me," he said quietly. "But I'm still having trouble believing this is real."

He watched something in her soften at that. Her smile changed, and there was a deeper sort of sheen in her gaze. She let out a sound like a sigh, then covered his hand with hers, guiding it to a different part of her belly.

It was like sorcery, he thought.

It was magic.

She talked softly, telling him which parts of the child he was touching. "She's just about ready to meet us," she said.

And it all shuddered through him. It was a complexity he had never imagined. He was touching a woman's belly, and within that belly was a child.

His child, no matter how this had come about.

She, Constance had said.

His daughter. Just there, separated from him and the world, by this fragile wall of flesh. By this surprisingly tough woman, who had not seemed to fight him at all—but had not backed down.

"Constance," he said then, urgent and low, but necessary. "I understand that this is strange. I understand that you don't know me. I understand there's no time for any of that. You have no reason to trust me at all and I am not sure that I would trust you, given the same circumstances. But it's true that I am a very wealthy man. And I cannot bear the thought that you and this child will not be under my protection in every possible way."

Something was different between them, then. Something he did not think he could put into words. It was the way their hands were still pressed together. It was the truth of this thing between them, that should not have made sense.

It made no sense at all, but it was beautiful—and theirs all the same.

She carried their daughter. A little girl, who he would meet. And soon.

"I'm sure there are implications that I need to think through," she said, her low whisper matching his. "But if what you're saying is true, I can't blame you for wanting to come here and do this. I would feel the same way. Anyone would. I'm sure we can work something out."

He felt something else wind its way through him, iron and dark, but shoved it down. There would be time for that. There was always time.

"I appreciate your generosity more than you know," he told her, gazing down into those marvelous eyes of hers. "But I'm going to ask you for something more. It will be a legal umbrella, that is all. So that you are safe. So that the child is safe."

She stared back at him, and Anax was aware of so many different things at once. It was the profundity of this moment, he was sure. His hands pressed against his own child, nearly ready to come out into the world when he hadn't known this possibility existed a scant fourteen days ago.

The fury was gone. Or at a low simmer.

Here, now, there was certainty instead.

"Constance," he said quietly, "I want you to marry me. Let me take care of you and this child in every way I can."

"My grandmother always told me that while she, for one, would not go around looking gift horses in the mouth, or any horse for that matter, it was a fool indeed who argued their way out of a good thing." Constance's voice sounded rougher than before. Beneath his hand, he felt a tremor. "I can't think of a good enough reason not to marry you, if it's just the legal thing."

"Of course it is," he said smoothly. "What else could it be? We're strangers."

"It is only for your protection," Vasiliki chimed in.

And he was glad that he and his sister were not looking at each other while they said these things. While they did what they always did—what was necessary.

No matter how it felt to him in this moment, it was necessary above all else.

He needed to remember that.

"If the Baby Jesus could handle three wise men and who knows how many shepherds, I suppose I can do the same," Constance said after a moment, and she let out a long sigh. "But you're going to need to hurry. Especially if you're concerned with legitimacy." This time, when she laughed, it was tinged with something like hysteria. "Because I'm pretty sure my water just broke."

CHAPTER FOUR

CONSTANCE MARRIED THE strange man who showed up at the back of the nativity play that very Christmas Eve, because it seemed like a good idea at the time.

Or that was how she remembered it, anyway.

She had no idea how even a man with his intensity and that *force* all around him managed to get a county judge to attend them in the hospital room. The hospital room Anax Ignatios had brought her to himself after her announcement in the classroom at the back of the church. It had been a whirl of the looks on the faces of the people she knew still milling about in the church lobby, then her awkward and inelegant attempt to climb into the waiting SUV.

But she couldn't care about gossip or her ungainly form. Not when the contractions started.

And so when the judge appeared by whatever mysterious means, she said what she was told to say and thought very little about it.

Because very early on Christmas morning, her sweet little Natalia Joy entered the world, the most perfect creature that Constance had ever seen.

She would have named her daughter Dorothy, but Grandma had been very fierce on that score. There were to be no Dorothies. Not in her honor.

I will rise from the grave and haunt you myself, she had told Constance a million times throughout her life. *The* Dot and Dottie *curse ends with me.*

And if anyone could manage to haunt her family at will, Constance knew it was her grandmother.

The events of Christmas Eve into Christmas were a blur to her, except for Natalia's actual birth. She knew she'd lived through it, obviously she had, but six weeks later Constance found that she was still trying to come to terms with all of it. The nativity play. The growing sense that *things were happening* inside her even as she'd met Anax and his ferocious sister for the first time, and led them back into a classroom, of all places.

She supposed she hadn't been in her right mind. That had to be the reason she'd agreed to marry him. Now she kept waiting for someone to ask her about it, because she had her answer all planned out. That she'd been overwhelmed and alone and he was the baby's father, after all.

It was true she hadn't seen any proof of that at the time. But no one needed to know that and besides, Anax's intimidating sister had furnished her with all the documentation anyone could require before Constance had even made it through her first lactation consultation.

And anyway, no one had asked. Not even Alyssa, her friend and midwife, who had met her at the hospital. It was as if Anax, the most compelling man she'd ever seen, had made himself invisible to everyone but her.

And, she thought now, as she rocked baby Natalia in her arms, all that mattered was this.

Her gorgeous little girl, even more perfect than she'd dared imagine. A living, breathing dream come true.

She had a rosebud mouth, and the darkest, silkiest eyelashes—just like her father's, though it made Constance feel funny to think about Anax's *eyelashes*. Or really anything having to do with Anax, come to that. Instead, she spent her exhausted, exhilarated, dazed days contemplating the fact that she'd found she could not kiss her baby enough. She could not stare at her enough, cataloging her features, committing them to memory. Sometimes the sheer depth and breadth of the way she loved her daughter made her cry. Sometimes it was the lack of sleep that did it.

But then, even that was far better than she'd been expecting.

Not because all of her friends had lied to her about what it was like in those first, tumultuous and overwhelming weeks, because they hadn't. She was, as promised, sitting in a body that didn't feel like hers with a piece of her forever outside herself now, which was an enduring heartache no matter how tempered by that fierce, deep love. Constance hadn't slept well at first, because how could she sleep? There was a tiny, brand-new human who she was feeding every couple of hours and responsible for keeping alive, and it wasn't that she hadn't expected that she would have to do that. She'd tried to make sure her expectations were absolutely practical and realistic. It was just that she hadn't fully understood how it would *feel*. As if, in a way, all the weight she'd put on during her pregnancy was to prepare her for the heavy weight of that responsibility ever after.

The truth of the matter was, she really had nothing to complain about when it came to sleeping or anything else.

Because Anax had taken her to the hospital, produced a judge, and then had not left...but had somehow managed to walk the line between involving himself in what was happening, without her feeling as if he was intruding. By the time it came time to actually push for Natalia's birth, she no longer cared who crowded into the room. The only thing she'd been able to concentrate on was the searing pain of it that was matched with her effort, and then, at last, that wriggling, absolutely perfect baby girl in her arms at last.

She had looked up at some point during that first meeting with her daughter—*her daughter*—and had caught Anax's dark gray gaze on her from across the room.

Now, weeks later, Constance still shivered at that memory.

She told herself she didn't know why. Possibly it was the embarrassment she hadn't felt at the time—that she had been in such a state in the presence of a man who, she was sure, was never in any kind of state himself.

A man she didn't know.

A man who had no place whatsoever in her life, except for the fact that clinic—that had gone out of business abruptly, she'd learned a few days after the birth—had tangled them together, permanently.

A man she was fairly sure she dreamed about, on the rare occasions she slept deep enough to dream.

Though it had taken her some while after Natalia's birth to remember that she really had actually *married* him. As the days passed, that decision became more and more opaque to her. She assumed she'd been overwrought by the nativity play and her role in it, and had decided it was the least she could do for a man in his situation, his *material* apparently stolen by a vengeful woman.

She had a lot of follow-up questions about said vengeful woman, actually, and the practical considerations involved in *stealing material* of that sort, but six weeks on, she had not seen Anax since the birth. When she'd gone home from the hospital, she had been greeted at her own front door by a smiling, cheerful woman of indeterminate age who had explained that she had been sent by Mr. Ignatios to pitch in where she could.

And what she was, it turned out, was a miracle.

Every time Constance turned around, the laundry was done, the dishes were washed, and the things she'd been about to look for were there before her, clean and ready for use. Maria was up at all hours, never seemed to need to sleep, and made the first six weeks of Natalia's life as close to easy as it could get for a first-time mother with a newborn.

Though Constance chose not to say such things to her friends. That would lead too quickly to questions she didn't want to answer.

If it hadn't been for Maria's presence in her house, she might have imagined that she'd fantasized the entire encounter with Anax and his sister in the church. Maybe it was a little-known pregnancy complication—wild delusions of marriage when, really, she'd been stuck on a bale of hay in the midst of a sea of toddler meltdowns and looks from her neighbors and old high school classmates that ranged from pitying to condemning.

What single mother *wouldn't* make up the whole surprise appearance of her baby's father?

Constance laid the baby down for her midmorning nap. She considered whether or not she'd like to take a nap herself, and sat on the couch in a heap of indecision when there was a smart knock on her front door.

Peremptory. Intense.

And she knew before she went to open the front door that it was him.

She knew she hadn't made anything up.

But still, she was unprepared.

Because Anax Ignatios stood there, in all his glory, in a way that made her want to shift and fidget like one of the little kids she tried to teach how to stand still.

"Oh," Constance said, though that felt inadequate. She tried again, but all she came up with was, "Hello."

He continued to gaze at her, then inclined his head in the direction of the house behind her. The house she was unconsciously blocking him from entering, despite the February weather.

"Perhaps you haven't noticed," he said in that rough, intensely dark and stirring voice of his that she understood had been echoing around inside her all this time, especially when she slept and dreamed, "but it is extremely cold out here."

"Of course it is. I'm sorry." She still couldn't seem to move for a moment, and that dark brow of his inched up higher, drawing even more attention to those smoky gray eyes of his. She had to force herself to step back, because her body did not seem to want to pay the slightest bit of attention to the order she gave it and she did not know what to make of that.

Just like she didn't know what to do with…*herself.* She was wearing what she considered a perfectly reasonable outfit for a brand-new mother with a six-week-old baby. Sweats. A T-shirt too faded and soft to read. Her hair piled on top of her head. And now, she couldn't think of anything else but how wretched she must look—

Except, of course, the last time he'd seen her she'd been wearing the cloak of the Virgin Mary, covered in hay.

Constance reminded herself that there was absolutely no reason to assume this man even noticed what she looked like, then or now. She took solace in that.

He moved past her, very nearly nudging her as he went to take off his magnificently sleek coat and hang it next to her puffy parka on the pegs in the hall. Their coats, together like that, struck her as an almost unbearable intimacy. Though how on earth she thought there was something *intimate* between her and this man while she had baby sick on one shoulder and undefined stains everywhere else, was a delusion all its own.

"How is our daughter?" Anax asked, in that way of his that sent sensation spinning through her and around her—but was also clarifying.

The baby.

He was here about the baby, *obviously*.

There was no other reason that a man like this would be anywhere near her, or Halburg, or possibly the entirety of the Midwest. She beckoned for him to follow her and then she was entirely too aware of him, prowling there behind her. Somehow silent on the old wood floors even though the faintest hint of the scent of him danced all around, teasing her senses. It made her think of cloves. And something else, something decadent and haunting, like a dark liqueur.

She led him into the little sitting room where Maria had set up a bassinet and Constance was known to nap, occasionally. Or lie there the whole time with her eyes squeezed shut, ordering herself to *sleep when the baby sleeps* like everyone else did.

Then she was standing next to Anax as he looked down at his daughter—*their daughter*—and found herself flooded with a kind of emotion she wasn't sure she'd ever felt before.

Constance snuck a look at him while her poor heart pounded hard in her chest.

He gripped the edge of the bassinet and gazed down at tiny little Natalia, who slept on her back with her little fists by her head and that sprinkling of dark hair on her head. She looked so much like her father it hurt, and as strange as all this was—this delusion that wasn't a delusion at all—Constance found she couldn't hate it. Maybe as time went on she would regret the circumstances that had brought her here, who knew, but right now she felt a fierce, primal sort of joy that she could look at the daughter she'd brought into the world and look beside her to see the man who had stamped her with his own dark beauty.

"She is beautiful," he whispered, the words sounding like an oath.

"She is," Constance agreed. "And more beautiful every day."

And when there came the sound of someone approaching behind them, they both started slightly. As if they'd been caught doing something…indiscreet.

Though Constance forgot about that strange moment almost at once, and the lingering heat it left behind inside her, because cheerful, bright Maria was bustling into the room holding a tray aloft.

"I took the liberty of making a light lunch," she said, because of course she had. "I'm sure you're both hungry. And this will make it easier to concentrate on the things you have to talk about."

And before she knew it, really, Constance found herself sitting on her own sofa, eating little sandwiches and trying not to stare too much at the man who took the chair across from her. It was her grandfather's chair. Grandpa Abe had not been precious about it and it wasn't as if Constance had kept it empty in some kind of vigil for him, but still. It made her feel prickly inside to see another man sitting there.

But not the sort of prickly that led to anger, she understood in the next moment. She was still feeling that heat. As if merely being in this man's presence left her... *flushed.*

"How are you holding up?" Anax asked her, the very soul of courtesy.

She doubted he wished to hear about her *flush.* "Very well," Constance said instead, trying to match his tone. "Maria is a godsend. I couldn't manage without her. Thank you."

"It is nothing."

He did not eat, she noticed. She was not entirely convinced that Anax Ignatios suffered the pangs of humanity or mortality that everyone else did. Perhaps he was above such things. Perhaps the demands of flesh and blood were beneath him.

She had thought that her impression of him, like some dark angel at the back of the nativity play, had been more of that same fever dream of a near-birth delusion. But if anything, she discovered, she had been underplaying the situation in her memory.

His beauty was almost brutal. It was a shock to her system. She felt *uncomfortable*, and too hot, that was how intensely attractive he was. Today he was wearing boots, jeans, and a sweater. It should have been unremarkable. But it was obvious that each one of those items was breathtakingly well-made, and no doubt priced accordingly. Or, more likely, made to his precise specifications.

It was also obvious at a glance that he was not from around here. That he was not even from this country. It took her a long moment to understand that it had something to do with how he was wearing that particular sweater, with its high collar. It had something to do with how he sat. With how he held himself. The sophistication in even his smallest gesture and the hint of Europe sunk deep into the fabrics that clothed him.

Another thing that felt ridiculous even to think, but that didn't make it less true.

"I'm afraid that most of what happened on Christmas is a blur," Constance said into the silence since she was terribly afraid that he would see right through her to all these likely offensive thoughts she was having about him. "I'm not sure I thanked you."

"I am not the one who was busy delivering a human being into this world," he replied at once, and yet something about the way he said that scraped at her, just slightly. It was the perfect thing to say, of course. It was lovely, even.

Yet there was something in his tone. There was something about that careful way he regarded her as he spoke. Maybe it was the stillness in him and the way he sat there, as if he was…waiting. If he was *holding himself back*—

Constance thought then that really, she needed to figure out a way to spend more time outside of this house before she really did lose the plot entirely.

"What I don't understand," she continued, because she was determined to talk her way out of this. Whatever *this* was. "Or, I guess, what I *missed*, is how you got anyone to marry us on Christmas Eve in the first place."

"I am very persuasive."

"I suppose you'd have to be, to get a judge to do anything, much less on such short notice. It probably wasn't legal anyway, because—"

"It was legal." There was something, then, about the way his mouth nearly curved. It seemed to scrape its way down the length of her spine. "That you can depend upon. My sister, in addition to her many other charms, is something of a legal scholar. She prides herself on being the final word in such things."

Constance opened her mouth to say something like *She seemed like a lawyer*, but thought better of it. And then was glad she hadn't started speaking, because she would have swallowed the words whole.

Because Anax stood and pulled a small pouch out of his pocket. She stared, unable to imagine what he could be holding there—and so she was completely unprepared when he tipped the pouch over and two rings landed in his palm with a soft, metallic sound.

"I took the liberty of finding some jewelry for this purpose." Anax's face was unreadable.

Constance worried that her face was anything but. "Jewelry?"

He set the rings down before her decisively, one clink and then the next. She stared down at them, sitting there on the coffee table that had sat in this living room for as long as she could remember. Though she was sure it had never been set with two gleaming rings of what she felt certain was platinum, one with an exquisite solitaire and the other etched in a sort of pattern she felt certain was desperately fancy. She'd never seen anything like it before.

"Rings do not seem like a little legal matter," she heard herself saying, almost desperately. "They seem... Like something else."

His gaze found hers and she watched as his lips curved again, and she found it...

Well. She wasn't sure what it was but once more, it wasn't a smile.

Yet in the next moment, she doubted herself. She didn't know this man. Maybe this *was* his smile, like the calm before a storm.

"Consider it a point of clarification, nothing more," he said after a moment, his gray eyes even smokier than before. "And a token of my esteem, if you will. You have given me a daughter, Constance. You don't need to wear the rings if you do not like them. Consider it a gesture of celebration, nothing more."

She thought about that quite a lot, after he left.

Weeks turned into months. Natalia changed so much that it seemed impossible to keep up with and yet Constance knew she was so little, so new, and had so far to go. Iowa winters were long and grueling, but she took advantage of every hint of decent weather she could. She bundled up the baby and went outside. To breathe. To move. To not stay in her house.

To walk down the length of her driveway to the main road, and sometimes into what passed for town.

Slowly, she started to feel like herself again.

Six months on, Constance was starting to not feel *quite* so panicked about things. She was grateful that Grandma Dorothy had taught her how to economize, as she'd been able to take a lovely, long maternity leave. She'd been able to spend all winter and the whole of the spring getting used to her new life.

And longer still if she'd taken Anax's offer of a hefty bank account to use as she pleased...but she'd declined.

He could create all the bank accounts he liked for Natalia, but *she* wasn't a charity case. Dorothy Jones would haunt her personally if she'd decided otherwise just because a gorgeous man was offering.

She'd be tempted to haunt herself.

"Lovely day," Brandt Goss said to her one day in June.

The weather had gone too quickly into the summer heat for Constance's peace of mind, though that might have been because she had a six-month-old strapped to her wherever she went. Today she had decided that she could pick up a few things at the Goss grocery, and get a walk in while she was doing it.

As ever, she had not been thinking about Brandt. Until it was too late.

"It's been a very pretty spring," Constance said, the way she would have replied to anyone.

But she should have known better, because Brandt shook his head, almost sorrowfully. "I'm sorry to hear this decision, Constance. Though it is only to be expected."

Natalia was singing nonsense words to herself. Constance smiled, and didn't ask Brandt to just ring up her three items already. "I'm sorry. I have no idea what you mean."

"The church." When she only stared back at him, he made a clucking sound that she found…deeply insincere. "Why, the nursery school. There was a vote, Constance. No one feels that it's appropriate to let you continue teaching nursery school. They're so impressionable at that age, you know. We wouldn't want to give them the wrong message."

"You mean, messages about loving people for who

they are, Christian charity, that sort of thing?" Constance shot back.

"You're an unwed mother." He didn't bother smiling then.

And Constance felt something almost alien take her over, it was so unlike her. She leaned in rather than smiling and walking away. As if she was Dorothy Jones's granddaughter after all. "I don't know how to tell you this, because I'm sure that it will spoil the glee you've been taking in what you think is my downfall, but I'm not an unwed mother. Natalia has a father. And I married him before she was born."

And to underscore it, she pulled on the chain she'd taken to wearing around her neck, so that the rings stayed close to her. Because they seemed so fancy, she'd thought. And she couldn't *wear* them. Just think of all the mundane things she did with her decidedly country hands. Like changing diapers. Or cooking. Or simply existing in the world, in Halburg, Iowa.

"See?" She shook the rings so that the diamond gleamed. "I'm sorry to disappoint you. Perhaps you need to return to the nursery school yourself, Brandt. We can talk about things like casting the first stone."

And that was so satisfying that it fueled her all the way home, where she immediately regretted the rashness of her actions. Because once her phone started ringing, it didn't stop. Everyone wanted to know if it was true, and why hadn't she told anyone, and was that why those big black SUVs were sometimes seen around town. Rumor had it that old Charlie Hannon had just been having those fits of his again.

Constance didn't know how to answer them. Because Anax had taken to dropping in with some regularity over the past six months, though he never did it unexpectedly again. He always gave Maria notice. He came, he saw the baby. He usually exchanged a few words with Constance, it was always strange and intense, and then he left again.

This time, she knew, she was going to have to confess to him that she'd let their secret out of the bag.

"What secret?" he asked when he arrived a few days later.

"The marriage," she said, and she wouldn't say it was *comfortable*, now, to stand in her house and feel the immensity of him and that *force* of his that filled every room. But she'd grown more accustomed to him even so.

Today he'd arrived as usual and Natalia had been awake and in one of her smiley happy moods, clapping her hands and blowing raspberries. Her dark hair was getting longer. She looked more and more like her father by the moment.

Constance had picked her up, gone over, and thrust her into her father's arms.

Natalia went to him with such delight that Constance lost the thread of the conversation entirely for a moment or so.

What was it about watching him care for their daughter? Why did it seem to wrap around her like that— so tightly she sometimes lay awake at night, unwinding those strings?

When she remembered herself again, she didn't tell him that her friends had been none-too-pleased to hear that she'd been keeping secrets. That was her business. But the rest... "It's just that Brandt Goss is everything that people imagine a small town is, and I hate it. Small-minded, moralistic, and always telling everyone else how to live. I shouldn't have said anything about you. I'm sorry."

"Why?" Anax asked. He looked over at her, and the open expression he wore for Natalia…shifted.

He was dressed in a more summery version of his usual sleek outfit. Jeans. A lighter shirt. Shoes that looked rugged and yet sophisticated at once.

But he looked at her the way he had in church last Christmas Eve.

"Why?" she echoed.

Anax returned to studying Natalia. The baby was studying him back. They both looked solemn, but his grip on her seemed firm. He settled her on his knee and she smiled at him, and then they were both smiling, and something in Constance seemed to…roll hard, and then keep on rolling.

"Why are you sorry? We are married. It is fact." His dark gaze found hers again, a quiet storm. "I have found that it is a deep waste of time, Constance, to trouble myself with apologies. You should not bother with them either."

She couldn't have said why that felt so much like a chastisement. But it did.

That kept her awake, too.

For weeks and weeks.

More months rolled by and soon enough it was fall again. Her favorite season and this year she got to enjoy it with Natalia, who seemed like such a big girl to her now. She was so alert and interested, into everything, and very much her own little personality. Constance also got to be done with summer, which had been less fun.

Because while fielding the usual confusing interactions with Anax, Constance had been on a local damage control tour.

Her friends had all expressed amazement and betrayal, repeatedly, that she hadn't told them anything about her lightning-quick wedding on Christmas Eve. Most of it joking—but not all of it. She'd had to explain that she still wasn't all that sure she hadn't hallucinated the whole thing.

Well, Kelly had said with a laugh, *those rings sure look real. Mike could never.*

The town found it harder to take. Or maybe it was that Constance had been naïve. She had truly believed that because she was *her,* people would accept what she was doing. What she'd done. She wondered if maybe they would have, if she hadn't thrown Anax into the mix. After all, she was hardly the first single mother in Halburg. And for all Brandt's big talk that day in the store, the fact was, they didn't have anyone else for the nursery school. During the months she'd taken off, it had floundered—because Constance was the only one who'd ever been so dedicated to it.

If she hadn't said anything about Anax, she could have become another one of those stories people told around here.

Always a bit of an odd bird, they'd say. *She lived with her old grandma all those years. Then she went and got herself a baby, but not the old-fashioned way. She did it on an exam table.*

But there was her mysterious husband. And her rings. And the fact that folks knew, now, that Anax kept turning up, but Constance never brought him around so people could get a look at him. It was a mystery that had kept everyone buzzing straight on through September.

What it was not, she supposed, was *grandmotherly*. Maybe that was what everyone found unforgivable.

Tonight was one of the town's harvest festivals. There were those that liked Halloween and those that hated it, but like most things in Halburg, everyone got a bit of what they wanted in the end. They called it a harvest festival, but there was trick-or-treating up and down the street, and half the town made no bones about the fact that all the decorations were Halloween-based.

Constance had dressed herself as a chicken and Natalia as a cutely cracked egg, and she felt that they were obviously the cutest joint costume around. As well as a little bit of pointed commentary. Grandma Dorothy would have cackled.

She walked with Kelly and should have been having a good time, but she couldn't seem to get past all the whispers that followed around after her.

"I hate that people are talking about me," she said, shaking her head when her friend looked at her with a query in her gaze. "I really do."

"You decided to have an interesting life," Kelly said, and laughed. "That's on you. You could have very easily coasted along the way you were. You could have kept your head down and no one would've had a bad word to say about you. But then, you wouldn't have Natalia, would you? Or a mysterious husband whose name you won't even share with your friends."

"That's in case it's really a delusion," Constance replied, grinning over her chicken feathers. "It would be so embarrassing if it turned out I made myself an imaginary friend, wouldn't it? I'd be worse than Charlie Hannon and his conspiracy theories."

As she said that, she felt a stir behind her on the main

street they'd blocked off to traffic, not that there was ever much in the way of actual congestion in Halburg. Still, everyone in the county was out in the streets tonight, enjoying the cool, clear night. Constance told herself it was that chill in the air that prickled over her, the cold creeping in. Winter on its way.

Even though the sort of string she untangled nightly after one of Anax's visits seemed to pull tight around the center of her.

Beside her, Kelly's eyes got round and she stopped muttering threats in the direction of her misbehaving, sugared-up children.

"I don't think you have to worry about your imaginary friend, Constance," she said in tones of awe.

"That's what I love about you," Constance said merrily. Or maybe hopefully. "Always so accepting."

"That's not it," Kelly replied. "He's here."

"What?" But as she asked that, she was turning.

And it was like something out of the sort of dreams she pretended she didn't have on those nights she pretended she didn't have trouble sleeping in the first place.

She turned and he was there, striding through the crowd as if he didn't see all the people who leaped out of his way.

Maybe he didn't. As far as she could tell, his gaze seemed to be trained entirely on her.

There was a lump in Constance's throat. Her mouth was dry. And every single part of her body, a body that was only starting to feel like hers again and even more so when he was near, lit up immediately.

Like she was nothing but a pile of Christmas lights, jumping too soon into the season.

"Anax," she said when he stopped before her, all that force and mastery of his beating back the night.

She could tell that something had changed. There was something about the way he was looking at her, something…but it couldn't be possessive, could it? Why would *he* look at *her* like that?

"Koritsi," he said, as if that was her name, and there was no mistaking the thread in his voice then, that dark current of victory. Triumph. It was lighting up his eyes. There was something dark in it, something compelling. "I have come to take you home."

CHAPTER FIVE

"I'M ALREADY HOME," Constance told him, though her voice was a bit faint and her eyes were wide. Always so *wide* and *wondering* in that mesmerizing shade, and Anax had waited long enough for this. Too long.

He took full advantage of her surprise. Of her *wide-eyed stare*. He nudged her aside as she did not quite gape at him, taking hold of the stroller with a curt nod to what he assumed was her friend. Though the other woman, mouth actually ajar, melted off almost immediately as if even she could sense the truth.

That this was a trap that he had set a long time ago and though he had let it run its course, it had done so. Now he was finished playing.

Though that, perhaps, was a little much to imagine was being transmitted to this parade, or whatever it was, that had brought out so many children and adults in various forms of questionable fancy dress.

Constance was the wife of one of the wealthiest men alive. Yet she appeared to be dressed as a barnyard animal.

He did not ask why. Nor what possessed her. He started walking back toward her house, pushing the stroller as he went. And he did not mind that she had to hurry—feathers aquiver—to keep up with his long strides.

"I don't understand what's happening," she said as she went, frowning up at him as if she couldn't decide whether to be annoyed or anxious.

"Yes," Anax agreed, with a dark sort of laugh. "That has been quite apparent for some time."

"Excuse me?"

But he didn't answer.

Maria, the spy he'd installed from the start because he was good at the games he played, had told him all about Constance's plans for the night and he'd decided that it would be the perfect opportunity to put an end—at last— to these trips all the way out into this hinterland. He had married her, securing his heir and locking her down in ways he doubted she could even imagine. Then he had spent ten months making certain that there was no possible legal loophole for her to wiggle out of, assuming she ever comprehended the danger she was in.

He had managed to secure both her and his daughter against any attempts to separate them.

Forever.

Though everyone agreed it would be far easier all around if Constance and the baby were not off in the abyss of America. Anax had agreed—but he had not achieved the success he had in life by failing to use the best weapons he had to hand.

Like, for example, lulling an opponent into a false sense of security to make sure that when he made his move, he could do so with surgical precision.

Maria was taking care of packing up the house. Vasiliki was overseeing the arrangements. All he had to do was get Constance onto his plane.

Anax had no doubt that he could. And once he did, once she was *handled*, he could put an end to the unacceptable *fascination* he could not seem to shake when it came to this woman.

He had it all planned out. He would install them on an island he owned in the Aegean, having bought it purely because it was the sort of unimaginable thing he'd never have believed was possible back when he was a boy. But now it was the perfect place to install a wife and a child.

If he took them to Athens, he would need to announce their existence to the world, sooner or later. And he was not certain that was something he wished to do. Not now. Not *yet*. It didn't matter if her neighbors here had been told she was married. It wasn't as if that Brandt Goss character could alter world events with a single phone call, or at all.

Anax's world was very different from what passed for life in Halburg, Iowa.

Until he decided how best to hard launch the fact of his marriage and the existence of his daughter, he needed Constance to stay out of view.

His view, specifically.

Particularly while dressed like a *chicken*, he thought as he pushed the stroller down the dark street. But there was no need to engage with that. With a patently absurd costume that cast aspersions on the Ignatios name by virtue of a member of his family parading around in it in full view of whoever cared to look—

Once she was in his grasp, he reminded himself, and settled in on an island that she could not leave without his permission, she could dress however she liked. With his compliments.

He could see his child as often as he wished, the lack of which had eaten him alive in all these months of carefully spaced-out visits so as not to alarm Constance or alert her to his ultimate goals. He could live his life as he always had, in accordance with *his* wishes and *his* schedule, not Constance's.

"Are those my things?" she asked from his heels as he reached her house. Even Constance, who he had noticed seemed perfectly capable of not noticing the obvious things before her, could recognize her own suitcases as they were loaded into one of the cars. "What on earth is going on?"

"I'll tell you," he said, with a swift look in her direction. "But we must hurry."

And Anax was no liar. He prided himself on that. Lies had always been his father's department.

But that didn't mean he was required to guide Constance away from jumping to the wrong conclusion. He saw the way she frowned at his security team. He watched her swallow, hard. If he had to guess, she was recalling the great many things his sister had said about his massive wealth and creating a narrative out of that. A whole story about why he would have to use his security team to pack them up in a hurry.

Then again, maybe she was simply that obedient. Either way, she did not put up any kind of fight. She settled Natalia into the car seat that was waiting in the SUV, crawled in after her, and didn't ask him another thing until they had boarded his plane.

Something that took her longer than it should have, as she'd had to wrestle her great chicken-feathered crest up the jetway and in through the door.

"Are we actually *flying* somewhere?" she asked with an odd note in her voice when the plane began to bump along the tarmac.

"But of course." Anax settled into his comfortable seat across from her. Maria had taken Natalia off to one of the staterooms to see if she would go down for a nap. Constance, he noticed, was sitting in a rigid sort of posture in her seat, her hands clamped down hard on her armrests. "Why else would we go to the trouble of boarding a plane?"

"I don't know. I thought it was some...rich person thing. Maybe it's bulletproof. Maybe it's a bomb shelter. How would I know?"

"I think you're describing one of those loud and overbright superhero movies. I do not wear a costume." It was possible he overemphasized the *I* in that sentence. "My plane is a plane, nothing more."

"That's a pity. I thought that's why we were getting on it. To keep us safe?"

"After a fashion." He studied her as the plane gained speed on the runway. More specifically, the way the color drained from her face. "Constance. Tell me. Have you never flown before?"

"Certainly not," she belted out in something of a high-pitched voice. "If human beings were meant to fly they would have wings themselves. That's what my grandma Dorothy always said and it always seemed like reasonable advice to me." The plane leaped from the ground into its initial ascent, and she yelped. Actually *yelped*. "Besides, where would I fly to?"

Anax almost allowed himself a smile. "Right now we are flying to Greece."

He had built himself up to this moment, he could admit that. He had decided it was a victory worth seeking. That he must win at all costs. And so he had.

But now that it happened just the way he'd planned it, it didn't change the fact that he was still fascinated by this woman. These months that he had told himself he needed simply to *get through* had made him...more *aware* of her.

He knew things about her now that only someone who had shared space with her could. The way she looked when she woke, dreamy-eyed and a little bit wild. The little songs she sang to Natalia to lull her to sleep. The way she laughed in sheer delight when the baby squealed out her excitement. The way she looked when she curled up on the sofa and slept, still glowing the way she had in that church when he'd first set eyes on her.

His fascination with her only grew.

And it seemed even more extreme just now.

She was dressed like a pale, rigid chicken. And yet that *yelp* got to him. It made him…

He didn't know what it was, that softening in his chest. That worrisome *warmth*.

"That's ridiculous," she shot back at him. He watched her whip her head around to look out the window, then whip it back so quickly that the chicken beak that poked out from her forehead didn't quite make it all the way back with her. And sat there, forlornly askew, as she frowned at him. "Why would we go to Greece? And more importantly, I don't have a passport. They're only going to send me back."

The warmth inside him intensified at this indication that even now, while scared and quite literally out of her depth, she was still concerned with the practicalities.

The fascination was bad enough, he lectured himself. Surely he did not need to *admire* her.

"I think you do not understand what it means to be a man in my position," he said, quietly enough. Because he could afford to be magnanimous in victory. No matter what strange sensations were battling it out in his chest, sending the strangest sensations deep into the center of his rib cage. "Your passport has been taken care of, obviously."

She squeezed her eyes shut and he watched her chest move rapidly, beneath what looked like a pillowcase with feathers stuck on. It occurred to him that he had seen this woman in a full-on, committed sort of costume more than he'd ever seen…anyone else in costume, ever. Even at the various masquerades and fancy-dress events he'd attended, it was always with the sort of people who expected that a gesture toward the idea of a costume would do the work for them.

That wasn't what Constance was doing at all. She wasn't dressed like a sexy devil, or any of the similar not-quite costumes that he'd seen in his time at the sort of parties he'd attended, where women tended to use the fancy dress requirement as an excuse to expose themselves as much as possible.

Constance wasn't vamping it up. She didn't look like a sex pot, which wasn't to say she wasn't sexy in her way. Mostly, however, he was forced to admit that she looked…*cute*.

As she sat across from him, pulling in breaths and letting them out, hard, Anax had no choice but to ask himself when he'd ever before considered a woman *cute*.

He hadn't. It didn't require any deep consideration.

Cute was the sort of word that applied to puppies and kittens, and possibly his own daughter when she smiled at him or simply *existed*. But not a *woman*.

Or not any other woman.

Just this one.

He was frowning back at her when she finally opened her eyes again, fixing him with that grave, smoky quartz gaze.

An upgrade from *cute*, he thought, though it seemed

that when it came to Constance, it was all tangled up into one. Into *her*.

"This is not a security situation, is it?" Her voice sounded calm. As if she'd never made that high-pitched noise. Though he noticed she did not look out the windows again. "You wanted me to think it was."

"My darling wife," he said, leaning back in his seat the way he did when the negotiations finally opened and the thrill of his imminent win moved over him like sweet, Greek sunshine, "I cannot possibly control what it is you think or do not think."

She did not so much as blink. "I don't understand."

"Natalia is just starting to walk," he said, very calmly. "You have had these ten months with her. I have had *visits*. I was happy to let this continue for a time, to encourage the bond that any mother and child must have, but that time has now passed. You are my wife and she is my child. Both of you therefore belong with me, in Greece."

To her credit, she did not break down.

Though…maybe he wanted her to. Maybe his pulse picked up the way it did because she didn't respond the way he'd expected she would. He was forced to remember that this was the woman who had gone into labor while standing quietly in a nursery school classroom in the back of a church, and had married him in between contractions. Why had he imagined anything he did could affect her when those things had not seemed to?

Her gaze was grave, and not so wide. "You said our marriage was a legality, nothing more."

"You have a choice, of course." Anax inclined his head. "I am a reasonable man. You are welcome to remain in your quiet little town forevermore, with my blessing. All you need do to achieve this is, naturally, sign over your parental rights."

At that, she cracked. But she didn't burst into tears or scream, as he'd half expected. Constance actually laughed instead, throwing back her head as if the hilarity was so great that she could not contain it.

"You must have lost your grip on reality entirely," she said after a moment, wiping at her eyes beneath the chicken beak, that seemed to point his way now in some kind of condemnation. "I assume these strong-arm tactics work in whatever it is that you do for a living, but I'm a real person. Not a billionaire. Not someone who has planes to fly around in, and whatever it was your sister was talking about that night." She laughed again. "Your *real estate portfolio*, wasn't it? I don't have a portfolio. I have one very old house that's been paid off for years. I have an ancient car that doesn't much like the winters anymore, but I keep it going just the same. I have friends and neighbors I've known all my life." She'd sounded as if she was warming to the topic but she seemed to slow a bit then, though her chin lifted. "Things might have changed a bit over the last year or so, but things are always going to change. What will never change is that I have a home, and my daughter will live there. With me."

He held her gaze. He waited until her chin sank down a notch.

"That time in your life is over," he said. Softly, but matter-of-factly. "I am sorry if this distresses you, but that is not a factor in what must happen now."

There was a different sort of color in her cheeks now, a flush to match the red chicken comb on the hooded thing she wore. "I never agreed to this."

"I have not asked for your agreement," he replied with

a shrug. "You married a very wealthy and powerful man, Constance. It was made very clear to you that you were giving birth to my heir. There was only one way this was ever going to end. Are you so naïve that you thought otherwise? I can't believe it."

"I don't think it's naïve to believe that a person's word matters," she shot back. "Apparently you don't share that belief."

"I am a man of honor," he told her darkly, not at all sure why he should bristle at the notion she thought otherwise. "But I did not pledge my word to you. My pledge was to our daughter, who will be raised as the heiress she is. She will not spend her days wasting away as a nonentity in the back of beyond."

"The back of beyond is a fantastic place to raise a child," Constance shot back, a flash in her eyes and a new lift to that chin. "I should know. That's where I was raised. That's why I went to all the trouble of going to a clinic for IVF treatments so I could have a baby there myself. You have absolutely no right—"

"But that is where you are wrong," he told her with a certain satisfaction. "I have all the rights. I have seen to it. Natalia bears my name. She already has dual citizenship. You cannot say the same. I believe you can submit an application for permanent residence in two years' time. And then attempt to become a naturalized citizen some five years later. As long as you are my wife, that is."

He didn't have to issue the threat. It sat there, between them.

She looked down at her hands for a moment. A long moment, where all he could see was that red comb trembling slightly to indicate that she was, too. And when she looked up at him again, that gaze of hers was troubled.

He might have felt a sense of shame. If he had anything to be ashamed about.

"Ten months is a long time to pretend to be someone you're not," she said, very quietly, that gaze unwavering. "To pretend to be kind. To pretend you intended to work things out with me. Why would you bother if this was always going to be the end result? Are you truly that cruel?"

There was something about her that got under his skin and he didn't like it. It was the way she looked at him, he thought, but dismissed it instantly.

Because he knew it was more than that.

It was the night she'd given birth. The way she'd worked and struggled to bring Natalia into the world and the truth was, he didn't like to think of it. It was... too much.

Too raw. Too real. Too starkly emotional.

It was all the days he'd spent with her since. The accumulation of hours here and there. The night or two he'd stayed over in that odd little house, in a bare little room close enough to the attic that should have offended his every sensibility and yet had been...*cozy.* A word he had little experience with in his life.

It was the fact that he'd seen this woman in every possible state and still couldn't shake his fascination with her. Up in the middle of the night, crooning to a fitful baby. Standing over her ancient coffee machine in the morning, bleary-eyed but still polite to him when he appeared.

He'd had entire affairs with women and seen less of them, less of their true selves, than he had of Constance.

And he liked Constance a good deal more than any of them.

But that was all in the realm of those feelings he preferred not to entertain. What good were they? What did they ever do but make bad situations worse?

"You want this to be about emotions," he told her flatly. Dismissively. "But emotions have nothing to do with it. This is about money, but not money the way you must think of it, Constance. Not a credit card or a paid-off mortgage to a small house. Vast, near incalculable wealth. The kind of wealth that cannot be protected in a village so tiny that it has neither a stop sign nor place to eat." He shook his head at that. "It is a wonder to me that anyone lives there at all."

She did not laugh the way she had before. She was also not gripping the armrests the way she had been at first. Nor were her cheeks still a match for the chicken head she wore. Anax could not tell if that was progress or not.

"It would seem to me that a town like that is the perfect place for a little girl that no one knows exists," Constance countered after a moment, still sounding calm. Very much the way she had in that schoolroom. Something about that poked at him, indicating he should pay attention, but then she kept talking and it was gone. "It's a place where no one will look for her. There being no spotlights, photographers, or whatever it is that happens when rich people go to the same places rich people always go, and then complain that they have no privacy."

He found himself tempted to smile again, somehow, and tamped that down. "I am not *rich people* in the way you mean. I made everything I have with my own two hands and my very own head." Anax found himself warming to the topic, likely because he had only had this conversation with his reflection in the mirror until now. "My child will not have to fight for things the way that I did. I will see to it, personally. She will have the finest education. She will want for nothing, ever. She will never be used as a pawn. Not by me, not by you, and not by the kind of unscrupulous people who would happily hunt her down and do their best to use her as ransom."

Constance looked alarmed at that, and he immediately regretted saying it to her. "Ransom? You think someone will kidnap her?"

"I don't," he replied, perhaps more tensely than necessary. "Because I have seen to it that she is no longer so exposed. You and she will take up residence on an island I own. I do not believe this will be much of a hardship for you, despite your protests. Perhaps you have heard that islands in the Aegean are widely praised for their beauty."

But his dry tone was lost on her. "I don't know how to swim," she replied.

That took him back a moment. "You do not fly. You do not swim. What is it you do?"

A hint of laughter and temper alike flared in her gaze, but her voice was cool. "I live a very happy life in a landlocked place where, if I feel the need to splash out on an exciting trip, I can drive all the way to Chicago in a day. No flying or swimming required."

"My daughter will know how to swim," he said, scowling at her in astonishment that anyone could imagine it otherwise. "She is a Greek."

"I understand you are a man used to things going a certain way," Constance said then, and there was a new kind of urgency in her voice. A different sort of gravity in her gaze as she leaned forward. Even the chicken on the top of her head seemed stern, then. "I know a little more about you now than I did when you turned up at the nativity play. I read all about your history. I know some of your accomplishments. I also know that all of this is something that was done *to you*. I'm sorry for that." She blew out a breath. "But I'm not the one who did it."

That hit him, hard. And it shouldn't have. He knew that already. Besides, he was not a vindictive man.

Are you not? asked a voice inside of him. *Have you not effectively kidnapped your own wife and child?*

He shoved the uncomfortable query aside. And in the next moment, he decided he was tired of this and stood. "I suggest you try to sleep," he told Constance. "As you have never flown before, you will find it easier to handle the jet lag if you sleep now. You can, of course, ask the flight attendant for whatever you wish. The plane lacks for nothing."

To his surprise she stood, too, catching herself with her hand in the back of her seat as if she thought the plane might topple her over by surprise though the flight was currently smooth. "You're punishing me for something I had nothing to do with. How is that fair?"

And Anax noticed too many things, then. She was standing so close to him. Close enough that had he been a different man, or this a different situation, he might have reached over and hooked his palm over the back of her neck to tug her close. That he should even imagine doing such a thing was...odd.

For a number of reasons, but high among them the fact that she was still dressed as a *chicken*.

He didn't know what to make of that. It confounded him.

And yet once he'd started thinking this way, it was all he could think about. Anax found himself looking at her differently as they stood there. Or perhaps it was that Natalia was not in the room.

He could not recall the last time that had happened. It had not been for a great many months.

Yet the woman standing before him in a feather-covered pillowcase and a chicken head hood, he could not help but notice, was no longer the outrageously pregnant Mother Mary in a stable in Bethlehem that he had met on Christmas Eve.

Her body shape had changed entirely since then. Had he not noticed it, despite the ways she fascinated him?

Or had he *decided* not to notice it?

She was now nicely rounded in all the best places, something he could not fail to notice even though he wished in this moment that he could. He noticed *too much*. He knew her breasts were heavy and round because she was still nursing their daughter. Perhaps he supposed her hips might always have flared like that. Perhaps she proved the point that a woman needed only to be herself, complete with a *chicken suit*, and that all the extraneous bells and whistles were unnecessary.

Anax was horrified. He had been too long without a woman, clearly. And even as he thought that, he tried to think how long it had actually been and…wasn't sure.

He considered himself a man with healthy appetites, but he was also quite consciously not the monster some other men in his position were. After the situation with Delphine, he had decided he could no longer trust his instincts where those needs were concerned, so had stepped back until he thought he could be certain of the people he involved himself with again.

But he could not bring himself to calculate the actual amount of time it had been since he'd touched a woman, no matter how something whispered inside him that it had been since before Stavros had walked into his office with the news that would change his life.

All he knew was that he could not touch *this* one.

Not even when she was staring at him with a look of such utterly *cute* confusion that he had the strangest inclination that she had no idea what was happening between them.

That she might feel the same compulsion, the same shock of heat he did—but *she* didn't know what it was.

Anax was forced to recall that in all the research his team had done on her, they had never uncovered even the hint of a man in her life. Not one hint.

Something in him roared then, deep and irrevocably male.

He was not certain he could tamp it down the way he should—

But he refused to be a man like that. He refused to give in to his urges. He knew where that led.

How often had he watched the way his father had treated his own mother?

Constance was clearly entirely unaware of the currents running there between them, obvious to any other naked eye. She stepped closer to him, heedlessly, and had to tilt her face up to keep looking at him so steadily.

That…did not help.

"I don't want to be hidden away on some island," she told him, and her voice was less steady than before, but still as grave. "How is that any better or any different from living in a small town no one's ever heard of? If you must offer your protection, why can't I stay in Iowa? Nothing happens in Halburg that everyone else doesn't know about by dark."

"I do not think that you know as much about human nature as you imagine."

Anax knew he needed to step away from her. She was too close. She had *freckles* dusted across her cheeks and he hardly knew what to make of them. Or that he found them *cute*, as expected, despite the looming specter of the *chicken suit—*

But *cute* was not the word he would use to describe what happened inside of him when he dropped his gaze to her mouth.

Anax had never spent this much time talking to a woman he did not have a clearly defined relationship with. Either she was a subordinate, his sister, his poor sainted mother, or a potential bedmate. He had always kept them all in their separate boxes, where they belonged.

But his wife didn't fit into any of those boxes.

He found he wanted to taste that mouth of hers more than he wanted to do anything else, including take his own next breath.

And he had never detested himself more than he did at that moment.

Anax moved away from her then, aware that he did it…jerkily. Almost roughly. He didn't like the way she looked at him, surprised and confused.

He didn't like any of this. He liked himself least of all.

"You and our daughter will have a lovely little life on the island," he told her, and he sounded stiff. Too close to *defensive* for his liking, when he had no reason to feel that way. "I will be able to see Natalia more often. As a father should. And if, in time, you cannot reconcile yourselves to this arrangement, I have already told you. You are free to go."

He turned to make his way toward the back of the plane and the stateroom he had made over into an office, so that he need not be in any particular geographic location to continue his business.

But he heard her, all the same.

"Over my dead body," she said, very quietly and very, very surely, "will I ever be separated from my baby. If you believe nothing else, Anax, believe that."

And he did believe it, he found—but the reaction that moved in him then, piercing deep and leaving marks, was something he did not intend to acknowledge.

So he left her there, because it was either that or abandon himself entirely. And he refused.

He would not be his father.

He refused.

CHAPTER SIX

ANAX'S ISLAND WAS like something out of a dream.

There had once been an old fishing village on one end of the bright little spit of land in the middle of the raucously blue sea. All that were left were the remains of colorful buildings, picturesque and lonely at once. The sands were blinding white and olives grew on the trees. There was an old temple in a forgotten grove, barely more than rubble and the hint of offerings long past.

On the other end of the island stood Anax's house. From a distance it looked like its own small village, with different levels and buildings scattered over a hill, with trees and views to spare. Whitewashed walls, red tiled roofs. Closer in, it was clear that all the buildings were connected by walkways and pools, patios and terraces and balconies to let the sky and sea in. The fall sun was warm and bright, pouring over everything, and flowers still grew.

It was objectively lovely, no question.

Constance hated it.

"Maria will stay with you," Anax had told her on the first day when she had been certain she would never sleep again, and had gone back into the stateroom to be with Natalia, shooing Maria away. She and her daughter had slept curled up with each other on the surprisingly comfortable bed, but that had been its own problem, because landing on the island in the glare of a new morning had seemed…impossible.

She'd pinched herself, certain she was still asleep in her bed back home.

But she'd been all too wide awake. Alert enough to look around her in a mix of wonder and anxiety, especially when the sprawling house came into view. She had visited whole towns in Iowa that were less expansive than Anax's house. This singular house in his vast portfolio, as he and his sister had been at such pains to tell her.

She had, accordingly, refused to comment on it. She had refused to acknowledge the sheer scale and glory of the place. After all, she reminded herself, she didn't want to be here. It didn't matter how pretty it was.

But when Anax told her, in his peremptory fashion, that Maria would be staying with her here, she laughed.

"You mean the spy who stayed in my house?" She did not look at the other woman as they all stood there in the shade of an outdoor space that flowed from eternity pool to sitting area to another sitting area inside actual walls. Maybe it was the Greek version of a front hall, she'd thought. How could anyone tell when everything, everywhere, was so *flowy*? "The woman who I thought was a friend? An ally, at the very least? No. Maria will not be staying. Not within my sight."

But when Anax's plane took off again, Maria stayed behind on the island all the same.

Constance told herself it was just as well to know precisely where she stood. To fully apprehend the shape of things, no matter how bracing it might have been.

"I'm sorry if you hate me," the other woman had said, though she had not looked sorry to Constance's eye. Or not sorry enough. "I love Natalia. And I think of the two of us as friends, too." She sighed. "But you must understand that Mr. Ignatios changed my life. He personally helped me out of a very bad situation and he helped my family climb out of a particular sort of hole, and I..." Maria squared her shoulders. "There's nothing I would not do for him."

And Constance could think of a lot of responses she could give to that, but she remembered her grandmother's sage advice.

Confrontations are for people who don't know the joy of a long-held grudge, Dorothy had always proclaimed.

Constance decided she, too, could choose the sharp joy of her people. "Natalia loves you," she replied coolly. "And now I know you. I only wish you'd given me that courtesy from the start."

And to her credit, Maria did flush slightly at that.

Which was as close to an apology as she was likely to get.

Then there was nothing to do but...settle into this dream she couldn't wake up from. After an admittedly self-pitying day—okay, two—Constance told herself, briskly, to get ahold of herself. It would be much like it had been these last ten months. She would focus on Natalia. Only now she would do it entirely without friends or even her nosy neighbors, trapped on an island she couldn't even swim away from if she'd wanted to.

The astonishing luxury that assaulted her at every turn might be a hurdle, she'd thought, but she'd handle it.

But the first thing that was different, immediately, was that Anax was back the next night. Constance had assumed that she wouldn't see him for weeks, the way it had always been before. She would have time to...prepare.

That was what was needed when it came to Anax, she told herself. *Adequate preparation.*

"What are you doing here?" she asked as she walked out onto the patio where her meals were served, complete with lanterns hanging from above, heaters should the balmy night grow cold, and a soft, admittedly beautiful view over the length of the island to the sea. She'd had to accept, reluctantly, that there was something to the whole *seaside* thing after all. But she had come prepared for more oceanic beauty, not the more masculine beauty of Anax. She frowned at him, because that was better than being flustered. "I thought you had important, billionaire things to do that would keep you chained to your desk. Doing them."

"Athens is not far." He lifted a brow, indicating that she must have done something with her face. "By helicopter, it is more or less an hour. I will be here whenever I wish."

They gazed at each other as the lanterns glowed and the stars above outshone them all.

"How wonderful," Constance said. It was not wonderful at all.

She skipped dinner and ate crackers in her room.

But it was a good reminder, she told herself sternly later that night, that she was not the sort of woman who wafted about from fainting couch to chaise, in a thousand pieces while her life did as it pleased around her. What she needed to do was spend less time contemplating the ocean and more time plotting her escape.

Yet that was a bit trickier than it should have been. It was one thing to imagine what *she* could do, if necessary, but she had to consider doing it with Natalia and that changed every far-fetched plan she came up with.

Constance was willing to risk herself. She was not willing to risk her baby.

Even if she could get around the Natalia factor safely... what could she do? Her first thought was that she would rouse all her friends back home in Iowa and see if they would come and rescue her. But how would she explain where she was? She could find the island on the map in her phone, but she had no idea how to tell someone to actually *get here*. They would have to rent helicopters or boats or planes.

Who could she ask to do such a thing?

Besides, her friends were a little too easily persuaded that she'd gone off with Anax...simply to go off with him.

As if that was anything like her.

You did just randomly decide to impregnate yourself last year, Kelly texted back when Constance pointed that out. You went from being entirely dependable to being a mystery, Constance. I don't know what to tell you.

Tonight she heard the helicopter come in as she walked from her part of the sprawling house to what she thought of as the dinner patio. And she absolutely did not walk any faster because of that, she assured herself.

But maybe she did, because when she arrived, he was already there. He was standing with his back to the house and his eyes toward the sea. And her breath seemed to be coming a little too quickly, all of a sudden.

"Sit," Anax said as he turned, though she hadn't thought she'd made any noise. He beckoned toward the table. "We will eat. We will be civilized."

She wanted to snap back at him and say something like, *That's what you think*. That felt unworthy of her. Because he already had all the power. She didn't have to act childishly on top of it. That would only give him more and he had enough as it was.

Constance took her seat at the table as gracefully as she could. And as she did, it occurred to her that all of this was a performance that he was putting on. An island that he owned. Private jets, helicopters. The mind-boggling luxury was the point.

He was wealthy and important. She wasn't.

But very few things put steel into her spine like being condescended to. Even obliquely.

The seat he'd indicated she should take was catty-corner to his. She sat there, ignoring what she felt inside, and tried to pay closer attention to the stagecraft of all this.

Anax was exquisitely dressed, as ever. Tonight it was the sort of bespoke suit that she had only ever seen on the pages of magazines that she, personally, would never buy herself. She only knew that word, *bespoke*, because of those magazines in the first place, because folks around Halburg put suits on very rarely. A prom, a wedding, or a funeral. And in all of those cases, they looked as little worn as they were. They were stunts. Costumes.

That was clearly not the case with the suit that Anax was wearing. She had a sudden understanding of what it truly meant to have something made *specifically* for a person. The suit fit him as well as a pair of jeans, and he wore it, jacket unbuttoned and no tie, as casually.

He exuded a kind of casual, yet cosmopolitan, elegance that she should have found off-puttingly showy. Because it was.

But she was not as put off as she should have been.

She watched the way he reacted to the dishes of food that his kitchen staff placed before him. She watched the way he scrutinized the wine that was presented to him.

How he tasted it, swirling it around his glass in what seemed like an offhanded manner until he nodded at the hovering servant, indicating that the wine was acceptable.

Then he sat back in his chair and focused on her.

And all she could see was that particular gleam in his dark eyes, which was not exactly calming.

Constance folded her hands on the table in front of her and smiled at him, hoping he really was paying close attention to her. And especially the cargo pants and slouchy sweatshirt she'd gotten from Walmart. There wasn't a single thing on her body that cost more than thirty dollars. Altogether, she doubted that it would tally up to the cost of one cuff of that coat of his.

She was delighted by the contrast. Just in case she needed reminding who she was.

"What's the purpose of all this?" she asked, and her voice was calm. At least she had that.

"Generally speaking," Anax replied in that low voice of his that seemed like a rebuke and a lure at once, "civilized human beings break their fast at the end of the day. Some consider it a convivial, communal experience. You're welcome to sit in silence, if that is what you would prefer. I understand that your will has been thwarted. That can be very upsetting."

"How would you know?" She let her smile widen when he stared back at her, his brows rising. "I was under the impression that no one dared thwart you. Ever."

"If it was up to me, *koritsi*, you would feel nothing of the kind." He didn't explain what that word was that he'd called her back in Halburg, too. She refused to ask. "It is obviously in our child's best interest to live where she is protected. Where she will want for nothing."

"And what did she want for back home?" Constance

asked. "You had a spy in my house from the start. If you had concerns about Natalia's well-being, you should have communicated them instead of all that subterfuge and drama."

"I permitted you to keep her in that place for nearly a year. That is certainly not something I was *required* to do, Constance. It was a gift."

"How thoughtful," she said, scathingly. "I don't know how I failed to notice that while being kidnapped and transported across borders without my consent."

She decided that there was no earthly reason why she should sit there and break bread with a man she would, all things considered, prefer to throw things at. So why was she doing it? She had agreed to legalities for Natalia's sake, not...*dinner.*

She stood up, regretting that she hadn't made more of a production out of it when all he did was gaze back at her mildly.

"Have a lovely evening," she told him. "I think, in future, I'll have my meals sent straight up to my jail cell."

And she felt that was satisfying, in its way. It didn't matter if Anax responded or not, what mattered is that she felt little more control than before. The only thing she *could* control was herself, so that was what she would do.

But he kept coming back.

Despite her claims, she did not take all of her meals in her room. For one thing, it was hardly a jail cell. It was luxurious in the extreme, past the point of embarrassment. She spent enough time in that room as it was. Why sign up for more?

Not that she intended to tell him that.

Besides, she liked that view.

"Does this constitute a prison break?" Anax asked one

night when she came down to find him sitting at the table as if he did that all on his own, whether she was there or not. She didn't care to examine the strange sort of feeling that gave her, deep inside.

"How could it?" she asked lightly. "When the warden is still here?"

He let out a low sort of laugh at that, she detested herself at once, because there was no pretending that laugh didn't affect her. She told herself it was another affront, but that was a lie. That was not at all the way the sound of it felt as it danced over her and through her.

But then, all of it felt odd. Sitting there, *eating*, felt like an unbearable intimacy.

Everything was inside out with this man. He had watched her give birth. She was married to him. Yet they had never so much as kissed. They had never *touched*.

They shared a daughter, but nothing else.

And yet she sat there as if they were, at the very least, friends of some sort. She told him about the successful weaning process she had just gone through with Natalia. She told him how she felt both liberated and nostalgic at this indication that their child was already growing up.

What astounded her more was that he was easy to talk to.

Shockingly so—when they were discussing *her*.

"I thought I read that you came from some pretty humble beginnings," she said when the first and second courses had been taken away. Anax was playing with the potent, dark coffee it somehow did not surprise her he favored after a meal. Constance felt overexposed, having talked too much about *weaning* to a man who was, factually, the father of the child in question.

But it had still felt a bit shocking to be *discussing her breasts*, essentially, with…some man.

And she didn't think she'd read that about his childhood. She knew she had.

"That is a very sanitized way to describe it," Anax said, after she'd started to wonder if he would reply at all. He did not look at her. It was as if he suddenly found his coffee fascinating. "I come from a long line of regrettable human beings who made their lives a misery, and made certain to pass that misery on to everyone in their orbit. This misery was always coupled with various addictions, very little money, and vanishingly small goodwill. So yes, I suppose you could call that *humble*."

That was supposed to shame her into ending the conversation, she thought. Or that line of inquiry, anyway, but it didn't. "I suppose we were poor," Constance said, almost musingly. "But no one ever called it that. And everyone around us seemed to be in the same state. So comparatively speaking, we always seemed fine." She considered. "My parents were both teachers. When I was little, we lived in my grandparents' furnished basement, which I thought was absolutely delightful. We all played games together, to see who could cut the most coupons and have the most money saved at the end of the week. When my grandfather died, he left the house to my father and the new game we played was to see how quickly we could pay the rest of the mortgage down. I never thought of these things as stuff poor people did. It was just what *we* did."

"What you are describing would have been a dream come true for me," Anax told her, in that same low voice, though he raised his gaze to hers. And she found herself somehow unable to move. Scarcely able to breathe. "My father was usually drunk. We preferred it if he was paralytic. That way we could pour him into bed and there would be significantly less violence. But we were rarely so lucky. My mother didn't make up games to play, she made do. It was a blessing when the old man died, in a gutter, as had always been his fate."

Constance studied him, not sure why that look on his face didn't warn her off the way it would any wise woman, surely. Instead, it made something inside her chest feel…softer. It was the way his eyes had gone from smoke to steel. It was the set to his jaw.

It was how hard she found it to breathe, still.

"My parents died when I was sixteen," she said quietly, because breathing seemed an indulgence. While telling him her story seemed…imperative. It occurred to her that she hadn't told anyone this story before, because where she came from everyone already knew. Somehow that made it both more difficult to breathe and more important that she speak. Her belly trembled from the force of both. "They were driving home from a weekend in Iowa City. They liked to go every now and again. Listen to some lectures, see some art, meet up with some friends. They both grew up in and around Halburg and knew each other, but didn't start dating until college. And it's a bit of a drive home, but they'd done it a million times before. Even in the snow. You have to come to terms with driving in the snow or you don't go anywhere all winter." It mattered that he was listening intently. That he did not interrupt, or even look away. "But that night there was a storm. It cropped up quickly and then turned into ground blizzards. They must have gotten disoriented. It would have been zero visibility." And now she could breathe, but it wasn't *easier*. She blew a breath out, hard, but she kept going. "They went off the side of the highway, into a ditch, and crashed into a tree. We didn't know until the next day."

"Did you mourn them?" he asked, something dark and electric in the question. In his gaze.

"I mourn them every day." She had no idea why she was whispering. "They were good, solid people. They deserved more time. I wish they'd had it."

"No one mourned my father," Anax said in that same darkly stirring way, as if he was as much a part of the night as the stars, the faint breeze. "If anything, people wondered why it had taken so long for him to meet the grim end he had always been courting."

Constance shook her head, not sure why it felt as if she was under some kind of spell, here. She picked at her plate, not certain when a sweet slice of baklava had appeared before her, oozing with honey.

"Is that why you think that all of this, all this excess, is better than everything else?" She ran her finger along the edge of the pastry, and then put it to her lips, not thinking twice about it.

Until she looked at Anax again and found him watching the movement with a certain hooded intensity.

Constance felt...stunned.

She felt it rebound through her, sharp and hot and unmistakable.

She felt herself flush from head to toe, and couldn't pretend for one moment it was hormones. Or a sudden fever.

And she curled up the finger she'd licked into a fist and hid it in her lap.

"Do I think that I am better than a monster?" Anax laughed, though the sound was...raw. A rough touch that did not help the heat swamping her. "I celebrate this difference. Every day."

"I suppose it makes sense that you think that what your daughter really needs are all these *things*." Constance waved her free hand around at the *immensity* of it all. The house that went on and on and on. The high ceilings. The art, the chic décor that she was afraid to sit on, the staff and their nearly unseen hospitality. "You do know, don't you, that it's not the *trappings* of things that matter?"

Anax stared at her for a long moment and she thought she saw his nostrils flare, just slightly. She became aware of the tension in his jaw and the muscle that flexed there, making him even more attractive. He picked up the small coffee before him, and tossed it back. And then it was his turn to stand up from the table with what looked to her a lot like his own dollop of melodrama.

"How would you know?" he asked in a certain silken *tone* that felt like an insult no matter how smooth it was. Or maybe it was how he looked down at her, as if pointing out their difference in station.

"How would I…?" Constance blinked and ordered herself to concentrate. "How would I know what matters?"

"How would you know whether trappings such as these make a difference or not? As you have been at such pains to tell me, your life has been happy, yet humble. I believe I am meant to take from this that you grew up in some idyllic state of being, merrily suspended in cornfields, taught the true meaning of things by the very earth below you and the sky above. Is that not so?"

His laugh was darker now, and she thought he knew full well that it danced all the way down her spine, then wrapped around to send heat spooling into the most fascinating places in front.

And he wasn't done. "This is nonsense. A farm is a farm, *koritsi*. A village is a village. There is no moral value assigned to either, there are only the banal home and hearth fantasies of those who live in them. And that is the difference, you see."

She had to tilt her head back to stare all the way up the length of him, and was aware that he wanted that. He wanted her to have to gaze so far above herself, at all his offhanded elegance and manicured perfection that should have made him look soft—but he was too masculine for that. There was too much belligerence stamped raw and unmistakable into all the rangy lines of his body.

And she still couldn't manage a decent breath. "The difference between what?" she dared to ask.

Anax's mouth curved in that way he had that was not a smile. It was nothing so soft or yielding. "The difference between your farmland, your cornfields, your microscopic village that no one has ever heard of, and the kind of neighborhoods that I called home. We did not fantasize, Constance. That was dangerous. And futile. We focused on making it through one day, then the next. No future, no past, no convenient virtue." He leaned in, and Constance felt her heart thump in her chest. Like a sledgehammer. She could feel the reverberations in her ears. "And yes, I think my daughter is safer here, away from all of that."

Then he left her there, and it was between Constance and the stars, how long it took to remember how to breathe again.

She thought about that conversation a lot more than she liked as the days slipped by. She found she truly loved the freedom of no longer breastfeeding, but also mourned the loss of that connection to Natalia. And despite her intention to freeze Maria out, it was impossible to stay furious in the face of all that relentless cheer.

Besides, she had no one else.

"I want to learn how to swim," she told the other woman one morning. "It seems prudent to learn how. Since we're on an island."

"And, of course," Maria said placidly, though there was a gleam in her gaze, "who knows? You might have to swim away from here one day."

"You never know," Constance agreed merrily.

But Maria began to give her lessons, every morning. They moved from one pool to another. Some were salt-water, some fresh. Some were heated, some cold. In every one of them, she learned to put her face in the water. To blow bubbles. To float.

Slowly, slowly, she learned to swim.

As November chugged along, Constance decided that the most diabolical part of this imprisonment was how easy it was to acclimate to it. It was sunny and warm during the day and there was a chill in the air at night, and it felt heavenly. Nothing at all like Iowa's slide into the dark season. And maybe, if she had been a different sort of person—even the person she'd been right after she'd had Natalia—she might have simply soaked it all in.

But she'd already had a break from her usual routine. She hadn't managed to restore her position at the nursery school, but she'd been making headway, and she'd started working at a day care in town in the meantime because she didn't like staying home.

She didn't like this idle life. It made her feel depressed.

"There are extensive libraries," Anax told her in repressive tones at dinner one night when she dared say so. They had moved inside to a room with art on the walls and a glass ceiling that brought the weather in. It was a stormy night outside, nearly December, and the staff had gone all around lighting fireplaces and candles so that everything glowed and very nearly felt festive. "There is no limit to how you might improve yourself."

Constance looked at him narrowly. She had taken it as a particular badge of honor to wear only the same Walmart sweatshirt and cargo pants when she saw him. No matter what else she might wear during the day when he was not around, the moment she heard that helicopter coming in for its landing, she changed back into the most trailer-park version of herself she could manage.

She'd tried to tell herself she didn't know why she felt this compulsion.

But that was a lie.

The truth was that she was Dorothy Jones's granddaughter. If necessary, she, too, could live on spite alone for years. And Anax might not admit it, but she could see that her uniform bothered him. She took a distinct pleasure in that shudder he managed to repress less and less every time he caught sight of her.

That shudder ensured that she would never stop her own pointless little protest.

In keeping with the Walmart outfit and synthetic fabrics that she was sure appalled him to even share space with, she made certain to keep her hair in the same messy knot on the top of her head. As if to suggest she never washed it.

She told herself it was all part and parcel of the same *resistance*.

But at moments like this, sitting at another intimate

dinner with this man who she would have sworn she did not miss—but raced to see when he came back each evening—she wondered. Because her whole body was lit up from the inside out, as if she was one of those fireplaces the staff had lit for them tonight.

She couldn't pretend it had something to do with his role as a father. That was its own sort of heat and tenderness, but this was different.

This was the flush that never went away.

This was an ache inside her body that woke her in the night.

These were the strings she never managed to untangle, forever wrapped too tight all around her.

If she was honest with herself, she felt that way in his presence...*a lot.*

It didn't matter how many times she sternly told herself that she did not wish to be seen as a woman, not by him. She was a woman. And she suspected there was a huge part of her that, tragically, wanted him to see her as a woman anyway.

That wanted Anax, specifically, to see her that way.

But Constance didn't want to have to dress to his standard for him to notice her.

There was a part of her, and, oh, how it shamed her, that wanted her husband to fall head over heels in love with the woman he'd seen in two costumes in Iowa and only this uniform here.

She knew it was delusional. Especially since, having nothing else to do, she spent a large quantity of time researching the man on the internet. She knew exactly what kind of woman he found beautiful and it certainly wasn't the image she deliberately presented to him.

It wouldn't be her even if she was dressed in her best,

but as she never achieved that standard nor cared to, she could pretend.

And that truth shamed her so deeply it seared into her like a scar.

Or maybe that was simply his effect on her.

Tonight Constance told herself that she didn't want him to see her as anything. She was wearing these things as armor, to make certain she would never lower herself to wanting the likes of him.

Especially when he spoke of her *improvement* as if that was something she should want above all else. As if that was something she sorely needed. She opened her mouth to announce that she would never read another book again as long as she lived, but caught herself just in time. If she said something like that she would feel honor bound to *do* it, and there was such a thing as cutting off one's nose to spite one's face.

"And what improvements do you think I should undertake?" she asked instead, looking at him without bothering to smooth out the expression on her face.

"We are all of us human, are we not?" Anax seemed unduly restless tonight and was not sitting in his seat. He was prowling around the dining room, glaring at the portraits on the wall. "Surely there is no one who could not use as many improvements as possible."

"What of you, then? In which areas do you think you need improvement?"

And maybe it was the storm outside, rattling at the windows. Maybe it was all those lit-up parts inside of her, blazing with that heat she didn't want to feel. Maybe he knew anyway, because he was the kind of man who *knew such things*. She didn't have to know them herself to understand that.

But when he turned to look at her there was something on his face, something stark that she didn't know had a name.

Does it need a name? whispered something inside her. *Or do you worry you already know what you would call it?*

And the starkness of it made her eyes felt damp with an emotion that felt almost too hot, too heavy, to bear. His eyes seemed darker. It did not seem as if there was a table and half a room between them. It seemed as if they were sharing one breath, as if all of these intimacies over the past months were embroidered into them, threaded through bone and flesh.

As if that storm beating down above was in both of them, too.

As if she'd been fooling herself all this time, pretending she couldn't see it—

But the door opened then, and Maria came in. She was carrying Natalia, who wailed when she saw her mother and held out her small, chubby arms.

"She had a bad dream," Maria said, apologetically, looking up at the glass ceiling to suggest the storm was the culprit. "And she would not settle. I'm sorry to interrupt your evening."

"Don't be ridiculous," Constance said, taking the sweet weight of her daughter in her arms. "Natalia is never an interruption."

She glanced at her husband while she said that and saw that odd, arrested expression on his face.

But it wasn't until later, after she carried Natalia back to the nursery, aware that he followed her. After she put the little girl down and sang to her, with a hand on her belly to keep her warm. After she kept going until the baby fell asleep.

It wasn't until then that she found herself standing in a dark hallway with Anax, as if they were still in that same, stark moment.

"You never answered the question," she said, and in her head, she wanted that to sound businesslike. Brusque and to the point.

But they were standing outside their daughter's nursery. It was later now, and this part of the house was not so gleaming or bright. There was only the two of them and too many shadows.

And that heat embroidered into everything.

Her eyes adjusted just enough so that she could see that gray gleam of his gaze.

"What question?" Anax asked and his voice, too, was altered. Lower. Like a rough scrape along the surface of her skin.

She told herself that was the cold outside, the storm that was still rolling over the island. "How would you improve yourself if you could?"

Somewhere in the distance, she could hear the wind outside. But deep inside her, she could hear her own heartbeat, loud and insistent and drowning out almost everything else.

He leaned forward, and his hand moved, and she had the most absurd notion—

As if the purpose of it all was to lower his face so they were at eye level—

Once again, she couldn't breathe. Her heart stopped, then slammed back into her ribs. Because she thought, she knew, she *wanted*—

That gaze of his dropped to her mouth, and everything

in her went still. Then burst into flame once more when he dragged that gaze back up to hers.

"What I need to remember," he said, very quietly, almost achingly, "is that I'm going to need to stop fighting monsters who aren't in the room."

She thought he leaned forward.

He did, she was sure of it. Her eyes felt weighted and heavy, and against her will, they fluttered shut.

When she opened them again, he was gone.

But Constance was not the same.

Because she'd made the very perilous mistake of desperately wanting her husband—the man who'd only wanted their daughter, never her.

And, worse, *showing* him.

CHAPTER SEVEN

ANAX LOOKED UP from a long, satisfyingly brutal stretch of hours at his desk to find his sister haunting his doorway.

He sat back, glancing at his watch to determine how long he'd been poring over the documents on his desk, looking for the sorts of secrets that he knew too well his opponents and their legal teams liked to hide in contracts where they thought no one would look. Throw enough clauses into the mix and people assumed they'd gotten the gist of all of them without actually reading them all.

Anax knew different. From experience on both sides of said clauses.

"You haven't heard a word I've said, have you?" demanded Vasiliki in her usual half-scornful, three-quarters disrespectful manner.

Truth was, he found it heartwarming. No one else treated him in exactly the same way she always had. There was nothing on this earth that affected his sister or her responses to things—except, perhaps, how discomfited she looked in the presence of Stavros, the security head. Anax assumed that was because she also disliked having her movements curtailed. No matter what good reasons there might be for it.

"Not one word," he agreed now, as close to *cheerful*

as he got, because he knew it annoyed her. "And had I known you were here, I would have ignored you even longer. To make a point."

She only rolled her eyes at that as she consulted the tablet she held. "All the holiday invitations are rolling in again. It's all the usual suspects, as expected." And then she rattled off a list of charities, holiday balls, events, and the like. "Your company is graciously requested and eagerly anticipated at all of the above, of course."

"Don't you normally answer for me without consultation?" He stood up from his desk and allowed himself to stretch, looking out at the bustling streets of Athens far below, gleaming in the December dusk. Something about the lights prodded at him, and he didn't like it. It reminded him of a firelit night, and a whispered question in a darkened hallway—in the promise he made himself that he had nearly broken. He turned back to his sister. "You are the one who tracks my contributions and packs my calendar with these obligations, are you not? Why is this discussion necessary?"

"This year is different." Vasiliki lifted her gaze to his with an air of surprise when he did not reply to that. "This year you have a wife, Anax, or have you forgotten that?"

"Am I known for being forgetful?" He was aware that she would not find that an adequate response, and sure enough, she frowned at him.

"Stavros says you haven't been out to the island in two weeks." Vasiliki lifted a brow in that way she had that suggested others found it precisely this irritating when he did the same thing. "Trouble in paradise, my brother?"

"What I cannot imagine is what you imagine you are doing with this bizarre conversational gambit." He considered her for the sort of long, thoughtful moment that would have anyone else at this company quaking. His sister stared back at him, immune. "Have you suffered a head injury?"

Vasiliki laughed. "Sometimes I wish I had, but then I remember, I am an Ignatios. It is a genetic injury." She tucked the tablet under one arm. "The fact remains, you have a wife. And that changes the conversation."

"Apparently so, and in astonishing ways. I'd like to change it back."

"Every year, you attend these balls and it is nothing short of mayhem," Vasiliki reminded him. "It doesn't matter how dire or sad the charity, the women are all over you. Old women, young women. You can't walk three steps without being propositioned. Perhaps you've forgotten that it was so bad last year they had to close down that one gala so you could be evacuated."

Anax rubbed at his temples with only slightly exaggerated impatience. "I was not *evacuated*. I chose to leave out the side entrance. It had nothing to do with me that the organizers chose to make a scene."

"This year," Vasiliki said, very brightly and very slowly, as if he was deeply stupid, "there is another option. You could present your wife to the world, which I feel quite certain would not stop *everyone*, but might put a damper on the usual stampede."

"Ókhi." He belted that out so abruptly, so succinctly, that he wasn't sure who was more surprised. Him or his sister. "No."

They stared at each other as the light continued to fade from the sky outside his office. The ancient city sprawled there before them, ribbons of lights leading to Syntagma Square, looking festive this time of year. Vasiliki, not one for atmosphere, reached behind her and slapped on the overhead lights.

"And am I to know why you refuse to take the life preserver that has been offered to you?" she asked. "It makes no sense. You have complained for years about these cattle calls."

"Think about what you're asking," Anax retorted.

And as he spoke he became more convinced that his gut reaction had been based on facts. On reason and rationality, having nothing at all to do with how close he had come to kissing Constance after watching her sing to their baby.

He didn't like to think of it. He thought of little else.

"How is it fair to throw Constance headfirst into a sea full of sharks? She cannot swim."

Vasiliki stared at him. "Is that a metaphor? Are you speaking in *metaphors*, brother? Has a Christmas miracle finally occurred before my very eyes?"

Anax thrust his hands into the pockets of his trousers and reminded himself that she *tried* to get under his skin as a matter of course. That she had been doing that since birth. Allowing her to succeed was on him. "The fact of the matter is, Delphine picked Constance for a reason. She knows nothing of this world and why should she? The American cornfields that created her are not simply far away from here, they might as well be on a different planet."

Vasiliki blinked. "The same could be said for your own trajectory, Anax, or have you forgotten what neighborhood we come from?"

He ordered himself to unclench his jaw. "Not to mention, she is my wife. I owe her my protection. I cannot in good conscience allow her to appear in front of the kind of people that run in these circles. They would eat her alive. Her wardrobe alone would make her little more than chum in the water."

"Again with the sharks."

"It is unthinkable," Anax said, warming to the topic, or perhaps he was simply letting his temper out to play here, with his perpetually unimpressed sister, where it could do no harm. "I cannot think why you would suggest such a thing. What has Constance ever done to you?"

His sister had eyed him for a long, uncomfortable moment. He thought that she would say something and braced himself, but instead she pulled her tablet back out, swiped at the screen, and moved on to other topics.

That night, though he had not intended on going out to the island, Anax landed there anyway. And found his wife, not in the dining room where they ate when he was expected, but in a small sitting room near her bedchamber that he could see, at a glance, she had taken over as her own.

And he could not account for the little pop of warmth in him at the sight. At the notion she was actually...settling in here.

"Maria did not tell me you were coming," Constance said in something like alarm when he opened the door and found her there. She stood up from the small table where she'd been sitting, and she looked...guilty.

Anax took in the pile of books beside her. The tray of food, a crock of soup and freshly baked bread in place of the usual delicacies.

"Would you have hidden all these books?" he asked after a moment. "For fear I would discover that you'd actually been reading?"

"You are a deeply annoying man," Constance told him,

but so very calmly, that he almost missed what she was telling him. "I have always read. Your suggestion that I should *try reading* as an activity made me want to never read another word as long as I lived. And yes, I would rather that you not see me doing it, because it would give me pleasure to read every book in your library and never mention it."

"What would be the point of that?"

"It doesn't matter if *you* know how wrong you are," she said, and smiled at him. A bit too piously. "*I* know, and I will nurse that flame for as long as I live."

But he was caught up on that smile. It was so *bright*. Festive, or near enough. He tried to imagine her smiling like this in the ballrooms of Athens, surrounded by those circling predators, and couldn't.

He had made the right decision. He was sure of it.

"Have you been complaining to Stavros about my not making it out to the island recently?"

He walked in further and threw himself down on the couch where she had clearly spent some time, if the cashmere throw that was tossed aside there was any indication.

She eyed him narrowly, breaking off a piece of bread with her fingers and dipping it into the crock of her soup. "I'm not much for complaining. My grandmother used to say that a complainer was a coward, too afraid to say what they really wanted until it was too late. I don't know about you, Anax, but I do *try* not to be a coward."

"That feels pointed."

She looked at him, then back to her meal, which rather dug the point in deeper, to his mind. "Besides, why would I complain to Stavros? He works for you. What would be the point?"

"My sister says that you did." He considered. "Or rather, she said that he had mentioned it had been a while."

"Has it not occurred to you that your sister and your head of security invent reasons to talk to each other?" Constance smiled again when she looked up and saw the blank look on his face. "Oh, come on, Anax. Where are those killer instincts you pride yourself on? You can't see that your sister and your head of security are enamored of each other?"

"Stavros would never—" he began. But then stopped himself.

Because he would not. But Vasiliki was bound by nothing at all—and least of all any disapproval from Anax.

Constance only shrugged. "Why? Because you would disapprove?" She did not roll her eyes. Not precisely. But the way she did not roll her eyes had the same effect. "You might not have any interest in being happy yourself, Anax. That's perfectly clear. But does that mean no one else can be, either?"

When he left later that evening, he could not think of a single reason why he had come, save the few moments he'd spent with his beautiful daughter after her bath. Much less why he would hurry to return.

But he found himself watching his sister and his security head over the following days, noticing that it did seem as if the two of them paid a bit more attention to each other than necessary...

And he hated that his secluded wife, who saw the pair of them far less than he did, had picked up on something he should have understood was happening before it started.

But there was little time to think too much of these

things. Because the holiday event season was beginning, and, as ever, it started off with a particularly ornate gala in the center of Athens. Vasiliki had made certain to block it off in his calendar in capital letters to remind him of their conversation.

He had to hurry out of a meeting to get ready the way he always did, because he put effort into the things he wore, unlike some. He had learned early on that the real secret of fashion was the way it was discussed, as if it was the sole province of empty-headed women, when the truth was that powerful men had whole conversations with their clothes alone. Sometimes these conversations took the place of other negotiations entirely.

It was the first foreign language he'd taught himself.

And yet tonight, instead of plotting out the conversations he wished to have and avoid, the photographs he would allow and those he would not, he found himself wondering why he'd been so adamant that Vasiliki continue to keep Constance's existence a secret. His sister had not been wrong. He had grown tired of these events long since. The same conversations with the same people, over and over again, were tiresome.

And yes, there were the women who followed him around, something the younger version of him would never have believed could prove objectionable. But then, Delphine had soured him on such experiences long before he'd learned of her vicious revenge.

In the car that drove him to the gala, he found himself thinking about his ex-lover, something he normally preferred to avoid. There was still such a huge part of him that wanted to enact his revenge upon her in a manner no one could mistake. So that no one, ever, would dare attempt such a thing again—on him or on anyone.

And yet...how could he wish his daughter out of existence?

He hated being away from her. That was the stark truth of it. Natalia had started walking. She was saying words, deliberately. Every time he saw her, she was a brand-new human. Even her face looked different, and he deeply loathed the fact that he could not be with her all the time to see these things.

He had been adamantly opposed to ever having children, and this was part of the reason why. Already he could feel it, this helpless certainty that he would raze the earth to dust and rubble for her. That he would never be happy if she was not. That everything he was, or would ever become, was wrapped up in two chubby fists, that stubborn little scowl she often wore, and that smile of hers that was already too much like her mother's.

What revenge could he take on Delphine for that?

Because this is what he knew about his ex. She was not a happy woman. It was not even *him* she had ever wanted, not really. It was what he had stood for. It was his status, his money. All the things it would have meant for her to become the wife of a man of his stature. That was what Delphine had wanted.

He could not even be certain that she had truly enjoyed the pleasure they'd taken in each other. Mechanically, he knew she had. But had she actually *liked* that kind of release? He had come to think that she hadn't and that was why he'd ended it.

It had become too difficult to see what part of Delphine was an act and what was real.

This all-encompassing, life-altering feeling inside of him whenever he so much as thought about his daughter was something else again. He knew people called it love, but it was far deeper than that. It was more terrible, more *total*.

It was something fused into his bones.

It was terrifying.

One moment he had been himself. And the next, his daughter had been born, and laid upon Constance's chest, and he had been changed forever.

He could not say he'd *liked* any of it.

But his life had changed that day and he had known, irrevocably, that there was no going back. He would keep his daughter safe. He would dedicate his life to her happiness, and it did not matter if *he* was happy in the midst of that.

He did not need to wreak his revenge on the woman who so richly deserved it, because she had ceased to matter. What mattered was Natalia.

And Constance, the woman who loved her as he did.

The woman he had very nearly kissed, and not because it was the end of a date and a kiss was called for. But because it had been dark in that hallway and she had smelled so good, and they had been standing close, and he had felt so *raw*—

Thank all the gods, old and new, that he'd remembered himself in time.

Another truth, he acknowledged as he was announced into the gala, was that he barely remembered what Delphine looked like any longer. He struggled to recall a single face of any woman he had known intimately. They all seemed to fade away, suggesting he had been as unengaged as many of them had accused him of being.

All he could see these days were eyes like smoky quartz, a spray of freckles across a pert nose, and that devastating smile.

He found himself particularly unhappy about that, but the more he tried to bring another woman's face to mind, the more he realized that it had been a very, very long time indeed since he had thought of any woman save Constance. And that truth was…unsatisfying.

Unwieldy.

And only half-true to begin with, something in him argued.

He ignored it as he walked into the throng of people, nodding at faces he recognized, but not wishing to stop or speak to anyone.

Until, that was, he found himself face-to-face with his sister and had no choice but to stop. And even attempt a smile.

"There you are," Vasiliki said, dressed splendidly. She swept a sharp gaze over him. "You look lonely, brother. More so than usual."

Anax decided he hated that she could read him. He supposed he always hated it—no matter how he relied on it—but today it seemed more offensive than usual.

"It is my natural state," he bit out, without the usual gloss of civility he tried to pull on at events like this. "It suits me. As it does you, or have I read you wrong, Vasiliki? Do you only pretend to be lonely out of some sense of solidarity?"

But if he'd thought that would land like some kind of weapon, he was mistaken. Vasiliki managed to give the impression of a deep, jaw-cracking sort of yawn without allowing so much as a muscle to move. Or her gaze to become any less withering.

"I will book some time in your schedule to discuss my loneliness, shall I?" she asked, sardonically. "I am sure you are precisely the therapy I need, brother. As you are so evolved yourself. In the meantime, let me present you with *your* date for the evening."

Anax opened his mouth to cut that off, and fast—certainly not to apologize—but instead it was as if all the air in the world...vanished.

His sister reached back and pulled the figure he had only half noticed standing behind her to the front.

It had been a very long time since anyone had kicked him hard enough in the gut for him to lose his breath. But that was not a sensation that a man forgot.

He felt it again now. Intensely.

"It is my pleasure to present to you, Anax, your wife," Vasiliki said, with a mock bow. "Constance Ignatios, this is your husband, little though you might know it after his recent behavior."

And then, whether because that had been her plan from the start or because she saw whatever look was on Anax's face, Vasiliki smiled as if she'd won a great prize—then made herself scarce.

Leaving Anax with nothing to do but gaze in helpless fascination at his wife.

His wife.

Who was, to his astonishment, completely done over.

Gone was his farm girl. Gone was any faint hint of the cornfields where he'd found her. And there was a part of him that missed the familiarity of that tragic tracksuit ensemble she favored. There was a part of him that longed for that coziness.

But then there was...every other part of him.

"I know," she was saying, with a wry twist of her lips. "Vasiliki would not be dissuaded. She descended upon me with a battalion of stylists and told me it was my Cinderella moment. So I suppose it's up to you if you'd like to be the Prince Charming in that scenario, or if you're feeling a bit more like the pumpkin."

But something was happening inside Anax.

A terrible illness, he thought, coming at him fast. His lungs hurt. His ribs seemed to be buckling in on his chest. His heart was pounding, too hard, and there was something wrong with his eyes.

He couldn't seem to tear them away from her.

And Anax realized something then, though it was lowering in the extreme.

Some part of him had preferred it when he could keep Constance in the box where he'd found her. Her terrible clothes. Her costumes. This was exactly what she'd been getting at, he realized in her talk of the kinds of childhood they'd had and the differing degrees of the poverty of their origins.

And he'd missed it because he'd wanted to miss it.

Because some part of him must have known the truth all along.

Because Vasiliki had taken that rough little piece of Iowa rock and polished her into the diamond that had been there all along.

She was buffed to a shine. Everything was done, from her nails to her makeup. The dress she wore, the shoes, even the bag she clasped in one hand.

Constance *gleamed*.

And Anax could not pretend that this was some costume she was wearing tonight. He knew too well the things fashion could and could not do. This was not a makeover—this was *her*. This was the Constance he had first seen in the back of that church.

It was just that now, here, there was nothing to detract from that beauty.

Her gown clung to her body in the richest hue of deepest purple. She looked elegant. Sophisticated. And he did not like the part of him that found it easier to recognize her beauty because of those things.

Or his sure knowledge that everyone else here would, too.

"Come," he said gruffly. "We should dance."

She laughed, as if that was a joke. "Should we?"

"If you do not, I will have to introduce you to all kinds of people who do not deserve to meet you. Not yet. Perhaps not ever." Somewhere inside him, the manners he had taken such care to teach himself over the years, so he could painstakingly make his way up into these higher echelons of society, stirred. Reminding him of the man he wished to be, even under duress. He extended his hand, and inclined his head. "If you would do me the honor, Constance."

Her smile widened, and he could see the delight that poured over her. And it occurred to him that she was simply…attending a party tonight. This was another fancy dress to her and she'd put as much concern into it as she had in the wearing of a chicken suit.

He was the one who was finding it hard to breathe.

Anax was the one who felt something inside of him seemed to change shape. When his hand wrapped around hers. When she leaned into him so she could slip through the throng of people and he caught the faint hint of a scent he knew was only hers. When he pulled her out onto the dance floor—a place he typically avoided like the plague—so that he could finally, finally, pull her into his arms.

Because it was as close as he could get to her here.

"Lucky for you," she said, sounding nothing but *merry*

as she tipped her head back to look up at him, "I actually know how to dance. My grandparents used to dance in the kitchen at night, listening to the radio and humming along. I would sneak up the stairs to watch them when I heard the floorboards creak. They always danced cheek to cheek. And they both knew all the words."

She smiled as if the memory brought her fresh joy and he wondered what that must be like, the kind of life where memory was a true blessing instead of a curse.

He moved with her and she flowed along with him, and Anax could not imagine ever dancing with anyone else. Ever.

"Eventually, my grandfather taught me, too," Constance told him. "My grandmother always said that knowing how to let a man think he was leading was one of the most important tools a woman could have in her arsenal."

"Your grandmother sounds like a woman I would have admired a great deal," Anax managed to grit out.

"Everyone admired her or feared her," Constance said brightly. "Often both, I think. But as for me, I just loved her. I still do."

Her memories were a fire she warmed herself by, he saw. His were a gas fire in a trash can.

And Anax could not keep up the conversation. He could not compare blazes, flame to flame.

All he could do was dance. Because Constance was in his arms, at last.

He did not have to pretend, not with the music soaring all around them, and his gaze locked to hers. He did not have to tell himself lies.

He did not even have to redirect his attention to his daughter, because the baby wasn't here.

There was only this. There was only her.

It was as if the fancy dress glow his sister had engineered had been a kind of stripping down, in the end. Because all he could see now was the truth.

All he could *feel* was the truth.

It was that truth he was thinking of as he danced her out of the ballroom and onto one of the balconies, in the dark.

Where, finally, he looked down at her and thought that he would count the constellations on her lovely face.

But that would have to wait, because she gazed up at him and he was hit with yet another truth that he'd been denying for far too long—

I want her, he thought, admitting it to himself.

Maybe he said it, too, because her eyes grew wide.

And finally, *finally*, Anax leaned down and took Constance's fascinating mouth with his.

CHAPTER EIGHT

ANAX'S HARD MOUTH descended upon hers, claimed it as if they had kissed a thousand times before, and everything changed.

Just like that.

Constance forgot…everything.

Where she was. What they were meant to be doing. The fact they were not in private, not even out here in the dark with only glass between them and the rest of the ballroom.

She forgot all of those things in a deep, hot rush, while at the same time there was a deep shock of what she understood at once was recognition.

A deep, intense, all-encompassing understanding of not only who this man was to her, but the responses to him she'd been pretending she didn't understand for almost a year now.

He held her in his arms, his mouth on hers, and it was as if she was falling. Soaring. Tumbling head over heels, back through time, as one image after the next scrolled through her mind.

She had seen him the moment he'd walked into the church in Halburg. She'd seen him, she'd *known*, and then her conscious mind had rejected what the rest of her body felt.

With the same intense throb of deep recognition.

Almost as if she had known who he was, there and then. Before he'd even come to speak to her.

As if somehow, cosmically, the baby inside of her had recognized its own father.

Or maybe it was simply that she had understood that for the first time in all her life, she comprehended precisely what her body was for.

Even ten months pregnant and about to give birth.

Even then, while she'd worked so hard to pretend all of those sensations were simply part of what it was to be so heavily pregnant, something deep within her had known otherwise.

His mouth shifted on hers, she was dimly aware of the change in the background noise on the other side of the glass doors, but not enough to stop. Not enough to keep herself from tentatively opening her mouth beneath his and accepting him into her mouth.

It felt like some kind of explosion. It felt messy and perfect. It felt like everything she'd ever wanted yet had never imagined she would feel.

Then he angled his chin, took the kiss deeper, and once again hurled her back into her memories.

The actual moment of giving birth. Of looking down the length of her own body, to see Natalia—tiny, alien and *hers*.

They had laid her daughter next to her heart and she had felt scraped raw, as if the process of labor was not simply to bring this perfect new human into the world, but to expand *her* from the inside out. To make it possible to contain all the love she felt, complicated and messy and almost as painful as the labor pains themselves.

Constance had looked up from that brutal, beautiful moment and he had been there. Waiting. Watching.

With a look of such extraordinary intensity on his face that she had not allowed herself to think of it since. It was too much. It was naked and unbearable.

It shook her, deep.

And that, too, was its own kind of recognition.

There on a balcony outside the ball, he pulled back. And once again, that look on his face was extraordinary. Impossible.

Once again, she felt as if his kiss was less of a surprise and more of an awakening—to a particular kind of daylight that had been pouring all around her all this time.

And now, at last, she could see it.

She wondered if he could see it, too.

Anax stared at her for what felt like a lifetime. Then he pulled her back inside and into the embrace of all that heat and conversation and music. He swept her out into the dancing once more, swirling them around and around, as if it was the most natural thing in the world for him to stop in the middle of a waltz to kiss his wife in the dark.

Constance looked over toward the balcony and realized that it was more lit up out there than she'd noticed. And that it was likely everyone here had seen that kiss. Surely that was something she ought to have been embarrassed about—

But she couldn't quite get there.

Everything inside her was sensation and need, wrapped all around each other with little barbs that sunk deep and confirmed for her that this had been what she'd wanted from him all along.

Without even knowing it. Not on the surface, anyway.

"If you keep looking at me like that," he said then, in

a deep, rumbling sort of way that she could feel beneath her hands even as she heard it with her ears, "everyone in this ballroom will think that my wife is a debauched libertine who thinks of nothing at all but taking me to her bed."

She understood something then, in another burst of clarity that she thought might have something to do with the fact she could still taste him on her lips. The Constance she had been before she'd gone down this road, before she'd decided to have a baby without waiting around for the right man the way everyone told her she should, was not the Constance she was now. The Constance who had soldiered on in the face of the sniffs and the raised eyebrows in town. The Constance who had lived the past year with this man in her house, who had spent many a sleepless hour telling herself that anything she felt about the situation was hormones, nothing more.

All of those versions of her made this version of her possible, but she wasn't *them* any longer. She was what they'd made her.

So she turned her head to look at him. She held his gaze, lifting one shoulder and then delicately lowering it again. "They would be correct."

And she had the very great pleasure of watching him… *ignite.*

It started somewhere in the backs of his eyes, burst into flame, and then took him over.

"Koritsi," he said, but it was like a growl.

And before she knew what was happening, he was taking her by the hand and tugging her through the ballroom once again. This time in the opposite direction. She saw him nod curtly to his sister, standing near a grand pillar in a knot of very well-to-do-looking people with the security chief at her side.

A car pulled up in front of them as he led her outside. And Constance did not question how it was that everything in this man's life seemed to work like clockwork, as if the earth on its axis rotated purely at his command.

Tonight, she would believe it.

And though she was sure it would shock her staid and quiet ancestors, she simply allowed herself to be swept up in all of this well-oiled wealth and consequence. She crawled into the back seat and sat there as if she was born to it, still buzzing from before. Everywhere he touched her she could feel it, like heat.

And her mouth was like a naked flame, hungry for more.

She heard him say something in Greek to his driver, then he was sliding in behind her. Sharing the back seat with her, so big and so male that he seemed to claim the better part of it, and it wasn't until he closed the door behind him that she noticed the car had a privacy screen. And it was engaged.

And that meant that there was no reason on earth that she should resist it when Anax pulled her onto his lap.

No nod toward propriety necessary. No need to concern herself with what anyone might see or say. There was no one around to gossip about it later.

There was only the feel of his hard body beneath her. And then, gloriously, his mouth on hers once more.

He immediately made it clear that what had passed between them in that ballroom had been an exercise of holding back. Of complete restraint.

Because this kiss consumed her whole.

His hands moved to frame her face between his palms and he took control, completely.

And then he set about teaching her... Everything.

Everything she didn't know about the ways that the word *kiss* was entirely too small, too banal, to encompass what his mouth could do to hers.

Everything about how to kiss him back until she made him groan, too.

Everything that built the fire higher, that made her ache, until she found herself squirming there on his lap because she couldn't get close enough. Because she wanted to... *Do* things with this body of hers that felt brand-new in his arms.

"Careful," he murmured. "Or we will give my driver quite a surprise."

She had no idea what he meant by that, but she could feel the hardest part of him between them, she found herself...fascinated.

Constance knew what it was when a man grew hard. She'd read about it. She lived in the same world as everyone else, even in her quiet life in Halburg, thank you. She'd watched enough television and film to fill in the blanks. But she had never understood how a thing that happened to *him* would feel inside of *her*. She had never understood that her own body could feel so jittery and liquid, hot and cold at once, simply because *he* was so unrepentantly hard.

Or that all of it was wonderful.

How amazing, she found herself thinking, *that people are wandering around the world feeling like this all the time, and I never knew.*

He muttered a curse against her lips, and then he was

lifting her up, settling her beside him, and looking at her in a way that she could only describe as baleful.

And yet her response to that was to feel inordinately proud of herself.

"You will make me disgrace myself," he said, as if he was offering an explanation.

"I can tell that that's meant to chastise me," she said, somewhat surprised that she could actually form words after...*all that*. "But I have no idea what you're talking about."

She watched as a certain sort of consideration moved over his face. A dawning kind of awareness.

"You are truly untouched, then," he said, but there was a note of something like awe in his voice, and as embarrassing as it was to be thirty years of age and untouched, of all things, she didn't mind it when he looked at her like that.

She wouldn't mind anything, as long as he looked at her like that.

"As of before this evening?" She nodded. "But I am... slightly more touched now, obviously."

That seemed to worry him, almost. He frowned. Something about that fire in his gaze seemed to shift.

She wanted to track that. She really did. But she wanted that fire, just the way it was. So she reached out a hand and smoothed it over one rock-hard thigh, then trailed her fingers along the seam of his trousers, right there where she could see the proof of all of this.

And he let out a sound as if she had punched him in the gut.

"Maybe," she whispered, "I can touch you, too?"

And the noise he made then was indescribable. Deep and low and guttural, and then his mouth was on hers again, and somehow it was even better. Even wilder.

The car came to a stop and she hardly noticed until he tore himself away from her, muttering darkly beneath his breath. So that all she caught were little scraps of Greek words she didn't know.

She *would* know Greek, she told herself then. Her daughter was going to learn it and she would learn it right along with Natalia, so one day she would know everything he said, not just half.

But she couldn't allow herself to think too much about language classes, because he was leading her out of the car and then into a strange building through what appeared to be some kind of private entrance. Then she was in a gleaming lobby, and wondered if they were in a nose-bleedingly fancy hotel. He herded her into an elevator, pressed the single button available, and then held her with a certain ferocity—and at a deliberate distance—as the elevator rose.

It felt the way she already did inside.

And then the sleek doors slid open, delivering them directly into the living room of an apartment that, at first, she thought was entirely made of glass. She could see Athens from all sides. She could see the Acropolis in the distance, gleaming atop its ancient rock in the night. Everywhere she turned there were more lights, and shadows that made her want to fly low over this age-old city to explore it. To relearn those old myths she'd pored over as a child, but from the inside out this time.

When she'd turned around in a full circle, she found Anax shrugging out of his jacket and tossing it to the side. Toward what she belatedly realized was some sort of piece of relentlessly modern furniture.

And then he was coming toward her once more.

"What is this place?" she asked.

"It is my flat, of course. What else would it be?"

"Some dramatic hotel. Open only to people like you, with secret entrances and private elevators and all this *glass*."

"Koritsi," he murmured as he stopped before her. "There is no one like me. Allow me to demonstrate."

Then he swept her up into his arms. And he kissed her again, deep and stern, and for a moment she couldn't tell if she was simply dizzy from the glory of it all—but then she understood that he was carrying her through this apartment made of glass, turning away from the windows at the last moment to lead her down a hallway, gleaming white and spare, until she found herself set down in a sprawling, rambling bedroom that was glass, still more glass, and chrome. With accents of the deepest onyx.

And there was something about all of that, anesthetized and pristine, that caught at her.

But she couldn't follow the thought because Anax was before her. And there was a look on his face that made her heart lurch. Because it was clear that for all these moments of recognition that she had ignored, for all the times she had felt she knew him better than she should, there was this part of him that she didn't know at all.

It thrilled her.

"All this time," she managed to say. "This whole long year, and I never realized…"

He stilled, even while that look on his face became starker, more intense. *More sensual,* something in her whispered, when that should not have been possible.

"I look forward to your visits," she confessed in a rush. "I even started missing you when you weren't there. Even now, when I should hate you for taking me away from everything I've ever known, I spend my days listening for that helicopter to land so I know you're coming. So I can pretend that I'm looking forward to showing you how little I care."

And he was so close, standing there in front of her in a darkened room with the lights of the city gleaming in. So she reached over, a daring act that felt like swinging on a trapeze or running full tilt along a high wire, and slid her hands onto his chest.

She felt something like a shock at the point of contact and pulled her palms back, swallowing the gasp that was surprised from between her lips. When she looked up, he was still gazing down at her in that same way, dark and hot and…encouraging.

That part felt like a balm…or perhaps more heat.

Either way, Constance put her hands back onto that hard, hot wall that was his chest. She cleared her throat.

And then she tipped her head back up to look at him again. "I wanted you the moment I saw you," she told him, like another confession. Or perhaps like a vow. "You walked in and I thought, *There he is*. And I've spent a long time pretending I didn't know what that meant. Maybe I didn't. Until tonight." And she wasn't sure she could say the last part. But the words were on her tongue and he did not look away, and her mouth tasted of him anyway. So she dared. "But now, Anax, I very much want to know everything."

"Then your wish will be my command, my darling wife," he gritted out, and the roughness of his voice made her skin seem to prickle with awareness.

She felt everything between them burst to life, alight and wild with flame. The next breath she took seemed to shake all the way in and then more on the way out. And some part of her wanted to career off into that feeling.

She wanted him to lift her up, toss her on the bed, and throw himself down beside her—

But what he did was far more devastating.

He reached over and ran his thumb over her lips, as if memorizing the shape. Then he slid his fingers back, deep into her hair. He kept on until the whole mess of it fell down around her and she could smell the fragrance that was caught in the heavy strands, flowers and musk.

His gaze dropped to her dress and his face took on a look of a kind of sensual concentration that didn't help her shivery responses any. But the fact they got worse felt even better, somehow.

He turned her around, his hands on her body and not a single word spoken, so that she was facing that great window before her. It felt as if, with one step, she could free-fall out over the city and soar down so she was one more gleaming old ruin, a song sung on the wind, a goddess in need of only this one man to worship her.

And slowly, almost as if he was timing it to her shaky breaths, he began to unfasten the back of her gown. And she heard his own deep humming sound, something deeply male and approving, when he finished and it pooled at her feet.

He turned her back to him. And now she was near enough to panting, because she was only wearing a bustier beneath and pair of highly impractical panties that she had thought were silly when she'd put them on.

Now she thought they were magic.

So did he. She could tell.

And Anax began to talk, then. Only occasionally in English.

His voice was like another touch, dancing over her skin, making her senses feel heightened. Making her *aware*. Making her moan and shiver and sigh. Because he took his time, unwrapping that last bit of her. He treated her like a precious gift for his mouth and his hands, and lit his way, one fire into the next.

His voice moved over her, too, using words she didn't know...but could feel in every part of her he touched.

She didn't have to know what he was saying to understand that he was worshipping her body, claiming it, exalting it. She didn't have to speak Greek to comprehend his deep male approval.

She gloried in it.

And when he was done he had tasted almost every part of her body, and stripped her completely naked.

It was only then that he lifted her and carried her over to the bed. He spread her out there and looked down upon her as if he had never seen anything so beautiful.

In that moment, Constance believed it.

He stripped his own clothes from his body, never seeming to take his eyes from her. And as he unwrapped his own male beauty for her to stare upon, it was as if more and more connections she'd never understood became clear to her. Why men were shaped the way they were. Why there was something in her that deeply celebrated the fact that his chest, for all that was hard-packed lean muscle, was also covered in a smattering of dark hair that she could not wait to put her hands on. To bury her face in.

She wanted to feel him, to breathe in his scent, to lose herself in his heat. She wanted to taste him, everywhere. She wanted to follow that hair-roughened arrow of muscle to its logical conclusion, down the length of his body to where the boldest part of him stood there, proudly, as if waiting for her attention.

But before she could follow that thought, as if he read her mind, he shifted forward onto the bed. Anax crawled between her legs so that her knees seemed to hook themselves on his broad shoulders, and that easily, she was wide open before him.

"I have been wanting to taste you forever," he growled.

And then he did.

For a time, then, Constance lost herself entirely.

There was no thought, no analysis, no contemplation of any kind.

There was only his mouth on that tender part of her, eating her alive. There was only the way he was looking into her, indulging himself in that most private part of her as if she was the sweetest dessert he'd ever tasted.

It seemed to take an eternity—and no time at all—before she was arching up against him, a thunderstorm pounding into her and then exploding back out, so that she could do nothing at all but let it take her. Until it was tossing her from one storm to the next.

Until she was nothing at all but heat and glory.

"*Koritsi*, you are perfect," he was murmuring, as he climbed up the length of her body, kissing her and tasting her.

He paused at her navel, and again at one breast. Then the next. Tasting them, weighing them, making her nipples ache so hard they pointed their way toward him. As if her own body was begging for something she hadn't imagined could possibly be so intense, so sensual, and have nothing at all to do with the way she'd been using those same breasts for the last ten months.

She wanted to tell him that bodies were amazing and his was even more so. But he was moving, until he could kiss her once more—deep and hard and intensely. Until she could taste herself, and him, and her body felt wild all around her.

And then, at last, she could feel him. The broad head of that silken, hot part of him, nudged against the sensitized flesh he had just tasted so thoroughly.

Even the feel of it made her light up all over again, and he was going so *slowly*.

She tried to move her hips toward him, but he laughed and adjusted the way he held her, so he controlled the way he eased toward her, one little bit at a time.

Constance opened her eyes to find him watching her, and then they were both there, suspended in that intensity. He slid inside her so carefully, so smoothly, both of them braced—together—for a pain that didn't come.

And he kept going.

Deeper and deeper, filling her up and making her body adjust to fit him. Her heart was pounding. Her breath was coming too fast. She found herself curling her hands into fists at his chest and then she was following the urge to lift herself up and press her face between the flat planes of his pectoral muscles, because she could smell him there. Taste him.

Because it felt right, and good, and hers.

Everything about him felt like hers, even this. Maybe especially this.

She felt him nudge the very deepest part of her. They both were still, for a moment. A breath.

He called her that name again. *Koritsi.*

If she could have answered him, if she could have spoken, she would have.

But then he began to move. And once again, it was as

if everything she thought she knew shattered apart, then came back, different. Better.

Because with every stroke, Constance finally understood.

Who he was to her. What she felt for him.

What this was.

Who she was.

None of it was verbal. None of it managed to come out as words.

There was only the way she raised her hips to meet his. There was only this old, deep knowledge within her, soaring up inside her as if her body had always known exactly what to do with this man.

The same way it had known what to do once before, on a primitive level.

This felt a whole lot better. She lost herself in the fire, the slick heat and the growing storm. But this time, all of that thunder and all of that rain, roared in both of them.

He told her to follow him, but she was already there, and together they shook apart.

Again and again, careening out there in the universe, dancing through the stars as if they had been made for this.

As if they had been waiting their whole lives, all that stardust trapped in bone, to make it back out to this place where they could finally be free.

It was hard to come back down.

It was hard to accept that she had to go back into her own body, separate from his.

It felt too much like grief.

But he was there beside her, then turned over onto one side so he could stroke his way down the length of her cheek, then back again.

"Again," Anax murmured. "How can I want you again, already?"

"And somehow it is not soon enough," she whispered back.

His laugh was dark, thrilling.

It was only the beginning.

And by the end of that night, by the time the glorious dawn crept over the city on the other side of the windows, Constance felt more like stardust and less like herself than she ever had before in all her life.

She thought that it made sense now. That they could fly if they liked, just like this. Whenever they pleased.

That it was all going to work out after all.

This marriage. This life. This situation she'd ended up in. She now knew that if left to her own devices, she would have chosen this for herself.

She would choose it, every day. She would have chosen it that night in the church if she'd thought she could. If she'd been able to imagine such choices were available to her.

But when she got herself out of bed to go look for him, to tell him all these magical things that were coursing through her with every beat of her heart…he was gone.

And when that helicopter landed it was there to take her back to the island.

Without him.

Like it had been nothing but that enchanted pumpkin all along.

And it was high time Cinderella got back to her unfancy clothes and lonely life, far out of sight of Prince Charming and his real life here in the city.

CHAPTER NINE

THE FIRST WEEK he stayed away from the island—and her—was torture. He barely slept. He hardly knew himself in meetings. He refused to look at himself in the mirror, for fear of what he might see. He even considered drowning himself in alcohol, something he never did, because surely there he might find oblivion.

He refrained from testing that theory, but detested the fact he'd allowed himself to toy with even the idea of such a descent—to a dark, low place he knew all too well.

By the end of the second week, Anax hated himself thoroughly. But there was no other choice. He had Maria call him on video so he could see Natalia. He pretended that he wasn't desperate for any hint about Natalia's mother. He refused to ask after her.

Though he had never been an overly superstitious man, Anax knew better than to welcome in the ghost that already haunted him nightly. And daily. And every second of every hour in between.

He threw himself into work.

He traveled the world too many times to count.

From one day to the next, standing before this window or that, it was difficult to discern what city he found himself in. One boardroom was very like the next. One set of negotiations led into another, and there was a point at which jet lag and exhaustion became so commonplace that he could almost convince himself that that hollowness within him could be explained by time zones alone.

And not the truth he did not wish to admit that he was running from.

The unpalatable, unacceptable truth that he had betrayed every vow he'd ever made to himself where Constance was concerned.

In this way, he was no better than his own father. Paraskevas had never met a promise he could not break, or a vow he did not rush to splinter into pieces. Paraskevas had laughed it off, his lies and his backtracking and his spontaneous retelling of histories they had all lived through, as if he could convince them it had happened another way.

He found himself doing something alarmingly similar, going over that night in his head again and again and again, trying to make it…something other than it was.

Trying to pardon himself for the unpardonable.

When he slept, it was fitful, and he dreamed of her. Of that night. Of the innocence she'd given him so sweetly, so fully. It never failed to make him hard. It never failed to wake him in the middle of the night, reaching for her the way he had that night—

Only to find an empty hotel pillow here, a cool bed there.

Even when he wasn't asleep, she haunted him.

All those things she had said to him. Going back to the very beginning, when that was the last thing he wished to do, even in the privacy of his own head.

Anax would prefer to pretend that he could not remember that very first night. The hit of all that heat, all that light, all those *people* packed into that tiny little church. And then Constance there, smiling serenely, pregnant with his child and more beautiful—yes, then, how had he convinced himself otherwise?—than he cared to recall.

It was bad enough that she was the mother of his child. That he had married her. That there was no possible way to remove himself from the situation that would not harm his child in some way.

Those things had already been true before the night of the ball. He had already been too fascinated with her.

"Are you fascinated with her?" Vasiliki asked archly after a set of meetings somewhere hot. That was all he retained about the place—the tropical heat. Heat which must have gone to his head for him to admit such a thing to his sister. "Or is it the fact that you've never had the opportunity to spend so much time *clothed* with any other woman? Because I think you know the answer, don't you?"

What Anax knew was that while his fascination with her *clothed* had been bad enough, now he knew what it was like without such considerations.

He knew *exactly* how it could be between them. And that was not better, because unlike every other woman he'd ever touched, he wanted her more, now.

His itch was not scratched. His fascination had increased tenfold.

He would rather die than say such a thing out loud.

"Tell me," he said to his sister, smiling at her in a way that made her eyes narrow. "Are you ever going to put poor Stavros out of his misery?"

She stiffened. "I don't know what you're talking about."

"He would never dare indicate his interest in you, lest it insult you." Anax eyed her, enjoying that the shoe was not on his foot just then. Enjoying it too much, perhaps. "Or maybe it is that you enjoy playing games with him. A little cat and mouse, is that it? Do you know who that reminds me of?"

His sister glared at him, but to his surprise, did not rise to the bait. "I'm nothing like our father, Anax," she said quietly.

Quietly enough that he looked away. Quietly enough that he regretted having said such a thing in the first place.

So quietly that he felt a hot wash of shame move over him.

"What's fascinating to me is that he is your go-to insult," Vasiliki continued in the same tone. "You were ready at a moment's notice to trot him out like a weapon. To bludgeon me with him. Perhaps it is not me who has to be concerned about taking on his characteristics."

It was, of course, no less than his worst fears, spoken aloud.

Because all of these endless nights and all of these weeks later and he could not accept the real truth. He could not run from it. He could not escape it no matter where he went or how many time zones he moved through.

He had forced his sister to lay it bare before him, and it was still the same truth.

No matter how he dressed it up and called it *passion*, he had lost control of Constance. He hadn't hurt her, thank God, but surely it was all the same sort of slippery slope.

He had vowed that he would not touch her.

Then one touch, one kiss, and he had been lost.

She was addictive—or perhaps it was simply that he was an addict. A bright, impossible flame that he had been utterly unable to look away from. Even now, just thinking of her, he could feel the lick of that flame moving over him, changing him.

Making him into the very model of the worst man he'd ever known.

Because Anax knew what was next.

He knew where this ended. The blood, the sobbing. The broken, ruined things in pieces on the floor. The injuries that never quite healed.

The monster looking back at him, ready to pounce.

He remembered his childhood with alarming accuracy.

And so maybe it was inevitable that when he got back to Greece, he did not go to that flat of his that now felt infused with her. As if Constance lurked there, beaming back at him from every shiny surface, as if she claimed the view outside his windows like she was Athens itself.

Nor did he head out to the island, though there was a deep ache in him to see his daughter that was nearly neck and neck with that intense desire to see her mother.

His wife, by his own command and decree, in case he wanted to blame her for that, too.

But there was another need in him when he landed, and this one even more inexplicable.

No matter what it was, or what it meant, he found himself at his mother's all the same.

He had wanted to set Evgenia up in luxury the moment he was able, but she had wanted none of it. She had eventually consented to a small house set there in the village in the foothills where she'd grown up, before her own father had surrendered to a set of bad decisions and moved the family into Athens. Before that had landed her in the kind of place where Paraskevas had seemed like a good idea.

Anax had grown up in the city and considered himself a city person, first and foremost. He understood Athens. It was why he liked his flat, with its bird's-eye view of the whole sweep of the ancient place, from the slums he had called home for so long to the rarefied air he could now afford to breathe.

His mother's little village seemed to get under his skin in ways he could not readily explain as he drove in, and more so than usual. It was not just that it was far away from what he considered the beating heart of things. That was always the case. Today it was something else. Something that moved in him like agitation.

When Anax made it a point of honor to never be *agitated* in his mother's presence.

He climbed out of the car in front of his mother's house and waved his driver off, knowing that his mother found his wealth embarrassing. In case he might tell himself otherwise, she had been sure to say so, more than once. She did not like that much money. And she certainly did not like to see it flashed about outside her cottage, where the neighbors would be sure to comment.

Anax stood outside in the cool sunshine. He did not have to turn to know that his mother's ancient neighbor was peering out her window. He knew that his presence would be shared round the whole village, likely before he said hello to Evgenia—

And that was when he realized that this village was not so different, really, than Constance's Halburg. There were more hills and goats and olive trees than cornfields, but the *feel* of each place was more alike than not.

He could not have said why that comparison seemed to slosh about uneasily inside of him.

And he might not know what he was doing here, but he had not gotten where he was by wasting time questioning his decisions. He strode to the door and knocked, not entirely surprised when there was no answer. He could have let himself in, because he had his own key—and suspected Evgenia did not bother to lock her door anyway—but he knew that there was only one other place his mother was likely to be.

Opting not to test her door to see if his unlocked theory was correct—a thought that would keep Stavros up in the night—he walked through the village, down to the small church at the base of the hill.

Anax had no particular reason to dislike this place, he could admit as he walked. It was lovely, especially basking in the sunlight on this near winter's day. It was colder than Athens, but that was to be expected, as it was at a higher elevation. As he walked, he could admit that it was charming and picturesque.

It was only that his mother loved it and so unreasonably, he thought. That, to his mind, she had shrugged off one foot on her neck for another.

An opinion she had not liked very much when he had shared it.

The church was old, and kept in pristine condition, something that made him tense all over again. Because he knew what he would see, and he did. He walked in the front doors and there was Evgenia Ignatios herself.

Though her bank account was now stuffed full and

every luxury on this planet available to her with a wave of her finger, that was not how she chose to spend her time. It was this. It was here, no matter how baffling it seemed to Anax. Cleaning this church as if it was her own home.

Something she did not have to do any longer either, because he had a service come into the cottage.

So she did it here instead. Every day. As if this was one of the flats they'd lived in when he was young and her actual health and well-being hinged on making the place sparkle.

Anax stayed in the back of the church and watched her as she moved around, concentrating fiercely on her work. It reminded him of when he'd been a boy. No matter what nightmare his father had unleashed upon them the night before, Evgenia would always be up with the dawn, keeping whatever hovel they lived in bright and sparkling.

He did not move from where he was, though he was aware that his mother knew he was there. She made no move toward him. She continued her work and when she was finished, she rose from the floor that she had been scrubbing on her hands and knees. She wrung out the rag she'd used and hung it on the side of her bucket.

Only then did she look at him.

It was quiet. Peaceful, he supposed some might say, though he was not likely to agree.

"What an unexpected visit that brings you not only to the village unannounced, but into the church." His mother sniffed. Her dark eyes seemed to pin him to the pew where he sat. "I can't imagine what could cause such an unprecedented event."

"Can a son not visit his mother on a whim?"

"Many sons do." A gleam in his mother's eyes reminded him a little too much of himself, just then. "But mine does not, as a rule."

She walked toward him, and it had been a long time since he had really looked at her like he did now. Without any preconceptions. To see what others must.

That she was, perhaps unsurprisingly, a beautiful woman. Yet if anything, her vanity moved in the opposite direction of most women's. She wore her dark hair scraped back into a bun, so that if there had been any gray showing it would be obvious. But there was still only the faintest hint at her temples. She wore no makeup, ever. He could recall his father shouting about a bit of lipstick here and there, back in the day, and wanted to wince as he wondered if that was why she preferred to keep herself barefaced now.

But he rather thought that it was a kind of armor.

She refused to hide from her past. She refused to hide in his money. If she was still beautiful, it was a simple gift from nature that she did nothing at all to nurture.

He knew from his sister that many men in the village had attempted to charm her, but she had only ever laughed them off.

I do not think, Vasiliki had said, *that our mother has any desire to ever enter the marital state again.*

Can you blame her? he had always responded. *It is a state of disrepair, at best.*

But now he wondered. "How many ghosts do you think we carry within us, you and me?" he asked Evgenia as she drew near.

She did not seem remotely discomfited by the question, which was an answer in itself.

"Even all your money cannot keep them at bay. Did you think otherwise?"

"Is this what keeps them at bay?" He did not need to wave a hand around the humble little church, or the village around it, full of simple people with simple lives. Or so he had always believed. "Is this what you do to banish them?"

He thought too much of his father when he thought of the influences on him. His drive, his focus, when his father had only ever truly paid attention to his vices. Somehow he always forgot that it was this woman who had survived.

The way she looked at him then, canny and knowing, with that interior core of steel that he knew had built him up from the start, made him wonder why.

But she did not say one of her enigmatic, usually dark little prophecies over him. Instead, she came to a stop in the narrow aisle and looked at him. "You are married."

He did not expect that. Maybe he should have. "I am."

"I do not seek out the papers, but I could not avoid them. They're filled with speculation about this wife of yours. This American. It is rumored you even have a child, though I know this cannot be true. Because I would be a grandparent, and I know that, surely, my own son would inform me if I had become one."

And despite himself, Anax actually felt…ashamed. Like the small boy he could barely remember being, trying to sneak a snack from the kitchen—back before he'd understood that all of them needed to follow the rules for their own safety. That even then, it wasn't all that safe.

"It was a complicated situation," he told her by way of an apology.

His mother nodded sagely. "So it is with ghosts, and marriages."

"You are the expert, I think."

Her mouth curved, though he was not foolish enough to think it a smile. "Your penance is an act of building yourself up so that no one can break you down again. I understand it. Mine is different. You think that I do this—" and she waved at the church "—because I wish to punish myself."

"I assumed," and he was careful as he spoke, "that there was a certain familiarity in the punishment. That perhaps you had grown accustomed to it."

She looked as close to *sad* as he could remember seeing her, at least in as long as they'd been free of Paraskevas. Then she shook her head. "You've got it wrong, *yiós*."

He could not recall the last time she'd called him *son*, either.

Evgenia sighed. "I wish only to humble myself some little bit. To remind myself that were it not for my pride, I might have saved all of us, long ago. When it was my job to do so, and I failed."

Anax stared at her, sure he couldn't possibly have heard her correctly. This was not something they talked about. Not so directly.

She smiled then, a real smile, as if she knew it. "I am an old woman, Anax. And I would like to see my grandchild."

"I am not holding her ransom," he said darkly. "You know where the island is, though you have refused every invitation to visit it. And what do you mean, your pride?"

"I mean exactly that," she replied, seeming to pull herself straighter and taller where she stood. "There was a time when I was the only thing that could soothe your father. And it took me too long to accept that I was not more powerful than his demons. Or his liquor. And in the meantime, I had two children who needed a better situation than the one I gave them. Who is to blame for that? Your father, diminished as he was? Or me, who stayed with him?"

"Him," Anax bit out.

His mother only gazed back at him for a moment. "Perhaps. And then again, perhaps not."

"You have a granddaughter," Anax gritted out, though there was a deep, pounding thing inside him that felt as if he was breaking open from within. "Her name is Natalia. She is…"

And that ache in him threatened to knock him over, though he was already sitting down. He hadn't seen her in weeks. He hated it. She was so young now. She might be someone else entirely by the time he went home to see her—

Anax stopped there because that island wasn't home. He had no home. He had many homes, and he prided himself on that.

His mother was watching him, far too closely for his peace of mind. "She's perfect," he said. "And her mother…"

But he couldn't finish that.

"The thing about ghosts," Evgenia said quietly, much too quietly, "is that they don't always haunt you in the dark of night, Anax. Sometimes they are right in the mirror, staring back at you."

And this was what he had always wanted to avoid.

This conversation.

This moment.

The truth he needed to know, no matter how terrible it was. No matter what it did to him.

No matter what became of him after.

"Am I him?" he asked, in a voice he barely recognized as his own. "Mother, you must tell me the truth, no matter what. Am I the same monster?"

CHAPTER TEN

"WHAT IF I wanted to go home to Iowa for Christmas?"
Constance asked one bright day toward the end of December.

Christmas was only a few days away, something that seemed impossible. The calendar marched on but here on this island it was all blue skies, sunshiny days, and very little hint that the year was ending.

She sometimes wondered if she was slowly going mad.

Though, as an upside to being completely abandoned by the husband she'd made the critical mistake of falling in love with right before he disappeared for weeks, she was coming along with her swimming. So at least that was one way she didn't have to worry about drowning. A person could float in water for ages.

Too bad the same couldn't be said about her strange, sad marriage.

Beside her in the pool Maria looked at her sharply, then away. "That wouldn't be up to me."

"I would ask my husband, of course," Constance said, with studied casualness. "But he is very busy. Very, very busy."

She and Maria looked at each other for a long while, there in the water. And they did not speak of it again while they stayed in the pool, practicing strokes and treading water and other ways to stay afloat.

But later that afternoon, Maria came into the room and informed her that the plane was ready and waiting.

"If Mr. Ignatios has any questions," Maria said mildly, in response to the question Constance did not dare ask, "I'll be happy to answer them for him."

"Wonderful," Constance replied in the same tone.

And that was how she managed to take Natalia back home for what was, technically, her second Christmas. But only her first birthday.

She spent the entirety of the plane ride mounting arguments in her head, though there was no one sitting across from her on the flight. There was only her, grabbing hold of her armrests and refusing to look out the windows for hours, until the plane touched down over the cold fields of home.

And she was happy to be back in Iowa, but she was coming back different. For one thing, it was all so easy. The privileges of Anax's wealth were evident everywhere. The car that met them on the tarmac. The fact that when they arrived at her house, it was warm and bright and welcoming, more than ready for them.

Constance felt guilty that she liked it.

"Mr. Ignatios has many homes," Maria said as they walked in to heat and light, a perfect welcome after a long trip. Maybe the other woman saw the look on Constance's face. Maybe she just knew Constance that well by now. "They are always made ready for his arrival."

Maybe, Constance thought, it was okay to admit that she liked it.

Maybe it was okay that not everything had to be hard.

Besides, it was the twenty-second of December. She

was finally back home in Iowa, no longer stranded on that island, trotted out only for the odd Cinderella moment before being stashed away again. More importantly, Natalia was a happy little toddler. She was still finding her legs, preferring to get around on all fours—but happy to stand if she was holding on to things. And today, she seemed delighted to find herself in a new place.

Or an old place she didn't quite remember.

Constance set out to walk into their little bit of town, prepared to be knocked sideways with all the nostalgia. She felt a bit groggy from the flight and thought a walk would sort her out. And she also expected that she would immediately feel right at home.

But that wasn't what happened. There was no sigh of relief as she and Natalia made their way into the center of Halburg. There was no sweet sense of homecoming.

Instead, she ran into a neighbor who made it clear, and quickly, that she knew exactly who Anax was, now. That everyone in the county did after all those tabloids had made a meal of Constance's appearance at that ball. Cheryl Fox, who had always felt she should have been the nursery school teacher and indicated that she had finally achieved that dream, straight out announced that she thought Constance had cleverly targeted Anax from the start.

As in, from before she'd even gotten pregnant.

"How would I have done that, Cheryl?" Constance asked, keeping one eye on Natalia as she entertained herself with standing up and sitting down at the edge of a bench near the church. "You do know that you're not actually allowed to know who the donors are at the clinic, don't you? It's all private. That's the whole point."

"I knew your grandmother," Cheryl replied, with a

knowing look that Constance immediately took exception to. She tried to check herself, because she'd always found Cheryl a bit of work...but had she always been so *smug*? "I wouldn't put anything past one of you Joneses."

She laughed merrily as if it was all a big joke, though the look in her eye suggested otherwise. And by the time Constance made it all the way into the main part of town, still and unchanged from the way she'd left it a couple of months back, she had similar conversations with three other townsfolk she'd once considered, if not friends, pleasant faces to interact with.

Not today, apparently.

This did not exactly put Constance in the holiday spirit.

She walked around in the cold for a while, but her *actual* friends—who were obviously not expecting her today—were caught up in their usual holiday festivities, or the preparation required for said festivities. She didn't quite feel up to a run-in with Brandt Goss, not if random neighbors on the street were so comfortable casting aspersions at a glance.

Even Natalia was fussing by the time they started home, though not because she felt judged harshly by the citizens of Halburg. It was far more likely that she, too, had gotten used to that Mediterranean weather.

The truth was, Constance thought a bit darkly as she trudged her way down the center of the snowy road, carrying a whiny Natalia, that she had somehow forgotten the truth about Iowa winters in a hurry. Maybe it was different when it was all you knew. Maybe it was different if you hadn't just spent weeks swimming in outdoor pools, bemoaning the beautiful sameness of the lovely weather that allowed for summery clothes by day and fires by night.

Whatever it was, the cold and quickly falling dusk seemed more oppressive to her than she recalled. She was shocked—and more than a little upset—that the Iowa blood in her veins hadn't kept the faith.

And, frankly, she was upset that her nostalgia wasn't kicking in the way she'd thought it would. It wasn't that she didn't love it here. She did. She always would. When she closed her eyes and thought of *home*, it would always be Halburg.

But today it seemed clear to her that the limitations she'd always put up with to live here were choices she'd made. Not facts of life she needed to come to terms with.

That meant she could choose *not* to put up with Cheryl Fox's snide comments. She could choose *not* to engage with Brandt Goss. She could *choose*.

It made her feel liberated, and very sad, all at once.

She made it back to the house, and that was where she felt that deep, inarguable surge of love and loss. That felt like the homecoming she wanted.

But the trouble was, she already knew that her grandparents wouldn't be there when she walked through the door. She'd known for far too long that her parents were never coming back. And now she knew that it was possible to go away and be, if not *happy*, necessarily, *perfectly able* to live a whole different life.

It seemed to make her more nostalgic, in a way, for the life she'd dreamed about when she'd decided to start the IVF process two years ago.

Last December, all she'd wanted was to raise a child the way she'd been raised. But now she understood something critical. She could stay here. She could raise Natalia here, just as she'd planned, and it would be a good life. But it wouldn't be *her* life.

And her daughter wouldn't get the same things out of it that she had.

The real truth was that Constance wasn't that poor, orphaned Jones girl who everyone felt sorry for any longer. She'd stopped being the town's favorite mascot right around the time she'd started showing. It had been obvious once the baby was born.

People had liked the girl they could pity. They weren't at all sure about the single mother she'd become, much less the glamorous Cinderella they'd seen in glossy pictures. That had all been made clear to her today.

Now she was notorious, people would treat her differently because of that. Inevitably, they'd treat Natalia differently, too. In her years here, she had always been loved and cared for by public opinion. She hadn't understood that that pendulum could swing for anyone.

She hadn't understood that there *was* a pendulum.

And besides, she'd been to Athens now. Vasiliki had taken her on a whirlwind tour the day of the ball. She'd seen as many wonders in the city itself as she had in that ballroom. Some faces she knew were renowned the world over. Scraps of intriguing conversations that had nothing to do with crops, yields, or the weather. All the practicalities she knew so well.

She remembered thinking to herself that it was funny how big the world really was. And how easy it was to forget that, living her whole life in a tiny farm town.

It was the kind of thing that now, having seen some of that bigness, she couldn't unknow. It was like the tiny bit of traveling she'd done had unlocked something inside of her.

"The poor thing isn't used to the cold," Constance said as she made it inside the house. She sighed happily as the warmth enveloped her, handing the waiting Maria the baby as she struggled out of her many layers of cold-weather clothes. "Neither am I, apparently."

"You are not Greek," Maria said with a smile. "You have no excuse."

Maria took the baby off, cooing to her as she went. That left Constance standing in the middle of the living room, feeling...harassed by her own expectations.

She sighed out a breath, and wondered what exactly she'd thought would happen if she made it back here the way she'd wanted to do. A parade? The ghosts of all her lost family members, lined up against the far wall?

Constance actually laughed at that image, and that felt better. Then she thought she might as well use Grandma Dorothy's tried and true remedy for a bruised heart, and set off toward the kitchen at the back to rummage around until she found the hot chocolate. Because there was always hot chocolate.

But just as she started to look through the cabinets, the front door burst open with a terrific crash.

Constance jumped, then went to peer out into the hallway, not at all sure what she thought she might see.

Her heart flipped over at once.

Because it was Anax.

And he was looking wild around the eyes and dark straight through.

"Did you truly believe you could run away from me?" he demanded.

"I did not run. I flew. Very sedately." Constance forgot about the hot chocolate and drifted further out of the kitchen.

Up above her, she could hear footsteps on the stairs,

and saw Anax shift his gaze. Then watched that gaze harden. "I will deal with you later," he said to Maria.

"You leave her alone," Constance threw out at once. "You're good at leaving people alone, Anax. If you were so interested in my whereabouts, perhaps you shouldn't have abandoned me on an island in the middle of the sea with no way to leave. It might as well be a prison."

"Yes, such a terrible prison. You are so mistreated."

But she had already had her fill of snide remarks this day. "Why don't we strand you on an island you can't get off of and see how you feel about it?"

She realized belatedly that Maria's footsteps had gone away again. And more, that she had somehow moved halfway down the hall. And he had moved, too, and now there they were, entirely too close.

Dangerously close.

"I don't even understand how you got here so fast," she said, because it was that or hurl herself forward—directly into his chest—because that's where she wanted to be.

It was an outrage she did not entirely understand that she could be mad at him, *because* of him, and still want *him* to make her feel better.

"I was already in Greece." He shook his head as if he didn't know why he was answering her question. Or maybe not, because then he said, "I was already making my way to you."

All the breath in Constance's body seemed to go out of her at once. The night they'd shared seemed to swirl around and around inside of her, the way it always did. She went over it and over it, every last detail. Every last touch.

"You couldn't leave me fast enough," she made herself say, and was happy that her voice did not shake no matter how she felt inside. "Why would that change?"

He reached out and slid his hand to her face, to fit her cheek. "*Koritsi*, if you hear nothing else I say to you today, know this. It had nothing to do with you. The monsters are all mine."

And she had told herself so many stories about how it would go.

Sooner or later, she'd been sure, he would return. Sooner or later, he would have to come back to the island to see his daughter. She had practiced whole speeches in the mirror. Stinging set-downs. Interrogations better suited to crime dramas. She had ripped him into pieces time and time again, but not once had she prepared for *this*.

For Anax in her grandmother's front hall, his hand on her cheek and his gaze on hers like this.

Honest. True.

Constance didn't really think it through. She lifted up her hands and slid them around the sides of his neck, and her mouth was moving before she knew she even meant to speak.

"I missed you," she said quietly.

And then she watched him come undone.

She watched Anax melt, but there was anguish in it, too, and then his mouth was on hers. First sweet, then wild.

Then he was backing her up, kissing her and kissing her again, his mouth drugging and desperate, seeking hers, finding her, and bringing them both home.

And she had no idea how long they carried on like that, wrapped around each other and kissing as if their lives depended on it, before she realized that they'd made it back into the kitchen. She pulled away, took him by the hand, and then led him down the cellar stairs to the finished basement where she'd lived with her parents so long ago.

Down in the basement, there were windows that walked out into the backyard, furniture covered in sheets and shoved back up against walls, but it still felt cozy. Close and warm, this close to the boiler that her father had used to call by a pet name, making up stories about its various noises all winter long.

Constance smiled at the memory as she took her husband by his hands. And she pulled him with her, over to the one sofa that was always left uncovered, because it was the place that she'd liked to come down to to sit and think about her childhood.

Thinking about Anax was better. Because he was here with her. He wasn't just a memory. He was hot and hard and *here*.

And it couldn't have been more different from Athens. There was a wall of windows, sure, but there was snow tugging down the tree branches outside. And the outline of her grandmother's old vegetable garden, a square set apart from the carpet of white.

Constance pushed him back on the couch and straddled him there, then forgot where they were.

Because here, in the space they made between them, nothing else mattered.

She moved over him, took his face in her hands, and kissed him. Then again, deeper and deeper. She angled her head in the way he'd taught her, and it felt like magic.

Like coming home.

This felt the way she'd imagined returning to Iowa would feel. But it was also harder. Deeper.

Richer, somehow.

And the more they kissed, the hotter it got. The deeper, the wilder it seemed to hum in both of them.

His hands streaked beneath her sweatshirt, then palmed her nipples. She rocked herself against his lap, pressing her breasts into his grip. Feeling the hard heat of him between them, and using his arousal to make that wicked, wonderful fire lick all the way through her.

And then it got even wilder.

Anax reached between them, and she was helping, and they both sighed a little when he pulled himself free of his trousers. He made a low, greedy sort of noise when her hands wrapped around him, but he didn't let her play for long. He picked her up, twisted her around, and then came down over her on the sofa.

And then everything was a tangle of maddening sensation, of removing clothes, of kicking off shoes. It felt foolish and unwieldy and impossible to stop or slow or *think*—

Until, at last, he thrust deep inside of her.

Constance shattered instantly. She bit down on his shoulder so that she wouldn't scream and rode it out as that lightning bolt tore through her, ripping her apart and rocking her down to the bones.

Only when she lifted her head and looked at him again did she see the way his eyes glittered. Fierce. Possessive. And something more.

Only then did he move.

Anax rocked them slowly, surely, to the very end of sanity, then back.

He brought her to that edge again, then danced with her there, as if he could dance forever. She wondered if he could, if they would stay like this, wrapped up in each other, reaching, driving each other mad with all this *want*—

But this time, he slammed his mouth over hers as they both tore off the side of the world, and found themselves nothing but stardust once more.

It took a long time for her to come back into her own body. She heard footsteps in the kitchen above and knew it was Maria, preparing some food for Natalia. She knew she should go up and offer to help.

But Anax was stretched out over her, and he was so hot, so warm.

He was *here*.

He had shifted to one side and was propped up on an elbow, playing with her hair. He drew it through his fingers, again and again, looking at her with a softness in his gaze that she had never seen before.

Maybe she was as selfish as she'd always thought she wasn't, not really, but she couldn't bring herself to move.

"Do not worry," Anax told her, his voice almost stern. "I will not leave you alone for so long again."

And it was tempting to simply float off into that. So deeply, wildly tempting. To take it for the kind of promise she wanted him to make to her. To let that be the end of it.

Maybe she would have done just that if he had said such things to her that morning after in Athens.

But she was lying on this couch, literally surrounded by the ghosts of everyone who had ever loved her. And she'd had nothing but time to think.

Here it was, almost Christmas, and while her world had changed unimaginably in the past year, there were some things that still needed changing.

Maybe it was that she'd been thinking about the woman

she'd been when she'd decided to go and get pregnant in the first place. She had wanted a family.

She still wanted a family.

Back then she'd looked around at a life that was perfectly fine and had thought, *Fine isn't good enough. I want more.*

Why should this Christmas be any different?

So she pulled away from him, sitting back so she could look him in the eye. So she could stare back at him just as sternly.

"It's good that we have chemistry," she began.

One of his wicked brows rose. "Chemistry? Is that what you call it? I would consider it more of an atomic explosion, myself."

She didn't fall for that, though she wanted to. "Everything is inside out with us and that's part of the issue. We had a whole baby before the one-night stand. I don't think that's how it's supposed to go."

"Nothing about you is how it is supposed to go, Constance," he murmured, and she couldn't tell if that was a complaint or an endearment. She couldn't tell if she minded either way, and she didn't like that.

She sat up then, reaching for the sweatpants that were inside out on the floor and pulling them on, one leg at a time. Anax did not do the same. He lay there, looking debauched, like some feudal lord reclining on a pile of skulls and furs, not that such an image was at all helpful in her present circumstances.

Constance stood and let her hands find her hips. She looked down at him, and she knew—from somewhere deep inside and from the stars she'd just tasted again— that she would never forgive herself if she didn't take this chance for what it was.

"I want a real marriage, Anax," she told him, matter-of-fact and to the point. She thought he froze at that, but she pushed on. "And what I mean by that is that I don't want to be secluded away somewhere, an afterthought that you can only trot out as it suits you. I don't want to be speculated about in all those tabloids, images of me pored over as if I'm a mystery to solve, if there isn't something real between us. It's not worth it."

She thought he would argue. She braced herself as he sat up, but he didn't speak.

Constance decided to feel emboldened, and pushed on. "I want to live with you. I want to go to sleep with you at night and wake up with you in the morning. I want to raise our daughter, together. I want to give her sisters and brothers. I want to fall in love with you, Anax."

She saw him swallow, hard.

So she stuck that knife in. "If I'm honest, I'm in love with you already. I want you to fall in love with me, too. I think you can. Or you could. I want you to try."

"Constance." Her name on his lips then was barely a whisper.

"I don't want to play games," she told him, and she found that the more she said the things she wanted out loud, the more powerful she felt. The more *sure*. "And I'm not saying that it will be easy, or perfect, or that we won't get it wrong a thousand times. But I want to *try*, Anax. It doesn't matter how we started. I want to try to make it right. To make it work. To make it be…" She tried to indicate the two of them, the space between them, the *entirety* of this thing between them. "I want to make it everything it can be. Because why not?"

She wasn't sure if the drumming sound she heard was her heart or something more like a heart attack.

She wasn't sure she was breathing, or had even taken a breath since she started talking like this.

What Constance did know was that she had no choice here. It was stand up for what she wanted or give it up forever. The choice was that stark.

And now she'd said what needed saying. It was on him now.

She could see he knew it.

Anax took his time standing. Then carefully, almost too deliberately, putting his clothes to rights.

Only then did he look at her and when he did, she had to fight to keep her knees from buckling. Because once again, there was so much anguish in his gaze. So much pain.

All of that mixed in with the fire she could still feel inside of her.

"I don't know how to want those things," he told her, but he sounded…careful. And somehow, that gave her hope. "And I certainly don't know how to give you those things. What worries me, *koritsi*, is that I do not have that within me to give."

And she wanted to melt, right there where she stood. She wanted to rush to him, take him in her arms, and assure him that whatever he could give, whatever scrap of what she'd asked for, it would be all right.

But something wouldn't let her. It was as if her parents and her grandparents had fused together to make her spine like steel.

It was Grandma Dorothy's voice inside her, reminding her that strength only bothered the weak, so what was the point of hiding it?

Or maybe it was that little girl upstairs with Maria. The baby who Constance intended to teach to ask for what she wanted. And not to rest unless she got it.

Then again, maybe it was simply Anax himself. Because she looked at him, and that same knowledge that she'd finally accepted had been with her from the start swamped her all over again.

He was the one. She had been waiting for him her whole life. And she wanted more than this.

"You are Anax Ignatios," she said quietly. "You can figure anything out, and have. As a business proposition, you've done such things a hundred times or more."

"Constance," he began.

But she lifted a hand. "You have until Christmas," she told him, her eyes steady on his. Not an order, but a statement of fact. "Until Natalia's birthday. Figure it out, Anax. We're both counting on you."

CHAPTER ELEVEN

"I DO NOT care for ultimatums," Anax growled at her, down there in that basement that was only half below ground. Right then he felt as if they were stuck in a pit that got deeper by the moment.

Or perhaps he was the only one stuck—and it was quicksand.

Because Constance was changing, right there before his eyes. *She* looked as bright as that smile of hers. As if the sun poured in and lit up only her and near enough to blinding.

She aimed that smile at him, though there was still that challenge in her fascinating gaze. "How fascinating, when you so enjoy delivering ultimatums to others."

The man he usually was would have responded to that at once, and in a manner calculated to end the conversation in his favor, but he…couldn't. It was the quicksand. Or it was her, and the faith she put in him to become… something other than who he was.

He wanted to tell her that was impossible. That he knew who he was and that was trouble—

But Constance did not seem inclined to stand about, watching a man go to war with himself. Her smile never slipped as she turned away and glided back up the stairs toward the rest of the house.

Leaving him there beneath her house in Iowa, of all places. To figure out what his next move should be.

To figure out who he really was, once and for all.

His mother had cast less light on the subject than he might have wished.

Who among us cannot find a monster deep within? she had asked, with an expression as close to sad as he'd seen it in years. She had leaned a bit closer, there in that tiny church. *This is the real trouble. You choose, Anax. We all choose. So if you look in your mirror and see a monster looking back, it is not your father. It is you.*

Thank you for this pep talk, he had replied dryly.

Evgenia had laughed. *I have never been that kind of mother,* she'd said. *But you should know that it is a gift, that the thing you fear most is in you. That you have chosen it, in one way or another. Because what you choose you can change.*

He thought about that now, in this lonely basement with discarded bits of furniture and windows blocked in by drifts of snow. He thought about the particular despair of having choices and all of them bad. Or with unknowable outcomes.

Anax had not taken a leap of faith in a long, long time.

He thought about other things, too. About indulging his temper, his fury at her dictates. About how he could do that and claim it was justified. About storming away from this place, but what would he gain from such a display?

It would not give him more time with his daughter.

And it most certainly would not give him his wife.

Anax stood there in this quicksand of his own making, aware that he was breathing too heavily. That his blood was rushing too hard, too fast, too intensely through his body. And he understood that the truth of the matter was that he wanted the same things that Constance did.

The only difference was, he was the one who needed to provide those things, and he was not certain he could. He was not sure he was *able*.

He wasn't sure that she truly thought they could happen either, those rose-colored dreams of the life they could live together. The difference between them was that Constance chose to hope that the things she wanted were possible.

Anax had somehow lost his ability to do the same.

It was that thought that animated him, washing away all that quicksand.

Because once, when he'd had far less than he did now and no reason at all to believe he could change his life in the slightest, he had *hoped* he could. He had *decided he would*, and thrown himself into it. He had not been afraid of failure—and that was a good thing, because he had failed again and again.

The difference was that younger, hungrier version of Anax had taken each failure as a lesson. As an opportunity to shoot even higher the next time.

Was he prepared to admit to himself that the fortune he'd amassed and the empire he'd built was more important to him than his family?

In what way, he asked himself then, *are you any different from Paraskevas? He used alcohol. You use money.*

After he thought that, in precisely those words, he had to stay there a minute with that thundering, pounding thing going wild in his chest.

His heart, he supposed.

And though it felt like it was breaking, he had the strangest notion that what it was really doing was *working*.

At last.

Because Constance was his family. Natalia was his family. He had always treated his family the way he treated his mother and sister. Close enough to care for, but distant enough to make sure that he could get away with the kind of care that came in the form of financial support and little else.

He had assumed that was how they all wanted it. That the arm's length version of familial harmony suited them all, when it occurred to him only now that it was him. It suited *him*.

Because he thought he could control it. And they'd let him.

Or rather, they'd allowed him to do what he liked and had maneuvered around him. Anax had always considered his mother and sister disrespectful and troublesome, in their different ways, as they each pretended to listen to him and then did as they liked.

It only dawned on him now that perhaps *he* had been the disrespectful troublemaker all this long while.

"I'm sorry," he blurted out to his sister when he called her, still down there at the bottom of Constance's house.

"I beg your pardon? Who is this? What have you done with my brother?"

"I think I have not been the best brother to you," Anax said stiffly, ignoring her incredulous, amused tone. "That has only very recently become clear to me."

Vasiliki was silent for a long, long while. He heard a voice in the background and almost smiled, because he recognized it. But he did not ask after Stavros. She would tell him if she wished.

"Thank you," Vasiliki said to him, after some while. "I think that you have always been the best brother but this is because I, naturally, have always been the very best sister possible."

"That is the truth," Anax agreed.

They quickly turned to business matters, but he thought she sounded as rough-voiced as he did when they ended the call.

And then he stood there in that basement a bit longer, because he did not have the slightest idea how to go about proving that he could be the man that Constance wanted him to be. Over the course of the next two days, if he wished to meet her deadline.

But one thing Anax knew he was good at was the impossible.

He walked up the stairs into the kitchen. He had the strangest sensation that he was catapulting back through time to this same town a year back, when he had opened that door to the church and stepped inside to a place that was warm and bright and filled with emotions he did not understand.

This felt very much the same. Now, as then, he found Constance immediately.

She was at the stove, stirring something in a big pot. Maria was singing to the baby, who sat in a high chair and was making a mess of what he assumed was a dish of pureed carrots, given the shocking orange color. Outside, the snow was beginning to fall again.

No one was cowering about. There was no whispering, no covert glances, no jostling for position—because there was no one in this room playing the part of a ticking time bomb. No one had to creep around, hoping not to cause the next explosion.

This, a voice in him whispered, *is what family is* supposed *to feel like.*

And maybe that was the point of all of this *hope.* All these messy, quicksand-like emotions that served no purpose except to lead him here. To a moment like this, when he could decide who he was.

So in that moment, though he had no idea how to do any of the things Constance wanted from him or even if he *could,* Anax took a leap of faith.

He closed the basement door behind him and he walked into the kitchen. He shrugged out of his jacket that was far too stuffy for the moment at hand. He nodded at Maria, and took the spoon from her that she was using to feed Natalia.

And then he played the role of the father.

Anax had observed the men in this town in all his previous visits, and had often thought it was like visiting a different planet. But he had visited, and he had studied, so he knew how it was meant to go. He'd known a lot less when he'd decided to jump face-first into finance.

That night, he took a page from Constance's book and made certain he had the appropriate costume for the part. A flannel shirt. Jeans and clunky boots. In fabrics he could not recommend, but certainly would not make him stand out—a common complaint in this town, as he knew very well.

When he came down from the room that he had always taken as his when he was here, both Maria and Constance stared at him like he was some kind of apparition, which he chose to interpret as a round of applause.

He pretended he didn't see it, either way. He went to

his daughter instead, whisking her away from the commotion as Maria set about serving dinner to play with her instead. So that when it was time to sit around the table, she was tired enough to allow it.

That night, he crawled into bed next to his wife and pulled her up against his body.

"We are not having sex," she told him fiercely. "It's too confusing."

"Whatever you wish, *koritsi*," he replied, like the angel he was not. And he did not convince her otherwise, as he knew he could. But he also did not leave.

And they slept like that, tangled up together, as if they had never spent a night apart.

That, too, felt like hope.

In the night, he heard Natalia making noise. He went in to soothe her, shooing Maria back to her bed when she came in. And when the baby would not settle, he brought her into the bed he had left, where Constance was stirring.

"Is she all right?" she asked, instantly awake and alarmed.

"We will sleep together," he told her gruffly, and lay the baby down between them, where he and Constance curled around her like they were making her a crib of their own bodies.

And in the morning, they were woken up by a delighted Natalia, who squeaked and crawled all over them and made it clear that as far as she was concerned, this family thing was heaven.

That next day, he trailed along as Constance went and saw her friends. They all greeted him with wide eyes and some suspicion, so he did his best to be charming. He spoke to their husbands. He was halfway through a discussion with one man, the genial Mike, before he realized that the man was discussing a backyard grill with the intensity that Anax himself reserved for high-level corporate negotiations.

He drank mass-produced beer. He made encouraging noises when sports were discussed.

"What exactly do you think you're doing?" Constance asked as they walked back in the cold, with more snow coming down. He watched his daughter try to catch snowflakes with her tongue. Then he looked at his wife.

"I am blending, *koritsi*. Was this not what you wanted?"

"I'm not sure I wanted the one and only Anax Ignatios dressing like a country song," she muttered.

"I will take that as a resounding show of support for this costume, thank you," he said blandly.

The next day was Christmas Eve. He took it upon himself to go out and find the Christmas tree he'd heard Constance tell Maria would be too much trouble. He brought it home and set it up in the living room, so that Constance could play happy carols and bring out boxes of decorations, all of them careworn and handmade.

They made her eyes shine, so he hung them without complaint.

He spent some time in the kitchen that afternoon with Maria, attempting to learn her tricks with dough and pie filling, though his creation was more theoretical than anything else.

Still, he felt a bizarre shock of pride when his wife deemed it delicious.

And that evening, they made their way to the tiny church where he had first laid eyes on Constance a year ago. This time, Anax sat with his daughter in his lap, and his wife sat beside him, no longer the Virgin Mary,

Mother of God. This year the role was played by a young girl with several pillows stuffed beneath her shirt.

And he was not sure he heard a single word of the service.

Because something was building up inside of him, like a terrible song he was not at all sure he could keep within his chest. By the end of the play, he thought it might have leaked into his bones, and he was surprised that he could stand.

When everyone started filing out, he did the best he could to keep up conversation with that strange old shop-keeper and the rest of these villagers who clearly did not know what to make of Constance, Natalia, or him.

Though he also made certain that if they had anything barbed to say, they said it to him—because, as ever, it turned out that most people were far more comfortable saying such things to women.

Maria took Natalia as they started back toward the house, out there beneath that wide-open sky. Anax took Constance's hand as the snow began to fall again, and kept her from going after them.

"It is Christmas Eve," he said.

"I know it is." She frowned at him. "Are you sorry you're here?"

"Constance." He shook his head. "Do you not under-stand? Do you not know how much my time is worth?" When her frown deepened, he growled at himself and pushed on. "There is nothing that I can give you that is more precious to me than my time. And if I'm honest, I expected to hate every second of this. But I was willing to do it for you."

She was fully scowling, then. "That's not really what I was looking for from this experiment, actually."

"If this is what you wish, what you truly want, then we will stay here," he told her rashly. But even as he said it, he realized he meant every word. "I can work from anywhere. If you want to live here, then it will happen. We will raise Natalia in this place, as you were raised. Because if she grows up to be like you, then I must assume that she will be perfect."

Constance looked as though she had started to respond, but then his words penetrated. "Perfect?"

He moved closer, as the snow floated down all around them, a hushed carol all their own.

"A year ago this night, I told myself that the reaction I had to you was simply because I knew you were carrying my child," he said, his voice quieter. But no less intense. "But that is not so. How could it be? Because you are like your name, Constance. You are steady. You are you, no matter what."

"Ask around and you might discover that many folks around here do not consider that a plus," she said.

He only shook his head, watching snowflakes melt against her freckles. "I cannot bear to be without you. It is torture. I will not suffer it again."

And he watched her as she breathed in deep, then let it out, making clouds in the cold night air.

"You don't have to," she whispered. "Anax. You never have to, if you don't want to."

"My chest hurts," he told her, because it did. Because he ached. Because he was wearing a costume but had never felt more like himself. "My heart pounds all the time as if I'm dying, and yet I live. After that night in Athens, I saw my physician, certain that something was wrong with me, but he said I was in perfect health." He let his mouth curve when she looked as if she might argue.

"It's you, Constance. You do this to me. You make me feel—"

But he couldn't seem to form the words to that terrible song that got louder and louder inside him by the moment—

"I think you are in love," she said softly. She took his hand, though it was covered in a glove and she pressed it to her own chest. And somehow Anax was certain that he could feel that same hammering from beneath her ribs, though they were separated by layers of fleece and down. Constance smiled, and it was brighter than any high noon. "Ask me how I know."

He let the song take him, then. He let the melody crash into him. He let it rush all over him and do as it would.

Once again, he leaped out into nothingness, hoping against hope that he'd figure out how to fly on the way down.

"I don't know how to be in love," he told her, with a deep urgency that felt like a part of the song and its own song, too. "I don't know how to feel the things that other people feel. I've always seen them as weaknesses. They were beaten out of me when I was young."

But she didn't take that as the warning it was.

"Says the man who keeps his sister close to him, closer to him than any other person alive." Constance laughed. "And who, according to your sister, visits your mother regularly. I think you do know how to love, Anax. You just don't know what to call it."

"I will call it whatever you want me to call it," he vowed. "I have built empires already, Constance. I will build you whatever you like. You can call it whatever you wish. I will do anything, as long as you're with me."

"Anax," she began.

"Just tell me what you want." And it was possible he was begging. Something he did not think he'd ever done before. Still, the shock of it did not stop him, because nothing could matter more than this. Why shouldn't he beg? "Please, Constance. Only tell me and I'll make it so."

She looked at him for a long moment, out there in such a dark, cold night. There was one streetlight down near the church, and it glowed. There were some twinkling lights on the trims of the buildings, only the twinkling visible through the snow.

But otherwise, it was as if they were the only two people alive in the world.

Anax was sure that he could handle it, if so. Because she was all he needed.

Just Constance, because from Constance came everything else that mattered.

She looked at him, then she smiled, that great, big, beautifully bright smile that made everything all right. It was like hope on earth and joy to all, like the words of the carol the congregation had sung on its way out of the church tonight.

It wound its way into that great song inside him and made it sweeter.

"What I want is simple," she told him, and she swayed closer to him as if she thought the snow might steal her words away. "What I want is for you and me to live happily ever after, Anax. Forever."

He pulled her closer then, and he held her the way he wanted to hold her for the rest of his life. And he smiled down at her, because he knew that given a task, he would not simply complete it. He would ace it.

And he would learn how to sing that song, at the top of his voice, if it killed him.

"Consider it done," Anax vowed.

And then he took his wife by her hand and walked her home.

CHAPTER TWELVE

THEY HAD A proper Christmas morning there in front of the Christmas tree in that house in Iowa, fire blazing and carols playing, and Constance pronounced it perfect.

Anax found he agreed.

They ate cinnamon rolls before the fire. They drank hot chocolate piled high with whipped cream and marshmallows. They watched Natalia play with the wrapping paper and ignore the gifts that Constance had set there beneath the tree.

And later, as Natalia napped, Anax held his wife close before that same fire. She put her head on his shoulder and his heart was still pounding hard, but at least now he knew it was a music they were making together.

"Would you really move here?" she asked softly. "And live here, forever?"

"Absolutely, if that was what you wanted," he said at once, without having to think it through. "I can live anywhere."

She shifted, turning so she could look at him.

"I promise," he told her. "All I need is you, *koritsi*."

"That is the most beautiful thing you've ever said to me," she told him with a smile. "But I don't think I belong here anymore. I wish I did. I expected to always feel at home here. Something changed in me, too, this last year." She blew out a breath. "There's a whole world out there and I know you've seen it. I want to see it, too."

He pulled her into his lap and kissed her thoroughly. "Then I will show it to you," he promised.

And that was what he did.

By Epiphany in January, the Greek Christmas, it was clear to them both that Constance was pregnant again. A test only confirmed what they already knew. So they made the most of it.

They traveled everywhere together for the first six months of her pregnancy. And then, for the last three months, they settled down in Athens so Anax could have his team of physicians see to her every need.

Though she insisted that they find somewhere to stay that was not a soulless set of windows with black and chrome accents.

"I love you," she said, "but that apartment is depressing."

The funny thing was that he agreed. Because he was a different man. She had made him see his life in a completely new way.

And when they went back to Christmas in Iowa that year, they brought their infant son with them.

They kept up the holiday tradition. Constance gave him three more babies, all of them boys. Natalia, as she aged, considered herself much more worldly and superior to her wild pack of baby brothers, though she could occasionally admit she loved them dearly.

On Christmas Eve, she lectured them all extensively on how they should stand quietly in the pew in the church in Halburg. How they should pay attention to the Virgin Mary especially.

"Because," she would tell her brothers loftily, "that was Mommy. And that was me."

Evgenia, though she perhaps never forgave herself for her role as a mother, more than made up for any shortcomings as a grandmother. She doted not only on Anax's children, but on the rough-and-tumble passel of babies that Stavros and Vasiliki produced, too.

They all spent many fine holidays on the island together, where the cousins raced about without a care, the way he and Vasiliki never had.

"Well done, brother," Vasiliki said on one such occasion. "You made us a family, after all."

Anax looked at her, and then at their mother, who was holding the youngest of the brood. He looked at his beautiful wife, who was talking animatedly to Stavros, still dressed as if she didn't have access to the finest wardrobe in all the world.

By now he knew she took a certain pride in that. In *keeping her head on straight*, as she liked to call it.

The ways he loved her astonished him daily. He tried to show her each and every night.

"We have always been a family, Vasiliki," he said then, slinging an arm over his sister as he guided her back inside to all that warmth, all that heat. That great and beautiful song they all sang together, season after season and year after year. "Only now, we can celebrate it."

And that night, that was precisely what he did with his beautiful wife, in their room with the door locked against curious hands, where he took her apart again and again.

She did the same in turn, rendering them both little more than stars out there in the sky.

Shining for each other for all eternity, as if they'd been made to sparkle.

And when they settled back down into flesh and bone, he did it all over again.

"This is it," she sighed into his neck. "The happiest of happy-ever-afters, my love."

"I love you," he said, the way he did so often now, holding her near.

And the real miracle, he knew, was that he meant it. That he had spent these years learning how to say what he loved, how to let his heart lead him, and how to accept love in return.

How to sing out that love at the top of his voice, every day.

And it was all because of her.

"I love you, *koritsi mou*," he told her then, as he built them back up again, and aimed them toward the stars. "And this is the happiest ever after that could ever be, or ever will be."

But he proved it every day for the rest of their lives, just to be sure.

Because Anax Ignatios had empires to run, rivals to decimate with his innate superiority, and whole worlds to claim—but he had only the one Constance.

And she was his everything.

* * * * *

ITALIAN'S CHRISTMAS ACQUISITION

MILLIE ADAMS

MILLS & BOON

To Taylor Swift—
for the music, the inspiration, and the quality time
spent being a fangirl with my daughter.

CHAPTER ONE

CHRISTMAS IN SNOWFLAKE FALLS, WYOMING, was Noelle Holiday's absolute favorite time of year. Not just because she was aptly named for the season—but being the daughter of two Christmas tree farm owners who also had a themed bed-and-breakfast might have contributed to it—but because it was just so…cheery.

The town was resplendent. There were lights strung on every available surface, the historic main street aglow with cheer. It was the calm before the storm for her, and like clockwork, she'd been craving her favorite Christmas drink this morning. So even though a trip to town hadn't been mandatory, it had felt vital.

The tree in the town square was vibrant, with large colored lights and brilliant rainbow ornaments. The tree had of course come from her farm. The one she selected to occupy the center of town was always her very best.

Even though it was early, the streets were bustling as people emerged from their hotels and homes to get caffeine.

Noelle was also on the hunt for caffeine. She dipped into her favorite coffeehouse, a little brick building at the end of the lane, and stepped up to the counter.

"Can I have a gingerbread latte, please?"

"Is it opening day?" her friend Melody asked, smiling from her position behind the counter.

Sweet Melody really did have the best coffee in town, but the fact that it was owned by one of her best friends made it even better.

"Yes," Noelle said. "How did you know?"

"The antlers."

Noelle laughed. She had forgotten that she wasn't wearing a regular headband, rather one designed as part of her reindeer costume. Her brown sweater dress and brown fuzzy tights, along with her brown boots, completed the look. She shook her head, and the bells on the ends of the antler tines jingled. "At least I don't have my light-up nose on yet," she said. "You can't drink a latte easily with a lighted nose on."

"You'll probably attract a lot of attention, too," said Melody.

"I probably already am."

"True."

Her friend turned and began to make her drink, adding flavoring to a brightly colored cup, steaming milk and making a shot. Noelle knew that she was attracting attention, but she also didn't mind. He family had owned the Holiday House bed-and-breakfast and Christmas tree farm for generations. Her name was literally synonymous with the season. Anyway, it probably wasn't even that notable that she was wandering around dressed as a reindeer. If she wasn't a reindeer, then she was an elf, when the farm was open. And this being the day after Thanksgiving, that meant the season was well and truly in full swing.

Many other places in the US had a different kind of consumerism in full swing on days like today, but not

Snowflake Falls. They didn't boast any chain stores, no massive Black Friday sales. Their little Main Street did come alive during the winter ski season. It had become an incredibly trendy place for people to stay, rivaling Jackson as the hotspot for Californians looking for snow. Some of the boutiques of late had become more chic, and there had been a few swathes of land bought with an eye toward making them into luxury resorts.

She tried not to think about that. She tried not to let that distract her.

Her mom was amping to sell the Christmas tree farm, and the B and B. Quite a few parcels of land around them had been sold to Rockmore Inc.

Noelle was opposed. Absolutely and wholly opposed. She didn't want her glorious, Victorian B and B turned into a soulless luxury resort made all of slate and glass. Need money. She didn't need to escape her life.

She didn't like that she had so much conflict with her mom now that her dad was gone.

Noelle's mother liked to remind Noelle that *her* name wasn't in this place. She wasn't a Holiday by blood, but by marriage, and she didn't want to stay in the little town forever. She wanted different things, and now that her husband was gone, she didn't have to keep living in this small town. She didn't have to confine her dreams to this mountaintop.

But Noelle's name *was* in this home, in this land. She wanted it more than anything. At the very least, she wanted the opportunity to buy her mother out. Of course, she didn't just have money. She would need time, a payment plan. She would need her mom to be patient. And to care, even a little bit about what mattered to Noelle.

It was just so frustrating. They had always had a some-what contentious relationship, but with her mom bound and determined to sell the Christmas tree farm and Holi-day House it had only gotten more strained.

Noelle didn't want to leave. She wanted to cling to this life, to all the warm, glowing memories she had here.

Life without her dad, life realizing that her parents' marriage hadn't been perfect, that her childhood wasn't quite so perfect, was just a little less cheerful than the life she'd grown up with. And if she wanted to cling to the past—with its warm glow of nostalgia and beautiful memories, who could blame her?

"You all right?" Melody asked as she handed her the latte.

"I'm fine," Noelle said. She forced a smile.

"No charge. You are officially bringing Christmas cheer to town, and I feel that you should be fairly com-pensated."

"Well, you don't need to do that," said Noelle.

But she would take it. Because she needed every penny that she could scrape up. She needed this year to be good.

That was the difficult thing. She needed the tourism. She realized that feeling grim and broody about advance-ments made in the town was... Ungrateful in a way. She needed people to want to come and stay at Holiday House. She needed an influx of travelers coming for Christmas. People who wanted Christmas trees, who wanted sleigh rides and to go through the elk preserve in wagons, she needed those people.

Because it was how she made money. It was how she continued to pay her employees. She might not be the owner of the B and B, but she managed it, taking a paycheck like everyone else with the rest of the earnings going to her mom.

Christmas was her stock in trade.

And the ski season was her best for obvious reasons.

But none of it mattered if everything she loved got leveled to make a new fancy hotel.

A strip mall.

The very idea. Strip malls in Snowflake Falls. What next?

The end of days.

She walked out of the coffee shop after bidding Melody a farewell, and looked down the festive main street again. And that was when she saw him.

He was taller than anyone else on the street, and he was dressed in black.

It felt like an aggressive block of darkness, right there in the middle of the well-lit street.

People bustled around him, in brightly colored knits, talking and laughing. In groups. He was singular, and there was nothing merry or bright about his expression.

But he was... He was the most beautiful man Noelle had ever seen. His hair was jet-black, as dark as midnight without stars. His eyes were the same sort of coal color, his jaw square, his mouth flat and severe. His shoulders were impossibly broad, and as he moved toward her, she felt her heart leap into her throat. Of course, he didn't see her. She was tucked beneath the awning of the coffeehouse, and she was... Well, she was a reindeer.

A brown blob in the midst of the seasonal glory.

He cut through the people like a blade, his every move efficient. Black jacket, black tie, black gloves, black pants, black shoes. She took in each and every detail as he moved closer and closer. Her heart felt like it would burst when he walked past. He didn't even flicker a glance.

She remained an unseen reindeer, standing there and sipping on her gingerbread latte.

Who *was* he?

She immediately started writing stories about him in her mind—how could she not. The town itself, and the citizens in it were always the same. Tourists were an endless source of fascination, but this man…even more so. Was he a man with a tragic backstory here to find his Christmas spirit. A widower? An investment banker from New York City who'd lost his way and needed a woman filled with the spirit of small-town Christmas to show him the right path?

Ha. Right.

He must be here with a wife, children. He was wearing gloves so she couldn't see whether or not there was a gold band on one of his large hands.

In many ways, he should look like anyone of the innumerable important executives who came to Snowflake Falls to ski, to eat local cuisine like bison Wellington and elk tenderloin. And yet, he didn't. There was something singular about him, and she couldn't put her finger on it.

You think he's hot?

She shimmied. She didn't think it was that. That would be very basic of her. Maybe she was basic.

She frowned into her latte. Then reached up and touched her antlers. She didn't think she was basic.

She cleared her throat and moved away from the entrance to the coffeehouse. She had to get back to Holiday

House. Because the madness would be starting soon. She was manning the Christmas trees today, as that's where all the action would be. She did have new guests arriving, but the staff at the inn would be managing most of that.

Often, the running of the inn was her primary responsibility, as she lived in the house year-round. But when the festivities picked up around the rest of the property, she relied more heavily on her seasonal support staff.

Many of whom had been working at Holiday House for years.

The idea of them not having jobs anymore, the idea of them not being part of her life, it was absolutely unconscionable. Surreal.

She wouldn't let that happen.

"Time to sell Christmas trees," she said to herself as she marched down the street and back to her modest little car. She started to drive out of town, and up the winding, dirt road that led to Holiday House. Fat gray clouds loomed overhead, but they didn't bother her. This was her favorite time of year. When fall turned into winter, when the leaves finally gave their last gasp and fluttered to the ground.

When the ground froze and was covered in snow. She loved the snow.

Of course, with her father gone, it was up to her to keep the road to Holiday House plowed. Her father had bought an old, giant snowplow fifteen years earlier, and had used it to make sure that their guests could always get in and out of their property. Her father had thought of every wonderful little detail needed to make it the most glorious place to be during the cold winter months.

She didn't take the road that led to the B and B, rather

she took the one that forked off and led to the little Christmas tree forest, which also boasted sleigh rides, hot chocolate, spiced cider, roasted chestnuts and various other forms of merriment.

The parking lot was already half full of people arriving from near and far to get their Christmas tree, and to have a festive experience.

She drove behind the parking lot to the employees-only access, and stopped in her small office, which was labeled: the North Pole.

She got out her card reader to help process transactions, and plugged it into her phone. Then she grabbed her light-up red nose and put it on, pressing the button so that it blinked merrily. She began to sing, a cheerful conglomeration of carols as she trundled about.

And that was when she saw a sleek black car winding its way into the parking lot. It was the strangest thing. She didn't have to see who was driving to know. In her gut.

Because the car was exactly like its owner. Sleek and sharp. Unerring. Dangerous.

What a strange thing to think.

She thought that he must be with a wife and children, why else would he be up here? Why else would he be getting a Christmas tree?

But then, he parked the car, and got out.

He was quite alone.

And he turned and began to walk toward her.

Rocco Moretti was not a man to suffer indignity. And this entire snow globe of a town was one indignity after another.

The roads were in a state of utter disrepair and the buildings were in a sorry state. And those sagging monstrosities were festooned from foundation to ridgeline with lights, ornaments and garlands. The entire thing was so sugary, it might as well be a gingerbread man's frosted armpit.

He hated it.

He hated Christmas.

He hated cheer.

He hated this place.

And yet, he had been advised that this was the smartest investment he could make at the moment.

He had already bought up swathes of land, and there was this one holdout. This rickety little Christmas tree farm.

The owner of the property had been communicating with him regularly about her terms, but had made it clear that her daughter had to sign off on the sale, or it couldn't occur.

Such were the terms of the property.

And right there, staring at him, was the tiniest little insult to injury he had ever seen.

A woman. With curly red hair, a blinking red nose, and antlers.

She might have been pretty, were she not ridiculous.

But then, he supposed that went for the entire town.

The glory and natural splendor surrounding it might have been awe-inspiring, but he could not overlook the adornment.

As was the same with the creature regarding him now.

He knew. Instinctively. That she must be the one. Of course she was. The one who was blocking his purchase of the last piece of land he needed in order to make the resort that he was bound and determined to have.

He knew all about the messy terms of wills. And he did not blame the woman desperate to offload this place left behind to her by her late husband.

Just as he had spent years cleaning out the mansion his mother had filled with her madness, he had also spent years trying to untangle the terms of her will.

Never a woman content with life, she had been quite like this whole town. Uselessly adorning each and every space with her influence. Collecting and collecting as if she would suddenly find the magic thing that brought fulfillment. Controlled chaos, she had called it, though he had never seen anything in it but chaos.

She had, though, proven that in her mind there was some form of control involved, by her utterly controlling last will and testament.

He must always keep building. You must always keep adding to the empire. New clutter onto the earth.

Or he must marry. Procreate. Before his thirty-second birthday. Worryingly close now.

A lovely parting gift from his mother, who had wanted to obsessively control everything for all time, and had succeeded in how she'd left the company to him, with a board of her own choosing there to make sure he complied.

But thankfully, he had it in hand. All of it.

He moved across the empty space, and approached the little indignity.

"Hello."

She only stared at him, aptly, as a deer caught in head-lights.

"I am hoping that I might be able to trouble you for a place to stay tonight? This is Holiday House, yes?"

Women found his accent charming. He had learned English quickly. And had decided that it was good enough. Partly because the accent was of use to him.

"Oh, Holiday House is full tonight I'm afraid."

Well. He would solve that problem.

"A shame," he said.

"Do you... Are you with your family?"

"No," he said. "I'm only in town on business. Just myself."

"Oh. Right. Well, I suppose then that you don't need a Christmas tree."

He never needed a Christmas tree. He could think of nothing more vile. A dust catcher, shedding detritus all over the place.

"No thank you. I have no need. I have heard though that Holiday House is very beautiful. Is it all right if I drive up the road to see it?"

"Yeah. Of course."

"Thank you. I shouldn't like to have come so far to not even catch a glimpse of it."

"Where did you hear about it?"

"I'm quite certain it's on a list. Of rustic inns."

"Oh, yes. *Home and Garden, Town & Country* and *Countryside Magazine* all did features on it."

"*Countryside.* That must be it." Did she really think that he read periodicals? Like a geriatric man sitting in a doctor's waiting room?

Her nose blinked as she regarded him. Yes. She really might have been pretty, though it was very hard to say in what she was wearing. The knit brown dress clung to her curves, and her eyes were a russet gold. Her lips were pink and full, but the nose. And the antlers.

"My name is Noelle. Noelle Holiday."

"Nice to meet you," he said.

So this was the woman he needed to charm. The woman he needed to wrangle into signing the papers. He would have to make her an offer she couldn't refuse, and what better way than by charming her.

"And you are?"

"Rocco," he said. "Moretti."

"Well, it was nice to meet you, Mr. Moretti. Why don't you have a complimentary cup of cider?"

She turned away from him and picked up a ladle from a slow cooker, dipping it into steaming liquid and pouring it into a paper cup.

His lip curled involuntarily, and he tried to turn it into a smile. It was wholly unhygienic. And yet, he had no choice but to graciously accept it. Charm. He was aiming for charm.

"Many thanks. I will not keep you."

"Oh. You aren't a bother at all."

A *bother*. Imagine. Someone calling him a bother.

He took the cup, and got into his car, and then he drove down the road, following the signs that would lead him to Holiday House. When he pulled up to it, everything in him recoiled. It was an old Victorian, as gaudy as everything else.

He got out of his car, holding the cup of cider. He poured it out onto the ground, and watched the steam rise from the frozen earth.

Then he crushed the cup in his fist.

He walked toward the front porch, and cast the waste into a bin that was placed there.

He brushed his hands off, and walked into the building. There was a young girl standing there, looking at the guest registry.

"I have a request."

CHAPTER TWO

By the end of the day, Noelle was exhausted, but she was still enervated by her encounter with him. Rocco ready. She was never going to see him again. He didn't need a Christmas tree, and the bed-and-breakfast was full. So, there was no reason that she would ever encounter him again.

Not ever.

Looking at him had been like being struck by lightning.

She had never experienced anything like it.

Of course, she had never experienced a day quite like today, and that was what she should be focusing on. The triumphant, rampant success of her grand opening day.

She hummed as she walked up the steps and into Holiday House.

The staff was already gone for the day, and it was quiet and cozy inside. She peered into the library, half expecting to see one of the guests in there reading or playing checkers. But there was no one there.

She frowned.

She was suddenly feeling exceptionally tired, though, so while she would normally linger to try and see if the guests needed anything, she was feeling like she needed to lie down more than she needed anything else at the moment. So she decided to head straight to bed.

Her little bedroom was in the attic, with a bathroom added, and a kitchen area. So that there were times when she could be contained just to herself even when she had a house full of guests.

That was when she had taken over as innkeeper. When her parents had decided to spend more time away from Holiday House.

Before her dad had died.

That made her chest feel sore. She was already achy, and grumpy, and she didn't want a sore chest on top of it, so she redirected her thoughts. Instead, she went over to her record player, and gingerly selected a Christmas album that her grandmother had left to her. She placed it onto the table, and put the needle on the cherished, antique item. The Andrews Sisters' voices filtered into the room, and she saw to her bedtime routine. She brushed her teeth, washed her face and put on a long cotton nightgown.

In moments like this she could still imagine that she lived in a simpler time. One where both her parents were still with her. Maybe one where her grandma was still here, even. Or perhaps, back in midcentury. When times had been hard, certainly, but Holiday House had been a sanctuary, and no one had been coming to knock it over.

Wyoming would have felt so isolated then. So separate from everything going on in the world. Sometimes, she thought it was a miracle that everything was so connected nowadays. But not now. Right now, she wished that she could cut her little house off from the rest of the world, from the march of time.

She wished. She really did.

She lay down in bed with the record still playing, and slowly drifted off to sleep.

When she woke up, it was with a start. Her alarm hadn't gone off.

She turned and looked at it, and saw that it was blinking there in the darkness. It was still early, thankfully. At least, judging by how dim the light was coming through the window. She got up, and threw the curtains open. Outside there was nothing but white. A whole blanket of it. She was going to have to get up and plow the road.

Because it had been a whole blizzard. Unexpected this early in the year.

"Fiddlesticks," she said.

But then, she thought it was awfully funny that she had just been thinking last night about how nice it would be if she could take Holiday House and separate from the rest of the world right now.

But not right now. Not while she had guests, and employees that needed to get up here so that there could be breakfast and clean rooms, and myriad other things.

She charged out of bed and down the stairs, shoving her feet into her boots in the cloakroom, and grabbing a long coat. Then she shuffled out to the machine shed. She pulled the doors open, and went inside.

The old snowplow was parked, ever ready to fulfill its sacred duty. Clearing the roads so that guests would be able to get in and out. So that her employees would be able to get in and out.

She sighed and got into the driver's seat. And turned the key, always left in the ignition, because why not?

But nothing happened.

That had never happened before. Usually, the machine roared to life, and she was off.

But not this time.

She growled, and tried to turn the key again.

Nothing.

"Start," she commanded, but still, nothing happened. She tried and tried, but the machine was dead.

Great. That meant she was going to have to wait until the city got around to plowing the road up here.

Well, that was a disaster. That could take ages. She wasn't on the general map for plowing.

She huffed, and slid out of the snowplow, trudging back through the snow and up the front porch, back into the house.

She was struck yet again by how quiet it was. And then by the fact that her head felt heavy.

She could not be getting sick. Not on top of everything else. It was the damn season.

She groused into the kitchen, where she decided she better make some coffee. She opted to do it on the stovetop, rather than in the Mr. Coffee, trying to make it feel… Festive, maybe. She could always hunt through the freezer to see if there was anything easy to bake.

She found sugar cookies. Not exactly the boon she was hoping for.

But she set about getting those in, so that there were some pleasant smells that could fill the kitchen when the guests got up.

She was still wearing the oversized boots, and her nightgown, when she heard the first sound of footsteps on the stairs.

She was going to have to apologize. Because normally there would have been a whole breakfast. But it was only her.

And she had spent too long wrestling with a snow-plow.

She walked into the entry room and stopped at the foot of the stairs. She could see a large, masculine hand on the railing, and she knew. The moment she saw those blunt fingers, she knew. Ridiculous, because the only other time she'd seen him he was wearing gloves.

But then he came into view, and there was no question. Rocco Moretti had somehow spent the night in this house last night.

"Good morning."

She looked up at him, her eyes wide. "What are you doing here?"

"I'm a guest in this establishment."

"It was booked," she said.

"Yes. It was. But I decided that I wanted to stay here, so I did."

"How?"

"I made arrangements."

She knew a sudden feeling of trepidation. She was snowed in with this man. Alone.

She was an innkeeper and she'd never thought too terribly much about guests and her safety or anything like that. She probably should have. But she'd grown up here and it had been an entirely safe situation one hundred percent of the time so she'd never worried.

Right now the whole room felt smaller. The whole house, the whole mountain. She looked at him and she shivered and it wasn't quite like fear. It was something she'd never really experienced before. A tension that

filled her lungs and her limbs and made her feel like
she might leap completely out of her skin.

"What arrangements exactly did you make?"

"I asked the girl who works at registration to give me
the contact info for the guests who had booked rooms
for the night."

"She can't do that. There's privacy and—"

"And they were entirely happy to take my alternative offer. Particularly when I told them that there was a
plumbing issue at the bed-and-breakfast."

"And why did you tell them that?"

"Because I wanted to say here. I may have gone over-
board."

"In what sense?"

"Well. I didn't have to buy out every room. But I did."

"I… I don't understand…"

"I offered the guests a refund, and then offered them
free accommodation at my resorts in Jackson."

"Jackson!"

"Yes. They were happy to take the offer. The rooms
are much more expensive than yours."

"How were you able to offer my guests a refund?"

"Well, I didn't give them a refund. I gave them money
from my bank account. So the truth is, you will be paid
twice. By them, and by me. I think you will find that to
be satisfactory."

"I… Are you telling me that you're the only one here?"

"Yes."

"But that's… That's psychotic, you realize that, right?"

"What is psychotic about it? What I wanted was to be
in control of this interaction."

"Why?"

"Because. Do you honestly not know who I am?"

"You said your name was Rocco."

"Yes. I'm Rocco Moretti. From Rockmore Incorporated. I am offering to buy this place."

Her stomach bottomed out. This was the man? Her personal nemesis. The man who was trying to ruin her life, her whole existence. It was probably why he'd stopped her in her tracks when she'd seen him on the street in town. Because she had sensed his innate evil.

"You're even worse than a serial killer," she spat. "You're a *property developer.*"

"I am that. A property developer, that is."

"Why are you… Why are you doing this?"

"Your mother told me that she was having no luck with you. I said that I would come speak to you. Also, I was informed that I needed to involve myself, as this was a very wise investment."

"It's not going to be an investment. Because I'm not going to agree to it."

"Really? You're not going to allow your mother to have this very generous offer of money?"

Rage filled her. Old rage from all the arguments she'd had with her mother about this very topic. She'd held herself back with her mom because she loved her mom. Relationships could be complicated without love being lost. But it was so, so difficult and it had made everything feel hard and anxious and she hated it.

And it was *his fault.*

"It's my dad's legacy," she said. "His family. Holiday House is our namesake. It means more than money."

"Not to your mother. Not at this point."

How dare he? With his whole handsome face, how

dare he? She didn't even reduce her mother's actions to anything that mercenary. He didn't know them. He didn't know how grief had changed her mother and made it so she couldn't stand to be here. He didn't understand at all.

And maybe she didn't either, but at least she had context for her mom. He was just acting like she was a greedy monster. Or maybe she was projecting that because she was desperately trying to not think of her mom that way.

She gritted her teeth and faced him down, and ignored the quickening of her heartbeat—it was just anger anyway. "Don't talk about things you don't understand. She's trying to make a new way of life and that's been a source of tension with us, but you don't know her."

"I don't need to know your mother, or you, to know that eventually you'll come around. People always do. You can continue to struggle here or you can take a payout and go off to live a very happy life."

"No."

"The truth is, Miss Holiday, if you don't agree to this, all the sales fall through, not just yours. You will impact the well-being of your neighbors. Because I cannot build around—" he waved his hand "—this. And many other properties wish to sell. Can you imagine the goodwill that you will extinguish in this town if you ruin this deal for everyone?"

She sputtered, "That's manipulative."

He grinned. "I am quite manipulative. Or so it's been said." He lifted his hand from the railing on the banister, and rubbed his fingers together, as if touching it offended him.

"This place doesn't need a big modern resort," she said.

"Many would disagree with you."

"Well, those people don't have a sense of history."

"History. What do you think you're going to tell me about history. You're an American. Your version of history on this continent is so new compared to my sense of history. I'm an Italian."

"Congrats on your frescoes, I guess. But you downplaying what this means to me is not going to change my mind."

"All right then, if not that, then what about this. I will offer you a very generous compensation package. And, if you do not want to leave here, I will offer you a job. Managing the hotel. Provided that I think you can handle it."

"I don't want to work for you. I work for myself. In my family-owned business. If you can't understand why that's different..."

"I understand." He walked all the way down the steps, and turned around the room, looking around them. "This is... Quaint. But you must admit, the appetite for such a place has never been lower than it is now."

Suddenly, she was seized by the urge to sneeze. She couldn't fight it. She inhaled, and then rocked forward hard, covering her face as best she could.

When she looked up, he had drawn back, his hands touching the collar of his suit jacket. The man was in a suit at six in the morning.

"Are you well?"

"I'm feeling a bit under the weather," she said.

"That is unfortunate."

"Well. The chores will not wait for anyone. I need to figure out how to fix my snowplow."

"If you worked for me, the chores would wait. You would have sick leave."

"Well, I wouldn't today, Mr. Moretti."

"You think not?"

"Yeah. I think not."

"I'm not sure exactly what game you're playing."

"Well, remind me again what game you're playing," she said. "Because I'm curious. What exactly was your name again?"

"I came up here to convince you that this place is not where you want to be."

"Ironic," she said. "Because now you're stuck here."

"Excuse me?"

"I can see that you're the kind of man who is used to getting his way. The kind of man who thinks he's in control of everything. But I regret to inform you, Mr. Moretti, that you don't control the weather."

CHAPTER THREE

ROCCO LOOKED AROUND the space, he felt an increasing sense of discomfort. There were things *everywhere*. The decor could best be described as dust catching. He was not amused. Nor was he impressed. The sooner a place like this was torn to the ground, all the better as far as he was concerned. It was the antithesis to everything that he created in his resorts. He strived for clean lines, for minimalism. Modern luxury, with no nonsense.

This place was entirely nonsense. And now, this... Sneezing creature in the nightgown was telling him that he was stuck here?

Then there was...her.

She was not dressed as a reindeer just now. But her red hair remained untamed, and her face was dotted with freckles. Her sweater was chunky and had a snowflake pattern and she had eyeshadow with glitter. She was maximalist, as a human.

And she was beautiful. Like everything he'd never wanted wrapped into an enticing package that should be as off-limits as it was forbidden.

He was not accustomed to that. The lure of the forbidden. His life was controlled. His space was his own and everything in it had been put there specifically by him.

This place was not his. The weather was not his to control.

And the way he felt about her was like all of these things that were so foreign to him wrapped up in lush, soft-looking skin.

What was this? If they were unresolved issues from his childhood come back to haunt him, he'd happily skip them.

It said a lot about him, perhaps, that he was suddenly afraid his childhood torment had manifested in his adult years as a kink for a woman who seemed to represent *chaos*.

There was a psychological breakthrough.

That which he could not control as a child, he wanted to screw as a man.

He would rather never ponder that again.

"I do not do *stuck*."

"Well, maybe not, but that does seem to be the situation. Stuck."

"What exactly do you mean?"

He went to the front door, and opened it. And saw that outside was nothing but white. It wasn't just that there was snow on the ground, it was falling thick and hard all around them, and the air was misty.

It was a total whiteout. He turned around to face her. "What do you normally do in a situation like this?"

"Normally?" She wrinkled her nose. "Well, normally, I plow my way out. But the problem is that there is no normal right now, because my snowplow won't start."

"Your snowplow won't start?"

"No—" She heaved back again, and wrenched forward with a giant sneeze. "No," she said. "My snowplow won't work. I've never had that happen before, I'm not a mechanic."

"How long do you think this will be?"

"I don't know. This is going to be part of the reality if you are buying property up here. If you really think that this is going to be where your big, sleek luxury resort is."

"I was easily able to lure your guests from here to my place."

"For free," she said. "And when you told them this place was a mess."

"This place is a mess. How long do you suppose it will be until you actually find yourself with some sort of insurmountable plumbing issue."

"I won't. Because it's actually in a better state than that."

A timer went off in the other room.

"Hang on."

She went through the door, and he followed her. There was a kitchen, large and clean, more modern than the rest of the house, updated he thought, to comply with code. So there was that. Not that it mattered in the grand scheme of things, since this place would not remain standing once he purchased this plot of land, but... Good for him now. Because otherwise he would starve.

She leaned down, and opened up the oven, covering her hand with a cloth, and taking out a sheet with cookies on it.

"What is that?"

"It's... Breakfast. Of a variety. I was trying to get something on the table as quickly as possible. Since I was out fiddling with the snowplow for so long."

"Did you make the dough this morning?"

"No," she said.

"I don't eat leftovers."

"You don't… You don't eat leftovers?"

He shook his head. "No."

He wouldn't explain himself to her. He didn't have to do that. That was what he chose to do with his money. He chose to make himself into an island. He chose to craft his surroundings into something that worked for him, and he did not have to explain it.

"I don't know that I have… All that much here."

He went to the fridge and opened it, and took out a carton of eggs.

"This will suffice."

She suddenly looked alarmed, then moved away from him, the tray of cookies and the oven, and sneezed again.

"I do not wish for you to prepare the food anyway. I will make some eggs."

"Do you know how to do that?"

"How hard can it be?"

"You don't know how to cook eggs?"

"I haven't done it before, that doesn't mean that I don't know how."

She sneezed again.

"You are unwell. I do not wish to have you sporing around my food."

She sputtered. "I am not…*sporing.*"

"You are," he said. "Sadly. For both of us."

"What do you want me to do?"

"Out," he said.

She obeyed him but not before grabbing a pot and two cups. But her general obedience was surprising, because she had been nothing but curmudgeonly from the moment they had encountered one another this morning.

She was quite ungrateful for what he was attempting to do.

Most people were happy to take the check. Living in places like this was not easy. There were few rewards for working as hard as people like her were working. There were few rewards for living such a hardscrabble life. In truth, as he expanded his resort empire, resistance was so unusual that he didn't even have an inbuilt method for dealing with dissenters. Usually, all he had to do was make it clear that he was sincere in the money that he was offering, and people took the check, and gave him the land.

This sort of thing was... Unwell. Mentally unstable behavior, in his opinion. People who were so attached to a specific place or thing that they couldn't bear to get rid of it... There was something wrong with them.

He looked around the kitchen, uncertain about where he might find a pan. He opened the drawers until he noticed one under the stovetop, and inside found a skillet. He was resourceful. It galled him to have to look up a recipe for eggs.

Surely it was *eggs*. What else could it entail?

But he did search for a recipe, because if nothing else, he was a perfectionist. And he found there was slightly more to it than he had imagined.

But there was a level of control with food that he required, and at least this would allow him to have that.

He spent longer than he would like to admit looking for a mixing bowl, and a whisk, but then he followed the instructions on the website that he had found on his phone, and set about to the task of scrambling the eggs.

He grimaced as he did so, but before he knew it, he

had a dozen eggs scrambled. He portioned them out so that he had the lion's share, and she had a bit, and then he added a cookie to her plate. Clearly she had been happy enough to eat the cookies.

He walked out of the kitchen, and did not see her. He moved down the hall, both plates in his hands, and finally saw a dining room, where she was sitting at the end of an ornate dining table with a lace tablecloth. Tablecloths made no sense to him. Better to wipe the hard surface of the table than add cloth to the top of it that you would have to launder after.

"Here," he said, putting a plate in front of her.

"Scrambled eggs and a cookie," she said.

"Yes," he said.

"Well, there's coffee in this carafe."

He was reasonably comfortable with that. He liked his coffee black and strong, and this would suffice.

"Why don't you eat leftovers? Are you too fancy?"

"I am not... Fancy."

"Then why? It sounded like an incredibly snobbish and wasteful mindset. Anyway, they weren't leftovers. They were frozen preshaped cookies ready to bake."

"Oh," he said. "That's fine."

"So why don't you eat leftovers?"

"Does it not bother you if you don't know the age of food?"

"I've never thought about it."

"You've clearly never eaten anything past its expiration date, then."

"Um... Well, no. I mean, I've definitely found things in the fridge that shouldn't have been there."

"Occasionally," he pressed.

"Yes, a couple of times."

"Yes. You might feel differently if it were a more frequent occurrence."

And that was all she would get.

"You aren't going to convince me to sell. We are at an impasse."

"Do you really think that's fair? Your mother is desperate for you to make a different choice."

"She's not desperate. She's grieving, and she's not doing it very well. She just wants to make it like he wasn't here. And that's not fair."

"Noelle," he said, her name strange on his lips. "Surely you must realize this is a foolish thing to go up against me."

"There is no against. I won't sell to you. And that's my choice."

"Surely you must have a price."

"Build somewhere else. Why does it matter so much to you that you have this?"

"Because I must keep building," he said. "And this is an excellent way to do that."

"Why do you have to keep building?"

"To expand my business."

"Aren't you like... One of the richest men in the world?"

"You didn't even know who I was when I introduced myself to you yesterday, and now you're talking about my status and wealth?"

"I googled you while you were making eggs."

"All right then. Yes. I am."

"Then why?"

"I must expand the company every year by two percent or it dissolves. Those are the stipulations of my mother's will."

"Really?"

"Yes."

"You just lose ownership of it if you don't…do that. Who's in charge of it?"

"There's a board. Who of course would love it if I lost control, because it would mean that they could have it. And I will not allow a board of my mother's enablers to have their way."

"Do you love the business?"

"Love the business? What does that mean?"

"I love Holiday House. I love it. I can feel the legacy of my family here. Memories of my father. I love this place. It means the world to me. Do you feel that way about Rockmore?"

"No," he said. "I don't."

"Then why does it matter?"

"Because I refuse to lose."

"What would you be losing?"

Why not tell her? This was an aberration and he was forced to exist in it, so why not talk to her? This creature he would never have spoken to as part of his normal life. Why not…indulge?

He did not do chaos or indulgence in his real life, and here he was, steeped in both. The snow making a mockery of the idea he'd ever had power over anything of note. It was perhaps more that his life had not encountered an act of God before now.

"The game. I do not cede control, *cara*."

She wrinkled her nose, and in spite of himself he found it…charming.

Had he ever been charmed before?

"You do not cede control or eat leftovers. So interesting."

She sneezed again. And he fought against his own distaste for anything germ related.

"You must go to bed," he said. "You are unwell."

"I've certainly been *more* well," she said, sounding flat.

"What would you do if you had a place full of guests?"

She looked slightly helpless then. "I don't know." She squinted. "I refuse to thank you."

"I do not require your thanks, though it is something to think about."

"Is there any way that you can... Stop ever?" she asked as she picked up her coffee, as if she was going to take it to bed with her.

"What do you mean?"

"I just mean... Is there any way... Another way that lets you stop the expansion?"

He mulled telling her this truth, as it was...like all things with his mother it was incomprehensible, and he found it humiliating in a strange way. Exposing the ridiculousness of the woman who had birthed him, raised him. But it was also the truth of her, and of his life, so what could be done?

"Yes," he said. "There is."

"What's that?"

"I have to get married. And have a child."

She blinked. "Your mom was kind of controlling."

"You have no idea," he said.

"Well, can you understand that I don't want my mother controlling me?"

"I can. Except this decision controls her also. As long as you have this place, she is tethered to it. It determines what sort of life she can live. My mother is dead. She is controlling me from the grave. Because she can no longer control everything in life."

She walked out of the room, and left him there to contemplate his eggs. He could see that he was in an uphill battle. When a person could not be manipulated with money, he simply had no idea how to proceed.

He wasn't used to being at loose ends. At least, not these days. During his childhood, he had often spent hours alone. Moving about in darkness. Living in tainted luxury where only one space was ever sacred.

His bedroom had been a necessary refuge. One that he had controlled fiercely.

The old manner home had secret passages, and they had allowed him to move through the walls, to access different portions of the house. So that he didn't have to walk down the cluttered hallways. But still, there were no other spaces in the house that his mother had not claimed with her illness.

He didn't like being trapped somewhere. It was too reminiscent of that time in his life. It was too reminiscent of days he would rather forget.

How he loathed it.

It was drafty in this house. And it was old.

Even though the manor home he had grown up in had been much more stately than this, it had still been old. And old equaled chill. Damp. Particularly where he had lived in the Italian Alps.

Many people thought of warmth when they thought of Italy. Not so where he had resided.

He could well remember winters where they had been blanketed in a deluge of snow. He had never liked it. It had increased that feeling of being isolated in the walls of their home.

And so it was now.

But he was concerned about his charge.

She had become his charge, somehow.

He did not fear illness, but he had a preoccupation with cleanliness and the control of said cleanliness, because in his childhood home he'd had no control of his surroundings. Still, it had become a fixation on cleanliness, and this was pushing against his comfort level.

But he would simply wash his hands more often.

There was no one else to care for her.

He had never cared for another person before. He had never had occasion to.

He had spent his life caring for himself. As a child it had often felt like a matter of survival. There had been two elderly household employees who worked for his mother, and they handled meals, such as they were.

As an adult, it felt like a luxury. To be able to care for himself, more or less, without the interference of his mother making it more challenging. Because that was how it had been. Ever and always. If he could find a way to ease things for himself, she would often make it more challenging with her impossible demands and needs. She wanted control. Over everything. Including him. When he had stopped being malleable, when he had stopped being a child, she had found all that much more difficult.

He decided that the best way forward would be to build the fire. So, he was going to take charge. And that was how it would be.

CHAPTER FOUR

HER HEAD WAS POUNDING. Or perhaps it was just a pounding happening outside. It was difficult to say. She sat up, feeling groggy, and wondered if she had fallen asleep, or if she had just drifted out of consciousness for a moment.

She looked at the clock. Only twenty minutes had passed since she had come upstairs. It was possible that she had dozed. She felt terrible. She rolled out of bed, and went over to the window, and what she saw outside made her brows rise.

He was out there. Chopping wood.

In a suit.

Without thinking, she opened up the window. "What are you doing?" She looked down at the man himself, knee-deep in the snow wearing clothing that probably cost more than she had ever seen in her life.

"Go back to bed," he said, looking up at her ferociously.

"Are you practicing to cut me into tiny pieces and take the house from me, or…?"

"I am not practicing the fine art of dismemberment. I am cutting firewood. That I might warm the library, seeing as you have a chill."

"Oh," she said. "Why that is very kind of you. Suspiciously so."

"I hate to be suspicious."

"Somehow, I don't think that you do."

"I promise, I do not wish to murder you."

"Well, *very* reassuring." But then she felt not so great, so as amazing as the sight below was, she ended up making her way back to her bed.

She must have dozed again, because when she opened her eyes, the door to the bedroom was open, and it had grown darker outside. "Here," said a very masculine voice.

She looked over. He was standing there holding a tray with a steaming bowl and a steaming mug.

"What is it?"

"I opened a can of soup. And I made tea."

"Oh. Well, that's very nice of you."

Still suspicious.

"Yes. It was." He sounded pleased with himself, if a bit surprised.

She looked around. "I don't want to be ungrateful, but I find that I don't really relish the idea of trying to eat soup in bed."

"I have built a fire," he said.

"Excellent," she said. "Maybe I'll eat down in the library. It's only a cold."

She sneezed.

"Yes. Let us… I will carry the food. If you sneeze whilst carrying the tray it is likely to cause a small disaster."

"I am nothing if not a small disaster." She got out of bed, clutching a tissue in her hand, and followed him out of the room.

"Are you?" he asked.

"Am I what?"

"A small disaster."

He was asking about her now? What strange dimension had she fallen into. He was cutting wood and caring for her and acting like...he cared about getting to know her, which couldn't be true.

She looked at his face—dear God he was handsome—and she tried to get a handle on what he was thinking. What he felt about anything.

He was a mystery, and she didn't think it was only because she had limited experience with men. He was... something else.

No leftovers. No experience making soup.

So cold in so many ways and yet...he'd taken care of her, so he wasn't entirely cold.

"It feels like it. Because how else have I found myself in this position? Snowed in on a mountaintop with a nonworking snowplow and a very large stranger who clearly wishes to be rid of me."

"Did I *say* that I wish to be rid of you?"

"You're trying to buy me out." She felt it prudent to point out—to him and to herself—that even though he'd been kind to her while she was sick he was still trying to fundamentally upend her way of life.

"That has nothing to do with my desires for you either way."

She felt a little bit warm suddenly. That was an odd collection of words for him to use in regard to her. Definitely a collection of words no man had ever used in her presence.

"Well, I'm only me. For all that it's worth."

"And you want to stay here. I can't say that I fully understand."

She led the way toward the library, but stopped at the entrance to the kitchen. She looked inside. It looked like… A disaster had occurred.

Not a small one.

"What happened in here?"

"I won't leave it," he said.

"You opened a can of soup and made tea?" It looked like he'd performed surgery.

Every cabinet was opened, and there was water all over the place. The microwave was open, and she could see a noodle hanging down from the top of it.

"I have never made soup before."

"You opened a can and warmed it up. That's technically not making soup. Not trying to be unkind."

He scowled. "I am not accustomed to doing such tasks."

"I bet you never cut wood either. But you didn't cut your hand off. So there's that. Have you ever boiled water before?" she asked him.

"Of course not," he said. "What occasion would I have had to boil water?"

"I don't know. We don't actually know each other. We're just stuck here, on a mountaintop. Because that's the way things are." She looked around. "Would you like a hand cleaning up?"

"Of course not. You're unwell. I want you to go sit and eat your soup. I will clean."

"I bet you don't know how to clean either."

His expression went thunderous. "I know how to clean."

She went into the library, and sat in a large chair, propping her feet up on a tufted ottoman. He handed her the tray with her soup and tea. It really was a nice gesture, all things considered. What a strange man he was. Not that she had any experience of men to compare him to anybody else. Not that she had any experience with men. She loved her hometown, but the men here were boring. She'd known them for too long, and when you'd known a man when he was thirteen there was little to make him interesting in his twenties.

And the good-looking, exciting men that came to town were either with their wives or husbands. That was just how it went. And there was a parade of very handsome men. Wealthy, sophisticated. Completely out of reach.

He was the first eligible man she had met around here. If you could call a towering inferno of rock, rage and capitalism *eligible*.

Actually, she didn't even know if the eligible bit was true. Maybe he was engaged to the woman who would free him from his life of eternal expansion. Though she couldn't actually get a read on if he wanted that or not.

He definitely didn't seem to like being under the control of anyone or anything, but she had no idea what he thought about that versus finding a wife. She had no real idea what he thought about anything.

Though she was unhappy to admit he was clearly more complex than she'd initially thought. When she'd told him he was worse than a serial killer.

He wasn't, obviously. Since, in fairness, a serial killer wouldn't have nursed her back to health.

She picked up a saltine cracker and ducked it into her chicken soup.

She heard a great commotion going on in the next room, and she ignored it deliberately as she chewed on the corner of the cracker.

He reappeared about twenty-five minutes later.

"Are you well?" he asked.

"I'm fine. Are you engaged?"

He looked stunned by the question. "No," he said.

"Just wondering. I didn't think you were."

"I'm not certain how to take that."

"Oh, at face value, I would suggest. There was no hidden meaning. I was only curious. Plus you know you mentioned that whole thing about your mother, and marriage and a child. I thought maybe you'd taken steps toward that. I thought it was funny, because you're the first eligible bachelor that I've ever met in this town—" She swallowed some of her tea, and her throat felt wretched. Then, she felt embarrassed, because she shouldn't have exposed herself in quite that way.

"I am not engaged. *Eligible* is another question."

She laughed. "That's funny, because I was thinking the same thing."

"Have you got a husband?"

"If you talked to my mother then you already know that I don't. And you already know that some of her objection to me staying in this place is that I'm not going to meet anybody." She frowned. "One of the worst things about my mother wanting to get out of here so quickly is that it makes me feel like she never actually loved our lives. That she never actually loved my father in quite the way that I thought she did."

He only stared at her. There was no kinship there. No understanding.

"Well, wouldn't you feel that way if you found out that your mother was desperate to escape the life that she had lived with your father?"

"I never knew my father."

"Oh. I'm sorry."

"It's fine. It means nothing to me."

"So you were raised just by your mother?"

"Yes."

"In Italy?"

"Yes. In Italy."

"Really only two people here. We might as well make small talk."

It was just a polite thing to do. And yes, sometimes the out-of-towners, the people who came from cities, they resisted it. They didn't really understand what the point of it was, or what she was doing in trying to engage them, but she was insistent on giving her guests the small-town experience. Plus she just liked meeting new people and hearing about their lives.

She loved her life.

But it was the only one she'd lived. Obviously. But she'd just never…gone away to college or lived in another state or tried life in a city or anything. So a window into how someone else lived always fascinated her.

"I was raised here," she said. "Obviously. This place has been in my father's family for generations. It means the world to me. My grandmother lived here as the innkeeper until she passed away, when I was fifteen. Then for a couple of years we had somebody else live here as a caretaker, and when I turned eighteen, I took the job."

"And your parents lived where?"

"Oh, in town. We worked up here, but we lived closer

to things. My mother already sold that house. To pay for her new condo in Florida. She likes it better where the sun shines all the time. But I don't."

"Have you ever lived where the sun shone all the time?"

"No."

"Then how do you know you will not like it?"

"Did you think that you would like making soup?" she asked.

"No."

"Sometimes you just know things."

They were silent for a moment. She wanted to push him. Press for more information, but she also didn't want to cause drama.

"So," she said. "You're from Italy."

"Yes," he said slowly, as if answering questions was a particularly strange thing for him. "From the Italian Alps. My mother is from a very old, very wealthy family, and she had more money than sense. She got herself pregnant when she was older. And decided to never reveal to anyone the identity of her baby's father. That was me."

"Oh. But she... She was very wealthy." Which she imagined didn't fix everything, but it had to fix a lot of things.

"My great-great-grandfather was a count, and also a real estate developer. The company had passed through two generations of our family before going to my mother. She did quite well in aspects of the job. Though, in the end, she receded from public life, and did most of her business online. Far before it was trendy for people to work remotely."

"Oh."

"There," he said, his tone definitive. "That is my story."

"That's *not* your story. That's a biography of your company, mostly. Why did she end up leaving you instructions like she did in her will? Why did you end up in that position?"

"She was eccentric," he said.

That only piqued her curiosity further. Because eccentric was not a word she would ever use to describe him. So how had he come to be? And what had she been like really?

"It sounds like it."

"At the end of her life she did not leave the house at all. We were very isolated. She liked to control everything." He stood there in the doorway, something reticent about his stance. "If I were a psychologist I would suggest that something traumatic happened to her. But I do not know."

"Oh."

Well. That wasn't fun eccentric.

He hesitated before speaking. "We were quite cut off from the rest of the world for the past decade of her life. It made things difficult. But she always wanted to maintain the level of control that she had in her home. And she wanted to make sure that she controlled me after she died. Hence the will."

"I see." She felt she had to stop saying *oh*. But she didn't really know what else to say to this…list of facts.

She could sense that he had compassion for his mother, but there was also anger. A lot of anger. She couldn't really blame him. She was frustrated that her mom was trying to control her life. That she was trying to take this from her. She could imagine that he didn't feel any better about it.

"Did you have staff?"

"Two members of staff. That had been with my mother for all of her life. They were elderly."

"So that's why you don't know how to make food."

"Yes."

"But you clean."

"I'm a man who has lived on my own for any number of years. And while I am happy to order food, I like to keep my surroundings in a certain level of order."

"You don't have a cleaning staff."

"I do. But you cannot have your home too clean."

He looked around the cluttered library, his expression one of pure disdain.

"I take it you don't like shelves packed full of books? And figurines and doilies?"

"No," he said.

"I do. It's history. Knowledge. A lot of this was collected over the years by my family. It's important to us. It's part of our story."

"I will never feel that way about dust catchers, I'm afraid. They do not appeal to me."

"Sorry," she said. "That's a little bit intense."

"I'm a little bit intense."

She laughed. "What are you going to eat?"

"I made myself a bowl of soup. I ate it before I delivered yours."

"Well, when I noticed the mess you really should have given yourself that credit. You made two bowls of soup. That's why it was such a disaster."

He didn't even seem on the verge of cracking a smile.

What a tough customer. He was gorgeous. Truly, the most incredible man she had ever seen in person, but he would be impossible to try to deal with on a daily basis. Or at all. Ever. She didn't know how anyone dealt with him. Maybe nobody really did. Maybe that was the perk of being a billionaire. Nobody really ever contended with you. They just sort of let you exist around them.

"I'm attached to this place," she said. "I love it."

"I consider that adjacent to mental illness," he said.

She gaped at him. "I'm sorry, what? People love their familial homes. You yourself were just talking about the fact that you descended from a long line of important people, you had a familial home, and a business. How is what I feel for this bed-and-breakfast different than that?"

"It simply is," he said.

"But that doesn't make any sense."

"It can cross a line, into foolishness. When you are so attached to a place that you begin to hurt yourself in the pursuit of hanging onto it, when you love things so much that you would choose them over the people in your life, then yes, I do believe it is adjacent to mental illness. And I will not apologize for that."

"You should. It's offensive."

"I don't care if I'm offensive."

She felt heat beneath his words, he was personally upset about this. Personally inflamed by it.

"You think that me refusing to sell this place because my mother wants the money is me choosing a place over my family."

"Yes," he said.

"It isn't. I would pay her for it. I would buy it from

her. But I either have to be able to get financing, or I have to be able to make payments to her. I need time. Also, I can't give her the exorbitant sum that you are. But isn't there a point where wanting more money is simply greed?"

"Isn't there a point where wanting stuff is simply accumulation?"

"I don't understand the difference in the two things."

"Money can afford you the opportunity to live somewhere with a view that you like. You can live in a sleek, clean surrounding, and money allows you to do that comfortably. With good food. Without the worry of scarcity."

"My mother is hardly living in scarcity. If that's what she told you, then it is a gross exaggeration. What she wants is to be done living what I consider to be a modest life. But I'm not done with it. I love it."

"Things are not inherently valuable. They have only the sentiment that you attached to them. You can simply carry a memory in your heart."

"Haven't you ever heard that home is where your heart is?"

"I have never had that experience."

There was something there that he wasn't sharing. And she wasn't sure that she needed him to. Nor was she sure she even wanted to hear about it. There was no point getting to know this man. Who was in opposition to her in every way. Who was insulting. Who was a threat to her way of life.

"Thank you for the soup," she said. "And the crackers. But I'm tired and I'm going to go to bed."

"All right then," he said.

She stood up, and brushed past him, and as she did,

she stumbled slightly, he grabbed her arm, and steadied her, and she found herself looking up, way up, into the fathomless depths of his black eyes.

Her throat froze, going tight. Her heart slammed itself against her breastbone like it was attempting a jailbreak. He smelled… Well, she could hardly smell, but from what she could tell he smelled of wood smoke and skin. She had never been close enough to smell someone else's skin.

"Oh," she said. "I think I'm delirious."

She practically windmilled away from him, and carried on up the stairs. And then she lay down on the bed, her hand pressed to her heart.

That was insanity. And she was not going to indulge it.

CHAPTER FIVE

THE SNOW DID not let up. The next day, it had piled up even higher than it had the day before. She called the local department of transportation and was told they couldn't plow up her way yet, as long as it wasn't a safety issue.

"No, we're just fine," she sighed, hanging up the phone.

But the good news was, her cold was much, much better. The bad news? Was when she heard Rocco sneeze.

"Oh, *no*," she said.

"I'm fine," he growled, his voice much rougher than it had been the day before.

"No, you aren't," she said.

She didn't need to know him well to know in advance he would be the worst patient imaginable.

"I never get sick," he said. "I am fastidious about germs."

She pinched the bridge of her nose. "As you pointed out yesterday, I was *sporing* in your vicinity."

"You can't get sick that quickly, can you?"

"I don't know," she said. "I'm not an expert in anything. Except maybe home remedies."

"We need a home remedy for your snowplow. So that we can get out of here."

Great. His response to this illness she very obviously had no control over was going to be him being growly at her.

How nice for her.

"Well, I am more likely to be able to help your cold than I am to deal with the carburetor or the starter or whatever is happening with that thing."

"*You* did this to me," he said.

She threw her hands into the air. "You just said that you don't get sick that quickly, or ever."

"Well, now I'm convinced *it was you.*"

She huffed. "Maybe it was somebody you encountered on your travels."

"I travel in a private plane."

"I don't know. Maybe it was your driver."

He looked stormy, and she went to get a cup of coffee from the kitchen.

"*You* seem well," he said.

And he seemed petulant, but she did not say that.

"I am," she agreed. "Which is good news for you. Because that means that you're probably going to be just fine in not very long."

"I should hope so. Also, I sincerely doubt that this is going to diminish me in any way."

"Oh. Do you?"

"I have business to attend to, I don't have time to be ill."

Of course, of course he had been working the whole time he was here.

"You know, sometimes getting sick is your body's way of telling you to rest."

"That is the stupidest thing I have ever heard." He was

thunderous, and he was ridiculous, and still handsome and she had no idea what she was supposed to do with this—the feeling inside her—or him.

Though one thing she was sure of was that no matter how handsome he was, he was annoying.

"Sorry. I'll try to talk to myself next time. I'm sure that I can come up with something even better."

"Why are you so relentless?"

"Am I relentless?" He looked infuriated. He looked ill.

"Go sit in the library. I'll start a fire, and then I'll bring you something to eat."

He felt terrible. He was quite certain that he felt much worse than she had, his whole body beginning to shake as hot and cold flashes racked him.

This was absurd. He couldn't remember the last time he was sick. Well. He could. But he deliberately pushed the memory aside.

Because he didn't want to think about being alone in his bedroom. He didn't want to think about going into the kitchen to try and find someone to get him some food. He didn't want to think about climbing over endless stacks of garbage and expired products...

So he didn't.

Except his head was swimming, and whenever he closed his eyes he saw his childhood bedroom. And then the rest of the house.

He stood, enraged when the floor dared tilt beneath his feet.

"What are you doing?" Noelle asked, sticking her head into the room.

"I'm going to lie down for a moment."

"You seem… You seem feverish."

She crossed the room, and before he could pivot away from her, she pressed her hand to his forehead. "You're burning up. You need to go lie down."

"I just said that I was on my way to go lie down," he growled. He could still feel where her hand had touched his face, cool and comforting. Softer than he would've expected.

Earlier, when he had grabbed her arm to steady her when she had lost her balance, he had felt a bolt of sensation, one that he was intent on denying now.

He did not engage in indiscriminate physical affairs. He certainly wasn't going to engage in one in this house. In this state. But this creature. He tried to picture her with the antlers, but he was unsuccessful. All he could see was her freshly scrubbed face, her sweet smile, her freckles.

"I'll help you," she said.

"I don't need help," he said.

"I think you do," she said, beginning to propel him from the room and up the stairs.

"You're tiny," he said as she grabbed hold of his arm and tried to move him.

"I'm not that tiny," she said, sniffing angrily.

And right then, he felt like he had been hit in the side of the head. Not from illness, from something else entirely.

This chaos, and she was chaos. This tornado of desire that was wholly and entirely connected to her.

"You are," he said.

"I think you're ridiculous."

She shifted, bringing herself beneath his arm, and that

was when he felt like he had been shot clean through with an arrow.

It was like the illness itself had stripped away something. Himself, maybe, because all he could see was how beautiful she was. It didn't matter that the first time he had seen her she had been dressed like a reindeer. And it didn't matter that her house was ridiculous, or that she was a barrier to getting what he wanted, which normally made someone his enemy and nothing more.

Suddenly, she was a beautiful enigma.

"I think my fever might be dangerously high," he said.

"Well, that's concerning. But I can take your temperature."

He narrowed his eyes. "How?"

She started laughing. "Oh, don't worry about that. There's no reason to get that medical. I'll just put it under your tongue." She guided him to the room that he was staying in. And then she disappeared.

He was suddenly overly warm, and he stripped his shirt off, then went to the closet where he had deposited his belongings earlier, and took out a pair of sweatpants. He put them on, then lay down on the top of the bed. This illness had come on like a freight train. And entirely without his permission. He was incensed. As he did not allow for things like this. And yet. Nothing was going the way that he wanted it to.

You cannot control the weather.

Hell and damn. He had controlled plenty enough for a good while now. Why was everything suddenly out of his hands?

"Oh!"

She sounded immediately like a heroine from an old

movie, offended and horrified all at once, when she stepped into the room and saw him lying there on the bed, bare-chested.

"I thought that I would get comfortable," he said.

"Of course," she said.

Then she seemed to avert her gaze as she came to the bed with a thermometer in hand. She knelt down beside him. "Open your mouth."

She slipped the thermometer inside, and he knew a sense of warmth and care like he had never known before.

He'd been sick as a child, of course. But there had been no hand on his forehead. There had been no concerned figure by his bedside. Maybe there would have been if he hadn't shut them all out. If he hadn't put so much distance between himself and his mother even then.

There was no way to know.

And he could not ask her now.

She put her hand on his forehead again. And he was… Undone. "You are very warm," she said. "I wasn't this feverish. I'm concerned that you have something worse."

"It wouldn't dare," he said.

"The virus?"

"Yes," he said.

"You are formidable, but I don't think you're that formidable. Sorry."

"All tremble in my wake."

Even he knew he was being ridiculous at this point.

"I am very sorry that you have been so sorely offended," she said. "But you have to stop talking, because you're ruining the temperature."

He stopped. It was an old-fashioned thermometer.

Glass. And it took minutes for it to get his temperature. He almost thought she was using it on purpose. To keep him quiet. But he didn't mind, because there was something somewhat comforting about having her there, kneeling beside him, holding the thermometer.

"Yes. You are quite feverish," she said. "It's over one hundred. That is concerning."

"Now what are you doing?"

"I'm going to get you some medicine. I'm going to get you soup."

"What if I don't want to eat it in bed?"

"I'm going to ask that you eat in bed," she said. "Because I don't want to have to maneuver you up and down the stairs every time. You can eat at the writing desk if you like. Otherwise, I'll bring you a little bed tray to prop your food up on."

She fluttered out of the room, and when she returned a little while later, she was fully supplied with anything he might need.

He took the medicine, and began to eat, but he felt like his thoughts were only becoming less and less clear. His throat hurt, his body beginning to ache fiercely. He soon fell asleep, but he was very aware that cool cloths were continually changed on his face.

He woke up when the sun was setting.

"How are you?"

"I've been better," he said.

"Well, I'm going to keep watch. Because… Well. I'm worried about you. I've been checking on you every twenty minutes or so, which is maybe silly but… I don't know. You just seem very unwell."

Had anyone ever worried about him before? It scraped

him raw, and he forgot why he ever held anything back. He forgot why he had fashioned himself into a fortress, because it was all too easy to forget the life he'd built in these past twenty years.

It was easy, right now, for him to believe there had only been his childhood, and this moment. Like all the space in between had evaporated. Been swallowed whole by his illness.

"I have never been cared for when I was sick. That's one reason I decided to stop being ill. It's very inconvenient when you still have to do everything for yourself."

He was only half aware of what he was saying.

"What do you mean no one ever took care of you?"

"Just that. But then, I didn't allow anyone in my room."

"When you were a child?"

"I had to make a boundary. I had to lock her out. And I could never go out the door. I had to use the walls." He'd maybe been…seven when he'd discovered that trick. He'd felt very big then, but now in his memory the boy was so, so small.

"I think you're delirious."

Maybe. But he could remember it so well. He described it to her. "One of the bookcases turned. I kept it empty. I didn't like all those books sitting there and collecting dust anyway. I always kept the door locked. And I don't think she ever knew about the passages. If she had known about them she would've filled them up. They were my secret. And they helped me get around the house."

"You locked your mother out of your room?"

"Everyone. *Everyone*. But then, she didn't take care

of me when I was sick. No one ever has. Who took care of you?"

He wanted to imagine her life. Not his. Not that little boy.

"Oh. Everyone. My grandmother. My mother. Even my dad."

"What was that like?"

Suddenly he wanted to know. He wanted to know what it was like if the people around you were... If they were normal. If they could care in a way that was normal. He just was very desperate to know.

"Well," she said. "They used to make me tea and soup. Wipe my brow, like I've been doing for you. Keep me cool. They'd rub menthol on my chest."

He looked at her, and then down at her delicate hands. And suddenly, his feelings were much less that of a child longing to be cared for. He didn't wish her to touch him in an abstract, caring way. He wanted those hands on him in a different way.

"Are you going to rub my chest?"

Her cheeks turned pink. He supposed it was very bad form to say something like that when she was trying so hard to take care of him. But he found he couldn't help himself.

"I think you can rub your own chest," she said.

"But it sounds nicer to think of you doing it," he said.

"Are you trying to flirt with me?"

He chuckled. For some reason that was funny.

"I don't flirt."

"No?"

"No. If I want a woman I simply tell her. And then I have her."

"I see. Do they need to want you to?"

"They always do."

She moved away from him then. He wished that she hadn't.

"I'm going to come and check on you again soon. I'll just…get more water. And get more cool cloths. Hot water and cold water. Everything."

And then, when she left, he found himself drifting out of consciousness again. And dreaming of her hands.

CHAPTER SIX

SHE COULDN'T BREATHE. Being in the room with him when he didn't have a shirt on like that was… It was terrible. Because he was half-delirious, it was obvious. The stories that he had been telling about his childhood didn't make any sense. She had tried to figure out what the truth of that could possibly be, what the whole truth could be from the little bits and pieces that he had tried to tell her.

There was something in his words that was just so tortured. Whether everything he'd said was true or not, she didn't know, but it made her chest hurt.

He was just so… He was so gorgeous and masculine and feral, and she had never seen anything like him. He was like an old-fashioned movie star. Broad-chested and muscular, dark hair sprinkled over golden skin. She had wanted to rub his chest. That was just a mess. She couldn't be lusting after a man who was half out of his mind.

A man she didn't even like. Yes, it was nice that he had taken care of her while she was ill, and now he was ill probably because of her, no matter that she had tried to blame it on outside forces, but that didn't mean that she should be… Thinking about him that way.

Her grandmother would be shocked. Shocked to know that her granddaughter was alone in a house with a man, first of all, and second of all, ogling his bare chest.

She had always been so well-behaved where men were concerned.

Because you never met one that you wanted.

Well, what good did it do to want this one? He might be beautiful, but he was… Incomprehensible. He thought that caring about things, that sentimentality was a defect of some kind.

He clearly cared for nothing and no one.

And then when he had talked about women…

They always wanted him? He was so incredibly full of himself.

And yet, she could believe it. That, she didn't think was from illness delirium. That, she was afraid, was the truth of it.

That women were quite interested in him, everywhere he went, always. And that if he said that he wanted them, then… Well, then he could have them.

What would you do if he wanted you?

She shoved that aside.

He couldn't consent right now. He was half out of his mind.

She tried to busy herself in the kitchen. She made homemade soup, and thought about him saying he didn't like leftovers. He had an issue with fresh food. But then he had said he was rich. And he had talked about locking his bedroom door and escaping through secret passages.

His story didn't line up or make sense, and she mused on that as she quickly delivered him soup.

She decided to google him. She didn't get any more

information from there. In fact, she got far less. The family was wealthy, Italian, and had been in property development for nearly a century. His mother had been a brilliant businesswoman. Beautiful, too. There were pictures of her online, but only to a point. He had said that she had retreated from public life. That they hadn't left their house.

While no articles stated that directly, it was definitely implied. But there were no further details. None whatsoever.

But if she connected the dots, and filled in the blank spaces using what she knew of him—sophisticated and wild all at the same time—she had no trouble believing...

That he'd been a child left on his own. That he hadn't learned how to connect with people, not really. That he was a man who needed control because his mother had controlled so much of his life until that moment.

She sighed and pushed back away from the computer. Then she went into the kitchen, and stood there at the counter. She shouldn't want to go back upstairs so badly. She shouldn't miss him. He was her *enemy*.

Except that didn't feel like the right label, and it should.

Was she that stupid? A man was handsome so it didn't feel right to label him the bad guy? He was the bad guy. He was a property developer who devoured adorable, unique places like Holiday House. He didn't care about her. He didn't care about what she wanted. Except he had taken care of her, even though he had no idea how to do it. And now he was lying upstairs all feverish. And handsome.

More than handsome.

She chewed on her thumbnail.

She made another cup of tea, and decided to go back upstairs. When she walked through his bedroom door, she saw him lying there on the bed, one muscular arm thrown up over his face, his body completely out of the covers, his chest bare. Every time he took a breath, the muscles on his chest and stomach shifted. She was fascinated by him. Surely there was no harm in looking, just for a moment. At the well-defined muscles, the tanned skin and dark hair that covered them. At just how very masculine he was. She had no experience of this. And she didn't wish that she did. Because it was a sort of magical thing for it to be him. Because he was so singular. So glorious.

She let out a sharp breath, and walked over to his bedside, putting the cup of tea down on the side table.

And she let herself take in all that masculine beauty. She felt outside herself in that moment, even in this very familiar room.

As she looked at every dip and hollow of muscle on his chest, his stomach.

Just looking at him made her feel…bold.

What if…

Her breathing quickened.

What if he was the first? What if he was…for her. Not forever, obviously, she wasn't that silly. But there had to be a first, didn't there? And he was definitely the only man who had ever made her feel like this.

She wanted her same life, she did.

But what if she could be different in it? Just for a while…

He shifted, lowering his arm. Sweat beaded on his forehead, and he looked… In pain. Which she hated.

She frowned, and put her hand against his face. He was burning. Without thinking, she let her hand drift down his cheek, the line of his jaw. The dark shadow of his beard was rough against her finger. He had been clean-shaven when he had arrived, but not so now.

She hadn't realized quite how fascinating men were. Quite how different.

Her admiration of them had always been distant. Mostly fictional. The problem with the men in town was that she had known them since they were boys. And they were distinctly uninteresting. It was difficult to see someone as sexy when you could so clearly remember them from middle school. Middle school was the least sexy phase of life.

And it had badly damaged the way that she saw every local guy.

It didn't seem to inhibit many of the people that she knew from school. So many of them had married each other.

It was just that… It had never been right for her. She was very clear on that. She'd wanted to find someone who captured her imagination.

So here she was, snowed in with a mysterious, handsome stranger. No one would ever think that would happened to Noelle Holiday. No, she was staid and boring. She was a homebody. She was old before her time, basically a cat lady without cats living on top of the mountain by herself.

And she was happy with that.

Mostly.

She realized that she was still touching his face. He moved without warning. Like lightning. And suddenly, his iron grip was around her wrist. She gasped and tried to pull away, but with his eyes still closed, he yanked her toward him. "Why are you so far away?" he asked.

His breath was hot against her cheek, and her breasts were crushed to his chest. She didn't even know if he was conscious of what he was doing. Or if he was absolutely and completely delirious.

"Rocco…"

"You smell good," he said.

She shivered. He was so hot. And she knew it was because he was feverish, but this felt… It felt like more. It felt like something else. Something that it wasn't.

She couldn't let herself get carried away by this. It was a sickness. Psychotic.

But her heart was pounding wildly, and it wasn't because she was afraid.

"You should be in bed with me," he said.

And any resistance that she had access to before was gone. She felt herself melting into him, and then he shifted, and his mouth connected with hers.

She had never been kissed before.

It was so… Disruptive. She had always imagined that a kiss would be sweet. That it would be a lovely, comforting sort of thing.

She did not feel comforted.

His mouth took no prisoners, it moved over hers with expert precision. And she found herself parting her lips for him, allowing him to push his tongue between her lips and stroke it over hers.

She gasped, and that only let him take the kiss deeper.

And she wanted it.

What did that say about her? The man was in a delirium. A feverish haze, and he also was supposed to be her enemy. No matter that she couldn't seem to cement that idea in her mind.

Enemies.

But he kissed like every dream she hadn't been experienced enough to have, and she couldn't bring herself to move away from him. She let him claim her. Let each pass of his tongue make her into something new. Into someone she didn't recognize.

She wanted him. She wanted this.

He moved his hand to the back of her head, holding her to him as he kissed her, on and on. She shivered, the sensual haze spreading from where his mouth met hers, through her limbs. She felt drugged in the most delicious way. Like she had just had a hot toddy by the fireplace, and everything in her was languid and warm.

She moved her hand down to his chest. Remembered what he had said. About wanting her to rub his chest.

She let her fingers drift over him. The prickly hair, firm muscles, hot skin…

What are you doing?

She gasped, and ripped herself away from him.

"Don't go," he said.

"You're sick," she said. "You don't even know who I am. You don't even know what you're doing."

"Sure I do," he said.

But he never opened his eyes.

"You can't consent," she said.

His eyes did drift open then, dark and furious, and connected with hers. "Excuse me?"

"You're out of your mind. You're on cold medicine, and you have a fever, and I'm taking advantage of you."

"I think you will find, *cara*, that I am more than able to consent and to act."

She shook her head, and took a step away from him, she bumped against the side table, sending the cup of tea down onto the floor, the porcelain clattering, thankfully not breaking, but the hot liquid going everywhere.

"Oh, fiddlesticks," she said. "Now look what you did. Look what I did. I… I'm sorry. I'm very sorry. I… I've never done this before, and I don't…" She picked the cup up. She would come back with a cloth. Her heart was pounding so hard, humiliation, thwarted need, and everything else, leaving her completely out cold. She went back down to the kitchen, and put her face in her hands.

She had kissed him.

Or she had let him kiss her. It wasn't entirely material, she didn't think. Which thing it was. He had a cold, a fever, and she was supposed to be taking care of him.

Does it feel better, if you make it your fault, if you make yourself feel guilty?

Tears sprang into her eyes, and she dashed them away.

Maybe it did. Maybe it felt better to make herself feel like she was some undersexed virgin who had taken advantage of a man in her care, rather than a woman who had responded to mutual attraction. No. Because that was too dangerous. The whole situation was far too dangerous.

They were working in opposition to each other. There was nothing that could be done about that. He wanted to try and manipulate this property away from her. She was refusing.

And if she showed him she was attracted to him, well… he'd undoubtedly think he could use that against her.

Her cheeks suddenly went hot. Because she worried he might actually be able to use it against her.

She was a virgin after all, and woefully inexperienced with men and even though it had been a choice, even though she wanted to believe that she was savvy...

There were no guarantees that an actual real-life love affair wouldn't change her, just enough, that she could be manipulated in ways she couldn't foresee now.

There was no compromise to be had there.

She let out a long, slow breath. She would make dinner.

And she would hope that when he woke up he didn't remember what had happened.

CHAPTER SEVEN

ROCCO GOT OUT of bed, and grimaced when he stepped into a cold puddle.

He looked down, and saw that it looked as if there was a spilled drink there on the floor, though there was no cup. It smelled of tea. He wondered if he had knocked it over in his half delirium.

He felt better. As if the fever had broken. He looked out the window and saw that it was dark. He wondered how long he had slept.

It took him a moment to find where the clock was in the room, and the digital readout indicated that it was only six o'clock in the evening. At least, he assumed it was the evening.

He turned the light on, and found a T-shirt, shrugging it on before walking out of the bedroom. He felt driven to find Noelle, though he couldn't say why.

He paused. The memory of her hands on his face, of the way she'd cared for him stopped him cold. His chest felt sore, his body suddenly immobilized. Why was it like this?

He had never…felt sore in his heart like this thinking about a woman.

But then, no one had ever taken care of him like that before.

He was familiar enough with sexual touch. But the way she'd touched him, the way she'd soothed him, that was something else entirely.

His stomach growled, and he thought perhaps he wanted to find her because he needed food. That was reasonable enough.

He made his way down the stairs, and didn't see her. He walked into the library, and there she was, sitting in a chair by the fireplace.

"I'm hungry," he said.

She startled and turned. She was looking at him as if he had grown a second head. It was possible that he was being rude.

"I made dinner," she said.

"Thank you," he said, those words felt so foreign to him, and yet he had found himself saying them to her often.

"You're welcome," she said.

She was staring at him. He couldn't quite work out why.

"Are you well?"

"Perfectly," she said.

She stood up, and attempted what he could only describe as a scurry when she went past him. He reached out and took her arm. Forcing her to face him. Her eyes connected with his, and his gaze dropped to her mouth. And suddenly he remembered.

He had kissed her. He had pulled her down onto the bed, and he had...

He let go of her and took a step back. "I'm sorry," he said. Those words really were foreign on his lips. He never said them. He never had occasion to. He was never wrong.

But this had been wrong. He had been half out of his mind, he hadn't made sure that she even *wanted* to kiss him, he had held her to him, and then she had run away. She had spilled the tea. That was what had happened.

The touching had not been comforting, it had, in fact, been sexual and while he felt like a brute for how it must have occurred there was something placating in the realization that it was sexual, and familiar to him for that reason.

It wasn't different.

It wasn't singular.

"I was… Not thinking."

"Oh, I know," she said.

"No, I mean… I had a fever and I…"

"I know," she practically wailed. "And I feel terrible."

"You feel terrible?"

"Yes," she said. "It was wrong with me to do that. I took advantage of you."

He barked out a helpless laugh. "You took advantage of me?"

"Yes."

"You are tiny. And the first time I saw you, you were dressed as a deer. You are hardly a seductive siren. I am the one that took advantage."

"Now you're insulting me on top of everything else."

"Nothing that I said was an insult, it was simply true."

"Well, it was bracing," she said. "And not fair."

"What do you not find fair about it, little one?"

"It's… Okay. Maybe it's true. Maybe I'm not a seductive siren. But I knew what I was doing. I mean, I meant to kiss you. You didn't force me to. But you clearly wouldn't have chosen to kiss me if you weren't out of your mind."

"That is categorically untrue," he said, feeling the danger rise up inside of him. Feeling the warning. He shouldn't be saying this, he shouldn't be drawing closer to her, none of this should be happening right now.

"Well, you didn't kiss me until you had a fever, so we can't prove it, can we."

"You are a silly girl, and unless you want to find yourself flat on your back in front of that fireplace, I suggest that you stop pushing me."

Her hands had been so soft on his skin. The way that she had cared for him… No one else had ever done that. It was that caring hand on his face, that was what had undone him upstairs. That sweet way that she had touched him. It left him feeling… Not himself. It left him feeling on edge.

Because he understood attraction. But there was something else with her. Everything he had said was true. She was tiny. And she had been dressed like a reindeer. Nothing about that should appeal to him. And yet she did.

The easiest thing would be to kiss her. The easiest thing would be to reduce it to sex. Because that was what he understood. That was the connection he always had with women. The only physical touch that had ever existed in his life.

Not this…soothing of his fevered brow. Not this…wide-eyed country girl care that she was forcing upon him.

"Who says I don't want that?" she asked breathlessly, her eyes round as copper coins.

"Do not push me," he said. "I knew exactly what I was doing. I am not a nice man."

"I already know that. You're trying to take my home from me. But you also took care of me when I was unwell."

"I am a man with a strong sense of honor, but that doesn't make me nice. And it doesn't make me good. Do you know how many women I've had?"

"No. Because you didn't tell me. And the internet wasn't really forthcoming with information about you."

He lifted a brow. "You googled me?"

"Well yes. Obviously."

"There is nothing obvious about that." Or perhaps there was, and most people simply wouldn't admit to such a thing.

"There should be," she said.

She was entirely artless. And he was a brute. But he was giving her a chance. A chance to turn away from this. To turn away from him. Yes. He was giving her a chance to make a wise decision, rather than a foolish one. And if she was a fool, then it was on her head. Her...antlers.

It was not up to him to protect her from him. He was giving her ample chance. Ample choice.

"I... I want you," she said.

Her face turned scarlet.

"Why?" he asked.

"You're... A handsome, mysterious stranger. Who wouldn't want that?"

That made sense to him. And he latched onto it. He wasn't special. She wasn't romanticizing this, not beyond the sexual fantasy inherent in sleeping with someone that you ought not to.

He wanted her, because he wanted this to make sense. And it did make sense. They were a man and woman snowed in together, so why shouldn't they?

She wasn't special. This was biology. He was not special to her. He was simply an object of desire.

He could understand that.

It pleased him.

He moved closer to her, and gripped her chin, tilting her face up and forcing her eyes to meet his. "That's what you want, then? The fantasy. Snowed in here at the top of this mountain? Does your snowplow actually work?"

She huffed a laugh. "I wish that I was that crafty, but I'm not. We really are stuck here. It's really... All of this, but my life is very unexciting. This is the most exciting thing that's ever happened. And I..." She looked up at him. "Am I worthy of a little bit of excitement?"

"You are worthy of being worshiped," he said. "Let me show you."

He dipped his head and kissed her lips. They were softer than he remembered. She was soft. He pulled her against him, moving his hands over her curves, bringing her flush against him. He held her tightly.

She was glorious. Everything he had ever fantasized about and more.

It was just sex.

What a relief.

Because he understood this. Because this made sense.

And he could have her. He could have this.

He kissed her, deep and long and endlessly.

He kissed her because he wanted her.

He kissed her until she was whimpering, until she brought her hands up to grip the fabric of his T-shirt. She was kneading him like a little cat, her nails sharp through the fabric.

"You do want me," he said, looking down at her.

She turned red again. "Yes," she said. "Sorry."

"Don't apologize for your passion. You're beautiful."

He was going to show her. He was going to show her exactly what he wanted to do with her. Petite and pretty and about to be his.

The snow would melt. He would buy this place, and he would level it. They would never see each other again. She would hate him after.

But she wanted him now. So he would have her.

It was that simple.

This was simple.

It would change nothing. Because nothing ever changed him.

He picked her up, and carried her over to the fireplace, laying her down on the plush rug. A kick of annoyance hit him in the chest. He didn't think he had any condoms with him. This was a business trip, and he was one to keep things compartmentalized. He thought it was perhaps a little bit too much to ask that the woman who had been dressed like a deer had condoms.

"I don't have protection," he said.

She looked confused for a moment. "Oh," she said. She frowned deeply. "I take birth control."

He was fastidious in all things, and he knew that he had nothing to worry about as far as cleanliness. Perhaps she made a habit of sleeping with men when she didn't have condoms. He doubted it.

"If that's all right with you," he said.

She nodded. "It is. It's okay with me."

The color in her cheeks was high, but it wasn't from embarrassment now. She seemed excited.

"Good. Now that we have gotten responsibility out of the way."

He stripped his shirt off, and the rest of his clothes. Her shoulders were scrunched up by her ears, and it looked as if she wasn't certain where she was allowed to look.

"What?" he asked.

"You just... Oh... You are... Impressive."

There was something so sweet, so guileless about the way that she said that. About the way that she looked at him. He couldn't help but be charmed. He couldn't help but be mesmerized.

"It's your turn now."

He knelt down beside her, and stripped her sweater off. The bra she was wearing was simple, pretty. White with a little bow in the center. Definitely not the kind of underwear he was used to seeing on a woman. This wasn't for show. But for practicality. He found himself transfixed.

"I'm not... I mean my boobs aren't very big," she said.

"They're perfect," he said, the understatement of the century. He unclipped her bra, and pulled it off, revealing small, perfectly formed breasts. The tips were rosy pink and beautiful.

His breath hissed through his teeth, tension gathering in his chest. "More than fine. You are beautiful," he said.

He leaned forward, and kissed the sweet curve of her neck, down to her breasts, taking one crest into his mouth and sucking hard. She arched against him, a rough sound in her throat.

And he found that he was driven for her to make that sound as many times as possible.

Yes. He was.

He hooked his finger in the waistband of her leggings, and her underwear, and dragged them down her body, leaving her bare for his appraisal.

He kissed his way down her stomach, down to the sweet center between her thighs, where he began to taste her.

She gasped, and he thought she even tried to pull away from him, but he didn't allow it.

"Let me pleasure you," he said.

He nuzzled her there, parting her legs for him as he began to lick toward her center.

"Rocco," she said, her fingers pushed into his hair.

Yes.

She arched against him, saying his name over and over again like a prayer.

Her hands moved through his hair. It reminded him of the way that she had touched him when she was caring for him while he was ill.

Maybe he was still sick. He felt dizzy. Dizzy with need for her. With the flavor of her coating his tongue. She was like a drug, one that he was more than happy to indulge in.

He pleasured her like that until he felt her body draw up tight like a bow. Then he pushed one finger inside of her, continuing to lick her as he did. And he felt her shatter. She gasped, crying out his name, forking her fingers through his hair and rolling her hips against him.

He growled, surging up her body and claiming her mouth with his, swallowing her cries of pleasure.

Then he positioned himself between her thighs, and thrust home.

She was tight. So tight.

And the way that she cried out didn't feel like pleasure now, but pain.

He looked down at her face.

"Noelle?"

"Don't stop," she said, arching against him. And he was powerless to deny her. He began to move, thrusting deep and hard. Until she began to relax, until she became pliant against him. He moved against her, again and again.

He wanted to take her to the peak one last time. He couldn't please only himself.

He moved his hand between them, began to rub her with his thumb, and she dug her fingers into his shoulder, crying out as she pulsed around him, and then he lost control. He thrust into her once, twice, surging inside of her, his orgasm overtaking him like a train.

He poured his desire out inside of her, kissed her lips, let her swallow his roar of need.

And they lay there like that, sweat-slicked. He was undone.

"You were a virgin," he said.

It didn't seem possible, and yet it did. She was the strangest woman that he had ever met. The only person that he had ever met who was as isolated as he was.

He let that realization rest heavy on his shoulders. He wasn't a virgin. He had traveled the world. And many women had touched his body. But no one had touched him deeper than that.

Her life was different. She was in this small town, where anyone you slept with, you would have to contend with again. He imagined it changed the complexion of how people did things.

Perhaps.

"Noelle…"

"Okay," she said, sounding grumpy. "I was. But… I don't expect anything from you."

She looked sad, though. And the trouble was, he now expected something. The trouble was, something had changed. This place, it didn't mean anything to him, not specifically, and it did to her.

Which was beginning to matter. She was not just a faceless person he could fling money at. Was not just a number or a statistic. She was a woman. Who had taken care of him.

Sex was one thing. It was everything else.

But he was caught. Caught in the web of his mother's making. In her game.

He had wanted to dodge it. He had thought that he could serve his own ambitions while completing the terms of the will, and it would never bother him. But it bothered him now.

There was only one other way to sidestep it.

He would have to think about this. Not what he was going to do. He was determined on that. But how he was going to do it.

Rocco Moretti had yet to enter into a battle that he hadn't won. But he had a feeling if anyone was going to challenge him in ways that he couldn't anticipate, it was her.

She had been pushing him from the moment they'd met. Refusing to give in to offers of money, caring for him even when she claimed not to like him.

But he would be able to win. He knew it.

Just then, the phone rang.

* * *

"Oh," she said, scrambling up. It was the landline.

"You have an actual phone?" he asked.

"This is a bed-and-breakfast," she said. She was naked, shivering, she didn't quite know what to do with herself, but she gathered herself to answer the phone.

"Holiday House."

"Is that you, Noelle?"

"Yes," she said.

"This is Fred, we're headed up to plow your road."

"Oh," she said. "Thank God."

"Everything should be open for you within the hour."

"Thank you," she said.

She hung up the phone. And suddenly she felt bereft. They were free now. They had... Cared for each other while they were sick. She had just lost her virginity.

And the roads would be open.

He could leave. She was suddenly seized with the strangest sense of grief. It didn't make any sense. She shouldn't be grieving.

She had known that this would happen. It was okay that it was happening.

Still, she felt overcome.

"I... The road is going to be cleared today," she said.

"Oh," he said. "Then we can go to town."

"Yes," she said. "You can leave—what?"

"We can go to town," he said. "Noelle, I want to see this town. The way that you do."

It was the nicest, most unexpected thing he could've said.

"Okay," she said.

That was how she found herself bundled up two hours

later, and headed down to town with Rocco. She hadn't really thought this through. She felt raw from having made love to him. She felt overawed by him in the entire situation, in fact.

And she was going to town, where she would run into people that she undoubtedly knew, and she would be forced to look at them in the eye and not announce that she had just had sex with this man.

This man who was now going to leave.

She ignored the lancing pain in her heart.

She had bigger problems on her hands. He was still going to try to take the bed-and-breakfast away from her.

That was a much bigger problem than him leaving. She felt torn in half, and she didn't want to examine it.

What if she'd played right into his hand? She was more afraid of the sex being an act of manipulation than she was of actually being manipulated by it.

Which maybe didn't make sense, but she wasn't sure she was thinking clearly.

He parked his car on the street, and he surprised her by taking her hand when they began to walk down the sidewalk.

"People know me here," she said.

"And? Do you have an attachment to them seeing you as Mother Mary?"

"No," she said. "I don't have an attachment to that at all."

"Well, that is good. Because you are decidedly no longer virginal."

"But people will talk," she said.

"And you care about that?"

She thought about it. No. Not really. But she was predictable. She'd always been Noelle Holiday of Holiday House and she'd never dated any men around town. So no one...thought of her like that really.

So nobody would see this coming. And they wouldn't be able to figure out what exactly it meant. She liked that.

Why not? Why not revel in walking down the street with the most handsome man she had ever seen.

So she did. From shop to shop. She took him to the ice skating rink that was put over the top of the parking lot every year in the center of town. They didn't skate, but they watched people. She took him to the town Christmas tree, and through any number of shops that boasted the best souvenirs in town. He declined to buy any. Not even the taxidermist raccoon holding a banjo. Which, if she were a billionaire, she probably would have bought. Because it was hilarious.

Everywhere they went, people said hi to her. And to him. They looked at them with curiosity, and she simply smiled.

Then they went into Sweet Melody, and she walked to the counter with him smiling, and ordered them both hot chocolate.

"Hi, Noelle," Melody said, her eyebrows rising up to her hairline.

"Hello," she said cheerfully.

"Who is this?"

"Melody Stevens, this is Rocco Moretti. We got snowed in up at the inn," she said.

"Oh," Melody said.

Noelle smiled cheerfully.

"We need to go out to dinner soon," she said.

"Oh, we will," Noelle said.

She walked back out of the coffeehouse holding Rocco's hand still, and drinking the hot chocolate. He grimaced as he said, "It's very sweet."

"Yes," she said. "It is."

They looked around, she wondered if maybe, just maybe, him having an attachment to the town would change the way that he saw Holiday House. If it would change his intentions.

"So," she said. "What do you think?"

"I hate it."

He took another sip of hot chocolate.

She simply stared at him. "You… You hate it?"

"Yes. Everyone knows you…they talk to you constantly. It is saccharine to the point of being sickening, and I am not talking about the hot chocolate. The decorations are too bright, and it is too much. But you clearly love it."

"I do," she said.

"You love it, and you would do anything to preserve your life here, yes?"

"Yes."

Her heart was pounding, she didn't know where this was going.

"I have something to ask you."

"Okay."

He looked around the street, and the Christmas lights reflected in his dark eyes. Then he looked back at her, and they were nothing but coal black. "Noelle Holiday, I want you to be my wife."

CHAPTER EIGHT

NOELLE WAS SHOCKED. Immobilized. Of all the things she'd expected from her first sexual experience—which had been amazing but clearly, clearly a one-off—a proposal hadn't been on the list.

She might have been only just recently a virgin, but she wasn't an idiot.

"Excuse me?"

She was so aware that she was standing out there on the streets of this town where everybody knew her. Where everyone had opinions on who she was, with this man. And it had been an extremely fun lark, until this moment. Until she had begun to realize that whatever she thought was happening, Rocco knew better. Until she had begun to realize that he never just did anything. This had been a calculated, coordinated move. He wasn't going to look at the town with her simply because he wanted to. No. Of course not. There was something else at play with him. She had forgotten for a moment who he was. Even though she had been telling herself to be conscious of it. To be aware.

"Why?" she asked.

Not the response she ever saw herself giving to a man

in her fantasies when he proposed. But then, the man had never been Rocco.

She couldn't have conjured him up in her fantasies no matter how hard she tried.

"Because. I either have to continue building, forever and ever, or I have to marry and produce an heir. You don't want me to build over the top of Holiday House. Increasingly, I don't want that either."

"Why not?" she asked.

"Because it would hurt you," he said. "And I don't want to do that."

She clung to that. Imagined holding it in her fist like a bright, shiny jewel.

If he cared about hurting her did that mean he cared?

Or was this the manipulation?

She didn't know, but she knew what she wanted to believe.

"But… But what would marriage between us entail?"

"I think we only just had a small sample of what it entails," he said, his voice low and seductive, and how she hated him for that. How she hated him for the ease with which he could take her back there. Could make her want to say yes regardless of whether or not it made any sense.

That bastard.

Was this what he had always planned on doing?

"You are looking at me as if I am a monster, and you did not look at me like that only moments ago," he said.

Her face went all hot and she resented it.

"You… Is that why you slept with me?" She was so aware that she knew the people who were passing by, at least by face, if not by name. So aware that she was playing out this intimate moment for all the town to see.

"No," he said. "Of course not. Of course that is not why."

"Was it your plan all along?"

"No. My plan was to bulldoze your bed-and-breakfast and build a hugely lucrative resort property. But this is another way forward. An alternative."

"What if I don't want your alternative?"

"Then I will proceed as I had originally planned. That is up to you. Though I do not know why you would want to make it so difficult."

She realized then that she was standing at the cusp of an improbable issue. An unsolvable problem. She couldn't go back to the life that she had known before he had come into it. That was the simple truth. She had been trying so hard to cling to her existence. To what she knew. And part of her had believed that once he left, as long as she won, as long as she was able to win this fight with him, then she would be able to go back to the way things had been. To that simpler time. Her simpler self.

But it wasn't true.

She was changed by knowing him.

It was an utterly horrendous thing to realize. She was altered for having met the man. Part of her would always be missing if he was gone from her.

No, she wasn't in love with him, but she felt something for him. There was no pretending that she didn't. And if he left, if he went away, it wouldn't be like he had never come there. Because she could never be untouched by him. Unkissed by him. She could never go back to how it had been before she was possessed by him. She was changed. Forevermore.

And always she would be living a half life. The one from before and the one after.

"So wait a minute," she said. "I marry you and…"

"I will give your mother the money that she wants. She will be cared for. The mother-in-law of a billionaire. You will have Holiday House, preserved, though you will not be able to be there all the time, you will of course be able to go there as you wish."

"But you and I will be married."

"Yes. And I live mostly in New York City."

She grimaced. "New York City. I have never been there, but it sounds vile."

He chuckled. "Most people are enamored of it. It is the greatest city in the world, after all."

"Subjective, I'm certain. Also, I love it here. I love it here more than I love anything else."

"How nice for you," he said. "I think you will find that isn't true for others. I for example, find that I am not so charmed by this place."

"No, of course not. That would be far too convenient. Can't you just fall in love with this place and decide not to build here out of the goodness of your heart?"

He shook his head. "I don't do anything out of the goodness of my heart. But the truth is, eventually, I will have to marry, and I will have to have an heir. You took care of me. When I was ill. You made me feel at ease. You are exactly the woman that I should want as the mother to my child. Yes, I find your house not to my taste, but it is homey. I think. At least, I suppose that is what others would say."

"But not you."

"I find it cluttered. But it is not dangerously so."

She didn't have any idea what he meant by that. By dangerously cluttered. What on earth could that mean?

"I think that you would be a good mother. I think that you could learn to be a good wife. We are compatible in bed."

She looked around, wildly. "I know everyone here."

"I don't. But in any case, you and I would suit."

"How? I hate the sound of the place that you call home, you hate the place that I call home. You think my house is cluttered. You think that I'm a silly small-town girl."

"You were also a virgin," he said, lowering his voice. "I take the gift that you gave me seriously."

"You make it sound like it's medieval times. Should I be grateful you didn't hang the bloodied sheet out the window?"

He frowned. "Did you bleed?"

"If so, not enough to worry about."

"I don't want to have hurt you."

"I'm a woman, Rocco, if I got wound up about a little blood I'd be beset all the time."

He considered that. "I don't mean to sound medieval. But perhaps a bit old-fashioned. I cannot help myself. I cannot ignore the fact that you have never been with another man, and yet you chose to be with me. There are things I cannot give, Noelle. I will be honest with you in that. I cannot give love. I will not give you a conventional life. I do not think that we will sit warmly around the dinner table all together, and talk of our day. I will come and see you, and the child. You will stay with me sometimes. You will be… The better parent, I feel, in the child's life."

"I didn't even tell you if I wanted children," she said,

even as she felt her stomach cramp low. The idea of carrying a baby… Of course she had always wanted a traditional life. It was the thing that she thought about often. Her family home, her family legacy. In order to truly realize that dream, she had seen herself having her own family. She had also seen herself living with that family at Holiday House. She hadn't considered being a part-time single mother.

But she couldn't go back to that simple dream. Because she could no longer put a blank face in the place of the father, the husband. The only man that she could imagine was Rocco. And she didn't have to be in love with him for that to be the case. She wasn't in love. She wasn't that naive, she wasn't that simple. But she also knew that attraction like they shared didn't just pop up all the time. In twenty-four years, she hadn't experienced it. Now that she knew it existed, she could never settle for less. Was she going to wait another twenty-four years for a man to show up who ignited her imagination in that way?

She thought of her mother, her father, who had clearly been incompatible in the end. They had loved each other. They truly had. But her mother had wanted to escape the life that they had built, whatever she had thought going into it. What that taught her was that you couldn't know for certain what you would want in the future. You could only make decisions as best you could right then.

It was all you could do.

It was the only thing.

She might be unhappy if she decided to marry him. But she would be unhappy if she didn't. She would still be in this fight. This fight to keep Holiday House, this fight to… To find herself. Because in the end, that's what she was trying to do. She had tried to do it by keeping everything the same. She had been lonely. Happy in so many ways, how she loved the Christmas tree farm. How she loved the house. How she loved the people in this town. But she was unsatisfied. She was unfulfilled. Maybe she could be half and half. The before and the after. Noelle, with her child, with her warmth and her Christmas, at Holiday House, and Rocco's wife in New York when he needed it.

Yes, what he was offering had a bleakness to it. But, she was happy with him now. She had been these past few days. He was a good man.

He would continue to be a good man. Who was to say that it wouldn't be enough?

Who could know for certain?

"I will marry you. But I need it in writing that Holiday House will be safe."

"It will."

"What will become of the other properties that you bought?"

"A preserve. For the local wildlife, and for the town."

She couldn't help herself. She threw her arms around him. "Rocco, that is amazing. The most beautiful gift that you could've given."

"You're very welcome," he said, his voice turning to stone. "Then we have ourselves a bargain."

"Yes."

"How long will it take for you to secure staff that can manage in your stead?"

"I do have staff. But…"

"Then it will work out. If I need to call someone in from one of my hotels to help manage, then I shall."

"I have a feeling they will feel that that is entirely beneath them."

"But I'm their boss, so they shall do as I ask."

"Oh."

She felt right then that she hadn't exactly understood what she was saying yes to. Because she knew the man in context of her life, she knew him in black-and-white on a Google search. But she didn't fully understand the place that he occupied in the world. How could she? How could she.

"We must leave as soon as possible," he said. "I have to announce my engagement so I can put a stop to my mother's expansion stipulations."

Her whole life was changing, and she could barely catch her breath.

But she realized it didn't matter.

Because she was prepared to follow him, breathless.

So perhaps his manipulation had worked.

She wasn't even sure she cared if that were true.

Rocco did not tarry. He called his people in as quickly as they could arrive and had them help pack Noelle's necessities. He asked that they outfit the plane with clothing and makeup suitable for his bride. She was cute in her normal attire, but cute would not be fitting for a Moretti bride.

Then she was bundled up and loaded onto his private plane, as he did his best to make sure that everything at the bed-and-breakfast and Christmas tree farm was secured to Noelle's specifications.

As they stood there in the doorway of Holiday House, all her things being put in the car caravan so that they could make the journey to New York with them, he palmed the jewelry box in his pocket. He had his assistant whisk the finest diamond she could get her hands on immediately to him. Because he would have this secured as soon as possible.

He held the box out, and opened it. "Here. Until we can sign a contract, this is my promise to you. There are expectations that come with it."

She was looking at the ring, boggling.

"Expectations?"

"When we get off the plane there will doubtless be paparazzi there. You must expect it. By now, the world knows that I have been snowed in at the top of a mountain. And I prefer to make the most of the story. I am considered a ruthless, heartless property developer."

"Yes. I have some experience with that."

"So you have. But this will change the story. Do you not understand all the ways in which you are perfect for this position?"

"You make it sound like a job."

"In many ways it is. For my wife, being married to me was always going to be a job. Not only will there be media attention it is…possible that the board of my company will be unhappy with the development."

"Why?" she asked.

"Eternal expansion suits them, of course."

"Right."

"I was content to continue putting marriage off. I am only thirty."

"Ah right, and sperm is everlasting. You could put it off until you were eighty."

He laughed. "I never had the inclination to do that. But I have been caught between two things all this time. The desire to be free from this excessive expansion my mother has commanded, and the desire to not yet marry. Neither option truly exists. But only when I met you did I see marriage as the more... Peaceful option. Why shouldn't I be a father? I would, after all, do better at it than my own mother. My own father being nonexistent, it would be impossible to do worse."

"Well, I don't think that's true. I think sometimes presence can be worse than absence. Depending precisely on how the presence manifests itself."

"Indeed." He thought of his mother again. Of the darkness of the house. The fetid smell. Of how she loved her things more than she had ever loved him. She could name the price of each one of them, where they had come from, the date they had been bought. She never even remembered his birthday.

"Will you wear my ring?"

She looked at him. "This ring exists so that you have a good story to tell. So that when your picture is taken as we get off the plane people will know that you fell in love with the innkeeper you were trapped on the mountain with."

"Yes. That is exactly why it exists."

She looked around. "I think this is the kind of thing I might've thought was romantic under different circumstances. I mean, if you had gotten down on one knee, and my family was here. If my dad wasn't gone. Oh, yeah, if we were in love."

She looked wounded, and what he didn't want was for her to have second thoughts, because now that he was set on this plan, he was convinced that it was the best way forward. No question.

He didn't want to continue on the way he had been. It felt like a life continually out of his control whereas…

One with her felt like it might, perhaps, be a path to a life that was much more his own.

Both were his mother's grand design, and he could not readily articulate why one felt better than the other.

Perhaps, it was Noelle.

"Would you like me to get down on one knee?"

"No. I don't need you to do that. Thanks, though. That's…"

He could see that he was losing her. He could see that she was afraid. That she was questioning things. He knew what connection they had. Where it was strongest. He cupped the back of her head and leaned down, claiming her mouth. He kissed her, deep and long until he lost himself entirely. Until he couldn't remember what he had been trying to do. Until there was nothing but her. Her softness. His need for her. Her lips, her sighs. Everything.

He was consumed by it, just as much as she was. He was caught in his own trap. It was a hell of a thing. It was unlike anything he had ever experienced before.

He did not know if he wished to drown in it, or turn away from it, never to touch it again. When he moved away from her, her eyes were still closed. She was breathing hard. So was he.

"It is not all a story," he said. "It is not all terribly unromantic."

Her eyes fluttered open.

"Yes," she said.

She put her hand out, and he took the ring carefully from the box, sliding it onto her finger. It glittered there. A promise of something.

And it was one of the few times he could honestly say that the addition of something made it better, and not simply more cluttered. Not worse.

On her, the ring was beautiful.

"Let's go," he said, gesturing toward the car.

"Okay," she said, turning to look back at the bed-and-breakfast.

"You will be back," he said.

"I know," she said.

"You look as if I'm dragging you away forever."

"You're certainly dragging me into the unknown."

"Didn't I already do that?"

Her cheeks went pink. "You can't make everything about sex."

"And why not? Sex is what brought us here. It is not a bad thing. It is our connection. It is certainly real."

"Yes," she said softly. "It is."

She was silent on the car ride to the airfield, and when they boarded the private plane, her eyes went round. "I… I had no idea that a private plane was this luxurious. But I've only flown one time."

"Really?"

"Yes. To visit my aunt in Ohio. I was a kid. I don't even really remember it. But I… This is incredible."

"It is a necessity," he said.

He didn't feel entirely comfortable with her all over the plane, and he wasn't sure why. He was used to being around people who were blasé about wealth and luxury.

Even if they were impressed they would never venture to behave as if they were. The disparity between the two of them was all the clearer here.

"It is yours now," he said. "What I mean is, everything that is mine is now yours."

"It… It is?"

"Yes," he said. "It is. We are sharing our wealth."

For some reason, that made him feel better.

"I… Good," she said. "I… I don't need wealth really. But it makes me feel better to know that you see me as a partner, and not simply an acquisition."

He didn't argue with her. He probably should. She wasn't exactly the same as an object, but she was primarily one. A wife that he'd needed to acquire in order to fulfill certain terms.

And yet, within that, she mattered.

Of course she did. It couldn't have been anyone, or he would've married already.

She was…everything he should not want, and yet he did want her. How could he let go of such a glorious mystery?

All his life he'd felt isolated. She made him feel something more.

He did not want to let that go.

"You got awfully quiet," she said.

"Do not concern yourself with my silence," he said, settling into one of the plush leather chairs on the plane, and inviting her to do the same. His stewardess bustled about the cabin, bringing them both drinks.

"Champagne?" she asked.

"Yes," he said. "To celebrate."

"Oh," she said, looking at her hand.

She looked back up at the stewardess and smiled. "Of course."

The stewardess beamed back, and then left the two of them alone.

"My staff sign ironclad NDAs," he said. "You have no need to put on a show in front of Elise."

"Well, I feel uncomfortable," she said. "Lying."

"It isn't a lie. I came to your bed-and-breakfast, we were snowed in. We were overcome by our attraction to one another."

"Were you?"

She was staring at him, with the intense copper eyes that he found so attractive, generally speaking, but a bit off-putting now.

"Yes," he said.

He felt pinned to the spot, but he also didn't see the use in denying it. "What is it you need to hear, Noelle? That I was attracted to you in a way that felt uncommon? In a way that tested me, and I failed that test?"

"What test?"

"It felt entirely ungentlemanly of me to claim you like I did when we were trapped in the way that we were. And yet I did, because I could not resist you. Because you were... Everything that I wanted and more. Because you are the most beautiful woman that I have ever seen. It doesn't even matter if that is strictly true in a measurable sense. You are the only one that I can remember. And I could not imagine not taking this opportunity to secure a wife when I found one who would suit me so well. You see how it is?"

"I... I suppose so."

"Is that what you wanted to hear? That you are special?"

"Not if you're only telling me that so that I'll shut up."

"I am not," he said.

He realized that this was the longest he had ever spoken to another person about something other than business in a very long time. But then, that was true of this whole lost weekend with her. She wanted to understand the way in which she was different? He couldn't begin to list a single way that she was the same.

"You have experiences that I don't have," she said. "It makes me feel… I wonder what you see in me, I guess. Is this obligation because you were my first or…"

"No. What I see in you is the ability to be a warm and caring mother. But also… I want you." He met her gaze. "I have never cared much about a specific woman. I have cared for my own pleasure. I seek out women who are the same. So that I do not have to think about them. They think of themselves. I think of myself. I have never been… Warm. You make me feel warm."

He didn't know if what he had said made any sense at all; he wasn't even certain why he'd said it.

"My whole childhood felt magical," she said. "Holiday House is the most wonderful place to grow up. I loved it so much. I always have. I imagined growing up there. Growing old there. Raising children there. I don't know where I thought I was going to meet a man. The boys that I knew in town never impressed me. Not because I'm a snob just because… Well. Maybe I am a snob. I never wanted them. I could never quite explain why. But I didn't. Still, I imagined a warm and happy life there. When my father died, and my mother left, I suddenly realized that the life that I thought was happening around me wasn't. My mother didn't love the bed-and-breakfast. She felt trapped there. Their relationship wasn't everything that I had believed it to be, and it made me realize for the first time that a fantasy, a dream that you have when you're a child, doesn't mean anything. It isn't guaranteed to come true. So I've been up there, clinging to that place, feeling more and more lonely. Wishing for a life I didn't have anymore. Wishing for the confidence that I used to have that my life was going to turn out okay. You disrupted everything."

"You do not find me warm?"

"I find you terrifying. The prospect of something that I never once imagined, but it seems like I would be a fool to say no. Not because you're a billionaire. Because it saves Holiday House. And because... I want you. That has to matter for something."

"Certainly."

"You said some things... When you were feverish. About your childhood."

"What things?"

"They probably didn't mean anything. You were probably completely out of your mind." She frowned. "Except you did remember kissing me. And I thought you might not."

"Tell me."

"You talked about traveling through a secret passageway. And always being in your room."

"That is true," he said. His chest felt icy, and he didn't like it. Because what he wanted was to forget his childhood had ever happened. That was what he wanted.

And yet... She had shared something of herself. And

he had already shared something of himself, even if he had done so when he hadn't meant to. Eventually, they would have to speak of it, because they were going to have to share a house and he was going to have to explain some of his eccentricities.

He had never considered that. What it actually meant to have to share space with another person.

Even while they had packed up all the things that she possessed to come to his penthouse in New York City, he hadn't fully thought all that through. He had imagined tucking her up in a space in the house, rather than integrating her. But then… Wasn't he simply treating her like his mother, only in the reverse?

"As you know, my mother reached a point where she could no longer leave the house."

"You did mention that, yes."

"There was nothing that could be done about it. She was a complete and total shut-in. Her phobias took over. She began to seek ways that she could control her surroundings. The way that she found peace…" He gritted his teeth. It was difficult for him to try and justify what his mother had done when he was so angry. And yet, he had done a fair amount of work to try and assign meaning to all that she had done. For his own peace, as well as her memory. Still there were times when all he wanted to do was rage.

This was one of those times.

Because having to expose it all again. To speak to somebody about it. To admit the truth to Noelle felt exposing, even if it shouldn't. Both of the conditions that he had lived in as a child, and of his mother. And as much as he often resented his mother and her memory, he still loathed exposing her. It went against his own need to also protect. Still, he did his best. "She began to collect things. Small things at first, but it grew. And the issue with something like that, when it becomes a compulsion, when it weaves together with all the other existing phobias is that it quickly takes over every part of your life. Every room of the house."

She was staring at him. "You said… You sometimes ate expired food."

"She would hoard food as well. There was no way of knowing, often, how old something was. And she did not like to throw it out. The two members of staff that she had enabled her. I don't know if they became used to the surroundings, or if it didn't matter to them because they knew that my mother would remember them in her will, and they would be paid handsomely for the trouble of living in squalor. But for whatever reason, they acted as if everything was fine. But I couldn't. I stayed in my room as much as possible, I locked my mother out. I would not allow it to become a dumping ground for her things. I could not allow it. The only measure of peace that I had in that house was my own space. And that is why when I left I would go through the secret passages."

"You… You were so isolated," she said. "When you said that you grew up in a wealthy family, that is by far not what I imagined."

"It is not what anyone imagines. But mental illness doesn't care if you have money. She could've had access to treatment, yes, but she didn't take advantage of that access. She didn't want to be fixed. She didn't want to be better. Perhaps she couldn't have been. Perhaps it was impossible for her to be better than she was, I will never know. What I know is she lived her last years in darkness, and isolation, and in secret. And then she wanted me to continue on in her quest to hoard things. In this case, property. And I have done so, because it has grown the business, but you can see, I hate this. This empty acquisition. This need to own. I keep very little in my home, you will find."

"Oh," she said.

"I like there to be space."

"It makes sense. All the… You're quite particular."

"Now that I can control my surroundings, I do so." He could hear himself. He could hear himself talking about control, and he could even recognize that was a close neighbor of his mother's issues. But he did not think it was wrong. He did not think that he was wrong. Not truly. What he did, he did as a matter of his own survival. His own mental clarity. He liked to feel as far removed from his childhood as possible.

"I thought my childhood was perfect," she said softly. "But, my mother ran away from it all as soon as she could. I thought that she loved our life. I thought that she loved me. But the truth is, if anything, she loved my dad. As soon as he was gone, so was she. And I know it's not what you went through. But it's just funny to me, how I'm clinging to my childhood as best I can, to the memory of what I thought it was. Trying to prove that it was perfect. And you're running as far away from yours as possible."

It was two different things. The opposite things, even, and yet there was something in the sadness in her voice that made him feel like they were connected by an invisible string. He wasn't sure that he liked the sensation, but there it was. Powerful. Intense.

"And yet here you are, in the midst of change," he said, and he wasn't sure if he was pointing it out to put distance between them or simply to see what she would do. She looked down. "I made my choice."

"You must admit, I steered you quite strongly."

She nodded. "You did. You also underestimate my ability to fight, Rocco. I am strong and stubborn."

"In my experience you are not so hard to persuade."

She shook her head. "I have been opposing my mother on the sale of that house for two years now. I am very hard to persuade. I live up there, in perfect happiness with my own company. You... Changed something in me. You made me see that something else could exist. I didn't quite understand what that might look like. I still don't. But I'm here."

"You should go and get changed," he said.

"My suitcases..."

"No. In the bedroom there is some clothing for you. You will have your picture taken when you get off the plane."

"And I have to look a certain way."

"Yes."

"Like I belong with you."

He paused for a moment. "You are in the midst of change, as I only just pointed out. I think it is only fair for me to acknowledge that you are the one that will have to change the most. I am bringing you into my life. You will accompany me to different events as and when I need you to. You will get off this plane and create the photo op that I want you to create. You will have my child."

"Presumably the child will also be mine."

"Yes. I have no desire, nor the inclination or ability to

be a full-time father. But these things… These changes, you're making for me. I am not changing. I feel that must be abundantly clear."

"Rocco, if you think that you can get married, bring a woman into your home, bring a child into your home and experience no change at all, I'm not sure you're living in reality. I think it's only fair to point that out to you." She stood up and stretched. "Now. I guess I'll go change." She laughed. "I only meant my clothes. But I suppose in reality it means… Everything."

CHAPTER NINE

SHE WAS LIKE a different person. Polished from head to toe. She had spent far too long of the flight on her makeup and hair. The clothes that had been provided for her were beautiful, she couldn't deny that.

But she felt a strange distance between herself and Rocco, because he had decided to put it there with his cold words about their arrangement. He had done that to them. And he had done it on purpose, she knew that. It was tempting to try and make it so he didn't win. But perhaps he was going to win just for a little bit. When she emerged from the bedroom, there was a strange light in his eyes, and she couldn't read it. She decided she wasn't going to bother.

The ring felt heavy on her hand, and the plane began to descend, which unnerved her, so she sat down and buckled her seatbelt.

Then, she took a look out the window. She could see the city off in the distance. A skyline that she had seen in movies countless times over, but had never imagined that she would see in person. She wasn't sure she had even wanted to. It was such a strange, surreal feeling. Before she knew it, the plane's wheels connected to the ground, and they taxied for a brief moment before they came to a stop.

"A car will drive up to the door to meet us."

She looked up at him. "I imagine this is quite a different experience to typical plane travel. I only vaguely remember."

"Yes, normally you must fight through the crowd like you're in a herd of cattle."

"So you've been told?"

"Yes. I've heard."

Her heart gave a little jump start. Because maybe they were back to being them. Such as they were. Maybe there was a little bit of a connection there still. Even though he was being difficult.

The door to the plane opened smoothly, and he took her hand. She couldn't keep any physical distance between them, he was making sure of that, and when the physical distance was erased, she found that it was harder and harder to maintain emotional distance. That was the danger of him. The physical connection was just so intense.

She was startled by the first flash of the camera when they got off the plane, by the crush of people who surrounded their car. He did not seem bothered by it at all. The click and pop of each picture felt like getting hit with a tiny boulder, and she started each time. But they made their way quickly to the car, the door shutting behind them. The windows tinted, hopefully enough to conceal them from view. She didn't know if she had done what he needed her to do.

"I'm sorry," she said. "I forgot to gaze adoringly at you."

"That's quite all right. It's all right if you look surprised, because you are definitely being positioned as my sweet small-town fiancée."

She frowned. "Shouldn't there have been security keeping them away from us?"

"Yes. If I wanted that. But what I wanted was photographs. I will not be making grand explanations about where I have been spending my time these past days. Nor will I be making an announcement or telling a story about how the two of us got together. The media will fill it all in as long as we make ourselves available. They will create the narrative. If we tried to make the narrative, then it would be questioned. The public likes to make a story for themselves."

"Oh," she said.

She didn't know how she felt that her naivety was being used against her. That he liked that she had been surprised by all of that because it would make her... Well, look like what she was, she supposed. Maybe it was a manipulation so much as a calculated lack of preparation.

He was so irritating.

But then, she was captivated by the cityscape, and forgot to be irritated with him as she gazed up at the impossibly tall buildings as they wound their way slowly through the manic streets. She had never seen anything like it. The sidewalks were filled with people, the road gridlocked with cars. The sky was nearly blotted out by those buildings. So tall that when she looked up out the window she couldn't see past the end of them.

They pulled up to a building that was all black glass and steel, and the car stopped. The door was opened for them, and Rocco got out, reaching inside and taking her hand, guiding her up out of the car and onto the sidewalk, where they were met by more photographers. He wrapped his arm around her waist, and instinctively, she raised her left hand to cover her face as they walked by the photographers. Once they were inside the building he looked at her and smiled. "You showed them your ring."

She looked down at her hand. "Not intentionally. I was just… Shielding myself instinctively."

"Well, your instincts are very good."

There was no one in the black foyer of the building, and she found herself confused by that.

"It is my building," he said. "For now, everything is empty. It requires security clearance to get in, of course."

They walked through the empty space, to the elevators, where he entered a passcode, and the doors slid open.

They got inside.

"You live in this whole empty building."

"It will be turned into luxury apartments for others to rent. But I have been enjoying the solitude. The top floor is mine."

She thought about what he had said. How he valued his space.

"Is this just you maintaining control of an entire building?"

He looked at her. "It does not make sense to continue to do it always."

"Right."

The doors opened, and there was a small entryway, and another door that required another code.

When they were inside, her jaw dropped. The space was expansive. And there was nothing in it beyond the necessary. The kitchen was black. The floors were black and glossy, the cabinets a glossy black as well. The countertops made of graphite-colored concrete. It was opulent in a way, but also spare. The materials themselves provided the cues of luxury. The couch that stretched across the living area was black, like everything, starkly shaped. And the view of the city below was stunning. It was beginning to get dark, and the lights glowed bright from the cars, the buildings, street signs and neon advertisements.

"It's strange to me," she said, "that you prize this level of spareness quite so much, and control, and yet you live in a city that is so… Loud. And cluttered."

He laughed. "I suppose so. And yet, it allows me to keep nothing. If I want something, I go out and get it at a moment's notice. There is no need to hoard when the world is at your fingertips."

"Considering that you're a billionaire I rather thought that you had the ability to do that even if you lived on a mountaintop."

"Perhaps. Although it would be inefficient."

"Ah. Efficiency."

"Come," he said. "I will show you to your room."

Her room.

"We won't share a room?"

She didn't know why, but the look on his face made her laugh. Well, she did know why. The stark horror there was just too funny. If a little bit insulting. "No," he said. "I prize my space."

"Right."

"We have an event tonight," he said.

"Tonight?" she asked, shocked.

"Yes. A charity event. There is a red dress in your closet. I want for you to wear that."

"You even get to choose what I wear."

"Did you want to stand there and dither over which thing to choose? Did you wish to wonder what might be appropriate?"

No. Dammit. The annoying thing was, she didn't want that. And it was helpful that he told her what she should wear.

"How long do I have to get ready?"

She would not validate him by indicating that she was grateful he had given her direction on her outfit.

"You have an hour and a half."

He opened the door to her bedroom, and clearly indicated she was to go inside. She did, and saw that her room was much the same as all the others, Spartan and spare. One wall was a window in its entirety. She stood there, feeling tiny and remote as she looked out over the city.

She took her phone out of her pocket, and FaceTimed Melody.

"I have a strange story to tell you," she said.

"What?" Melody asked.

She took her phone and turned it so that her friend could see the scene below.

"Where are you?"

"I'm in New York."

"New York City?" her friend asked, emphasis on each word.

"Yes," she said. "New York City. And… I'm engaged."

She flipped the phone around to face her again.

Melody's expression was wild. "Engaged? Not to that gorgeous man you brought into the coffee shop."

"The very same."

"No, well… You barely know him."

"I know parts of him pretty well," she muttered.

"You don't have to marry a man just because you slept with him," Melody said. "I don't care what the church elders say."

Noelle snorted. "That's not why I'm marrying him." Though, it was a little bit. Not because she thought she had a moral obligation to do it, but because she felt connected to him in a way that she couldn't explain. She wasn't even going to try. She couldn't even make it make sense to herself, much less her friend.

"So he's rich?"

"Yeah. Well, he's sort of the billionaire that has been trying to buy my bed-and-breakfast."

"No," Melody said.

"Yes. But we got snowed in together…"

"Real life is not a Hallmark movie," said Melody. "The evil developer stays an evil developer. I mean, the fact that he dragged you back there instead of moving to the small town is kind of making that point for me."

"Oh," Noelle said. "I know."

She went over to the closet and pulled out a red dress. It was satin and slinky, with straps that went… She didn't even know where.

"But you got engaged to him."

"I have feelings for him," she said. She sighed heavily. "I know. I know. And he hates our town. But he agreed to let me keep the bed-and-breakfast. He agreed to give my mom the payout that she wants anyway."

"What's he getting out of it? I mean, no offense. Not that you aren't a prize."

"I am definitely a prize," she said. Then she laughed. "No. I mean… He wants a baby."

Melody's forehead wrinkled. "Oh, I don't know what to do with that."

She imagined a baby. Soft and small, with Rocco's dark hair. "I've always wanted to be a mother," she said. "And… You know my mom leaving hurt. It broke something. I get to keep my bed-and-breakfast. I get to have a family. Unconventional, maybe. He's going to keep living in New York most of the year. But he says that I can go back home and stay at the bed-and-breakfast sometimes."

"So it's a marriage of convenience," Melody said.

She wished that it was that straightforward. That there were no feelings involved on her end. But there were. There were a lot of feelings.

"Yes," she said. "Of a kind. It's not that we don't have… A certain amount of passion."

Melody blinked. "Wow."

"I don't want you to think of me as some sacrificial lamb going to the slaughter when I go to his bed. I certainly went the first time with no coercion whatsoever, and no offer of marriage or saving my bed-and-breakfast on the table."

"Admittedly," Melody said. "He is the most handsome man I have ever seen."

"He really is," Noelle agreed.

She looked at the dress. "I have to go. I have to get ready for this… This thing."

"What thing?"

"A big party. Where everyone is going to be watching me and judging me next to this man, who is sophisticated and gorgeous. And deciding whether or not I'm good enough for him, I guess."

"Well, you make it sound very fun."

She suddenly realized what an interesting trap she had stepped into. Rocco had all the power. If he decided to, he could send her back home, demolish the bed-and-breakfast anyway. They weren't married yet. No agreements had been signed.

She could've come all this way only to go right back.

And it was even more impossible to imagine going back to the way things had been before now.

She had come so far, and yet, she still had nothing to hold on to, not really.

Except for him.

This wildly difficult man that had woven himself around her existence.

"I better look great in this dress."

CHAPTER TEN

HE WAS ABOUT to go in and fetch her when she emerged. And his heart nearly exited his chest, straight through his rib cage. He had never been affected so by a woman. And he couldn't quite pinpoint why it was happening now. But with or without reason she affected him all the same.

The dress was… She looked like a present. All red and satin and he wanted to unwrap her more than anything.

It was a complicated series of straps that crossed low in the front, showing her glorious cleavage.

The back was almost entirely bare, the satin hugging the curve of her rear, before cascading out around her feet like a waterfall.

She was… Everything.

"You will do," he said.

She looked at him like he was certifiable. Nobody ever did that. Nobody was brave enough. Nobody but her.

"You are beautiful," he said. "Does that fix things?"

"Why is it so difficult for you to compliment me?"

"What is difficult is finding words for what I feel." That was honest. He wasn't sure that he liked it, because he felt as if she had extracted a compromise from him. And he was determined not to be changed by this.

He wanted to build a hedge around his space, as he

had done when he was a child, to keep himself protected. Pure. Controlled.

Control.

A word that cut both ways with such precision. He did not care for it.

And yet, it was what also protected him. Even while it was what had victimized him. But his control, that never failed him.

And so, his control was how he would choose to live.

"You look all right too," she said, lifting a brow.

It astonished him, the way that she was so… Resilient. Even so soundly out of water as she was. A little fish who shone brightly in spite of it all. He thought of how he had tried to chop wood and cook at the bed-and-breakfast. The way that he had tried to bend himself to care for her when she was ill. He had made a mess of everything. It had been torturous. And none of that torture was visible here, now with her.

"Let us go," he said.

He was about to put his arm out, but she closed the distance between them and held his hand. "I will probably need a coat," she said.

"Yes, of course."

He knew that one had been placed in the coat closet by the door, and he opened it up, producing a white, faux fur dress that would fall nearly to her ankles.

He put it on her, slowly. Her scent mesmerized him. The way she looked up at him. He was held in thrall for a moment. Perhaps this was what it was like when one got to know a lover. He had no experience of that. Sex was a need that he wrapped tightly in control. Because to share with someone else was to engage in give-and-take. Never his strong suit.

But perhaps this was the other side of it. The benefit. He had always imagined that one would grow bored with a lover eventually, and yet he found himself growing more and more intrigued by his.

She held his hand again as they made their way down to the front of the building, and got into the waiting limousine.

"Very fancy," she said.

They had only taken a town car from the airport.

"It is meant to give us room," he said.

Her brows lifted. "For what?"

He chuckled. "I don't know. Perhaps you could think of something."

"I have only just put this dress on. I'm not taking it back off."

He growled. He hadn't even meant to do that.

Her eyes went wide. "Feral."

"I'm not feral," he said.

"You kind of are. Strange, feral man. In the most luxurious of surroundings. And yet… You don't quite know what to do with people. Do you?"

"I am very good with people. My position demands it."

"Are you good with people, or do you find yourself in a position of power over them and they respond accordingly?"

"What is the difference?"

She shook her head and leaned back against the seat. "Nothing of note to you, I suppose."

"You mean if I did not have power, people would not treat me with deference."

She shook her head. "No. They wouldn't. And that actually has nothing to do with your personality. That's just life."

He didn't like that thought, because it made him feel powerless. It made him feel like his position in the world was tenuous. It made him feel like a small boy again. Because he could remember well what it had been like when he had no influence in his life, in his house growing up. And for just a moment, he had the flickering glance that she would not be here if he didn't have power over her life.

If he hadn't manipulated her.

He pushed that to the side, because there was no benefit to the thought whatsoever.

None whatsoever.

The car pulled up to the gala venue, a stately museum with vast steps, and pillars.

He was gratified by the look on her face. Because he was giving her something. This was an experience far outside her own, and she might not have known that she wanted it, but he would see that she benefited from it. And it didn't matter then, why she was here. It didn't matter. Because the truth was, he had the control.

He had the influence.

He got out of the car ahead of his driver opening the door, and attended to it on behalf of Noelle, taking her hand and pulling her against him as he closed the door. "You do look beautiful," he said.

Perhaps to add more to the moment. Perhaps to make her remember that it wasn't only his offer to let her keep the bed-and-breakfast that had brought her here. It was the passion between them. That was real. It had nothing to do with his influence.

It certainly had nothing to do with his soup-making skills.

"So do you," she said softly, touching the side of his face. Then he felt as if she had grabbed the thread inside of him and pulled it hard, unraveling something. He did not know what to make of that.

He did not know how to proceed. Except to walk up the steps holding tightly to her, entering the building.

There were so many women dressed in colorful dresses, and yet they remained indistinct blurs to him. The trouble was, everyone did. Even people who held influence at the event, the people that he wanted to network with, and speak to, meant so little. Because what he really wanted to do was take that dress off Noelle. To the degree that he resented that they had to go out at all. Of course, if they hadn't gone out she wouldn't have put that dress on.

Whenever someone talked to her, monopolized her attention, he resented it. It made him miss the bed-and-breakfast. It made him want to go back to the top of the secluded mountain with her where he did not have to consider anyone else ever.

It made him want to reclaim her for himself.

He hated that town. He hated that mountain. There was no reason for him to harbor fantasies about returning there. To that cluttered old house filled with dust catchers that she called knickknacks. Filled with memories that weren't his own, and never would be.

He felt himself growing impatient. And perhaps it didn't really matter if he was here at all. The business was now his to run by his own design. He no longer had to engage in endless expansion. He could simply maintain what was. Make better what existed, rather than cluttering up the earth with more resorts that nobody wanted or needed.

That was his mother's grand design, of course. It was not his, and it never would be.

So maybe it was all right that he didn't want to network. Maybe it was all right that what he really wanted to do was take Noelle straight back to his apartment.

Though there was a small amount of joy to be had when he watched her interact with the people around him. She was entirely out of her depth, and yet there was a glow about her that people seemed to find irresistible. God knew that he did.

Even as he grew jealous when other men monopolized her attention, he also felt pride that they saw what he did.

He found it increasingly difficult to keep his hands to himself. He went from holding her hand to wrapping his arm around her waist. Pressing himself against her, moving his hand over her bare back, and then kissing her neck.

"Rocco," she said.

"What?"

"We are in public."

"I find myself bored of the public," he said. "Let's go home."

Noelle had had a lovely evening, but Rocco had clearly been growing impatient. And every time he touched her it felt like he ignited a spark inside of her. Realizing the

effect that she had on him, even in his environment…
It emboldened her.

When they got out of the building, and into the limo, she positioned herself across the way from him. "That wasn't very polite," she said.

"What? We stayed an hour."

"Barely," she said. "And I was having a lovely time."

"I'm glad for you," he said. "But I found myself growing exceedingly impatient."

"I gathered that."

"Witch," he said.

"Hardly," she said.

But inside she felt satisfied. That he was undone. That she had this much power.

The way that his eyes glittered when he looked at her sent a shiver through her. This handsome man wanted her.

She wasn't just the only woman available at the top of a snowed-in mountain. There had been beautiful women all over that gala. He was impatient to leave with her.

She needed to hear him say that.

Because she wanted… Something intense. Something reckless tonight. She felt like when she had slipped this dress on she had put on new skin with it. Like perhaps she had uncovered new depths to herself, new layers.

Like she wasn't just Noelle, with the Christmas tree farm and the bed-and-breakfast. Unassuming and sweet.

Trying to hold together the warm, glowing images of her childhood.

Wholesome. That was what she had always been. Trying to maintain this air of wholesomeness, essentially, as she clung to a two-dimensional vision of her past.

Of her parents.

She had kept herself simple because she resented the complexity of her mother.

That was a stunning realization.

And yet, not one she needed to deal with just at the moment. What she really needed was him.

"Do you want me, Rocco?"

"Yes," he growled.

"I don't mean opportunistically. I don't mean because I'm the woman who you decided to marry for your own convenience. I don't mean… You know, how I pointed out to you that people are nice to you because you have power over them. I don't want you to want me simply because this arrangement gave power to you. Or because we were stuck on a mountaintop."

"I could not even see the faces of the other women there. I could not track the shapes of their bodies. They were brightly colored orbs, orbiting around you. They meant nothing to me. No memory of sex means anything to me. Only the reality of you. You are correct, I am a man with exceeding power. I have trapped you with me, haven't I? Because of that, I do not have to give you my fidelity, do I? I could have left with one of those women. What would you have said? What would you do?"

"I would be hurt," she said.

"And that would only matter to me if I cared about your feelings. My point is, nothing is stopping me from taking another woman if I want her. But I do not. I want you."

That was what she needed to hear. She closed the distance between them, crossed the space, and claimed his mouth. She kissed him deep and long, as she had wanted to do all day, but had felt so disoriented, she simply hadn't. Or perhaps she had been protecting herself. But not anymore.

He was starving. She could feel it in every line of his body. The growl that exited his mouth, even though he was bound and determined to pretend that he was not feral for her.

He was.

She was.

They arrived at the penthouse too fast and too slow. And she moved away from him reluctantly, allowing him to take her hand and lead her out of the car.

She was covered by her coat. It felt cumbersome. Like too many layers, when she wanted to be naked against him.

What a strange thing to know exactly what she wanted. To be in this strange place, in a new situation, and yet to know this.

It was like an anchor, holding her fast to the earth.

What a glorious thing.

The trip up to the apartment was a blur. And when they entered, he pulled her hard against him, kissing her deep, letting her feel that iron hardness of his body, letting her feel exactly what she did to him.

He pushed the coat off her shoulders, as she began to loosen his tie.

They moved, in synchronous rhythm, to that expansive black couch.

They stood at the edge of it, her back to the window, and he began to untie the straps that held the dress to her body.

It fell away, leaving her naked except for the red high

heels she was wearing. She hadn't put any underwear on beneath the dress because it simply hadn't allowed for it. The fabric was to slippery and silky. And now she was grateful for it, because the look on his face was... That was a look that she wanted to pursue. Not just now, but maybe forever.

She felt like she was enough. She felt special.

Not just in the context of being the only woman on the mountain.

It was intoxicating.

He stripped his tie away, and shrugged his jacket off, then he began to unbutton his shirt, and she watched with rapt attention.

As he revealed that gorgeous chest, his rippling stomach. He cast the shirt to the ground, and began to undo his belt slowly, and she found her breath hitching slightly with each articulated movement. He stripped himself entirely naked, and sat on the edge of the couch, like an emperor. "Come to me," he said.

She was very aware that her back was to an open window, and that her front was to a naked man. That she wanted him, as fiercely as he wanted her.

The center of her ached. Felt hollow with the need for him.

She could feel how slick and wet she was with each step she took toward him. It didn't even occur to her not to obey. Not when obedience would lead her exactly where she wanted to go.

"Take your hair down," he said.

She reached up and quickly dashed the pins out of her hair, letting it fall around her shoulders in a wild cascade.

"Yes," he said, his voice hoarse. "Now you are feral for me."

She laughed. She couldn't help herself. Because of course she was. She always was. She had been from the beginning, hadn't she? After thinking herself tame for so many years, the truth of it was she had never met anyone who made her wild.

But he did.

And that was when she did something entirely out of character, without even thinking. She ran her hands over her aching breasts, summing the nipples, pinching herself, watching as his expression went from stormy to the black eye of a hurricane.

She let her hands move down her own waist, her hips, before pressing one down between the center of her thighs, where she touched her own slickness. Where she zeroed in on that beat of pleasure, and began to stroke herself.

"Noelle," he growled.

She didn't know who she was. Who was this woman? Bold and naked in front of a window, pleasuring herself as a man watched her. Who was this woman, in nothing but red high heels?

Who was this woman, in New York City, with a heavy diamond ring on her left hand.

She was her. That was the stunning thing. She was Noelle Holiday. All things Christmas and bright. And yet sensual and needy with him.

It was like finding herself. Like seeing herself for the very first time.

She continued to walk toward him, and she didn't have to be asked. She knew exactly what to do. She straddled his lap, bringing her slick center against his hardness. He growled, his large hands cupping her ass as he brought her forward, arching against her, rubbing himself through her slick folds.

"Mine," he said.

And she could only agree, in small, short bursts of need.

It was like heaven to have his hands on her. And she luxuriated in it. He moved them up her back, down her arms, around to cup her breasts, and his touch on her sensitized skin was so much better than her own could ever be.

He teased her, his thumbs moving over her aching peaks, and then he moved his head there, sucking her deep, biting her. She cried out, the pleasure/pain paradox making her head spin.

Making her ache for more.

He wrapped one arm tight around her waist, and gripped her chin with the other, making bold eye contact with her as he thrust himself up inside of her. She moaned, his possession thorough, complete and glorious.

And she began to move over him, as he held her steady, as he let her have the control. Was there any control to be had? She was this creature that he had made her. One of need and desire.

One of absolute earth and fire. He had broken something in her, or made something in her, she didn't know which. Perhaps it didn't matter.

There was nothing but them. All she could see were those dark eyes, gazing deep into hers. The sparkling ring on her left hand, his muscular chest, her hand against his shoulder. He whispered things against her mouth, dirty and beautiful all at the same time.

And when they went over the edge, it was together. Her nails digging into his skin as he poured himself deep inside of her.

She collapsed against him, and he lay back on the couch, still buried inside of her, his hands moving through her hair.

"Stay on the pill for a while," he said.

The comment jarred her back to reality.

"What?"

"There's no need for you to fall pregnant immediately. And... I think it would be better for you to become accustomed to this life."

Confusion twisted inside of her. "I thought that it was important..."

"This is important," he said.

The granite in his voice rebuilt something within her that had cracked only a moment ago. He didn't want to have a baby because he didn't want to be distracted from the attraction between them. She was actually happy with that. Happy to put it off for a little while.

"It would be better," he said. "Anyway. The optics. If you waited at least a year to get pregnant, there would be no question as to why I married you."

She nodded. Except of course, if people asked questions about why they got married, and came to the conclusion it was not for love, then they would be right.

But something had certainly shifted within her.

This thing that moved her further and further away from who she was. Further and further from home.

She clung to his shoulders then, desperate. Because he was the only thing keeping her here.

On his whim, the bed-and-breakfast could go away. On his whim this relationship could end. And she would be the one left picking up the pieces. It felt hideously imbalanced. Except he wanted her.

He had said it.

This was her power.

What a strange thing, for a woman who had never wielded power in any way, but least of all this way.

"Yes. We can wait."

"Good. I think that you should spend tonight in my bed."

So she did.

CHAPTER ELEVEN

When Rocco showed up to the board meeting the next day, he knew that he was going to be met with sterling opposition.

"This is how you tell us that you are engaged?" Jeremiah Ulster, one of the oldest members of the board, tossed his phone into the center of the table, pictures of him and Noelle plastered into a tell-all article. Of course, he and Noelle had told nothing. But everyone knew at this point he had been snowed in on the mountain, and they knew that she was the person he had been snowed in with. People wanted to believe in romance so desperately, that they fashioned one out of it. And that suited him just fine.

"It is not my fault that the press decided to fill in their version of the truth without my speaking to you. But, as you know, I was indisposed for a while, and could not communicate, and when Noelle and I arrived in the city last night we had an event to attend."

"You were making a show of it," Jeremiah said.

"Yes," he said. "Perhaps I was. And perhaps that will serve as a reminder that I am not a child to be scolded, whether or not my mother put you in your position or not.

This is my company, and I make decisions based on what I feel is best. The expansion ends. I am to be married."

"Surely we have to approve that," Jeremiah said, and he searched around as if he was hunting for a stack of bylaws.

"You don't," Rocco said. "I simply must wed within three months of informing you. Which I shall do. And then within a year of the marriage, my wife must be pregnant, or we must be in the process of pursuing surrogacy or adoption."

"You are quite well versed," Jeremiah said.

"Because it is my life," Rocco said. "It is my life, and I will do with it what I choose. I have chosen to marry Noelle Holiday. It is my right. She is the woman that I have chosen. And I am not building a resort in Wyoming."

"What?" This came from Rosalie, another older member of the board.

"No, I am not. Because my wife, Noelle, will be preserving her family home rather than agreeing to any changes."

"You've cut a deal with her," Rosalie said. "That much is obvious."

"And what incentive would I have to do that?" Rocco asked. "She is the one who benefits from it, not me. I found that I had a change of heart up on the mountain."

"I don't believe it," Jeremiah said.

"It is not for you to believe. It is what is happening. You were all happy with my mother's mental deterioration because she gave you more power. And the eternal expansion lines your pockets. But I do not work for you. And I am not someone you can take advantage of.

Perhaps it has not been clear. I am Rocco Moretti. And I will have my way."

He stormed out of the meeting, his heart hammering. He was furious. Every single one of them had a stake in the way that things had gone with his mother.

And they would pay for it. By watching their easy profits slip away. And once he had total control of everything, he would oust them. He also knew that they were going to drip feed terrible PR stories to the media. There were going to be competing narratives now. He called Noelle as soon as he got into the car.

"Oh," she said. "I didn't expect to hear from you."

"I just had a rather explosive meeting. You have to be aware that there is going to be negative press. Because the board is opposing this marriage. They have no control, but once we have a child, I can begin the process of replacing them, and they don't like that. They are going to make it sound as if this marriage is an entirely Machiavellian scheme on my part."

There was a short pause on the other end of the line. "Isn't it?"

For some reason he didn't like that. Not after the explosiveness of last night. Not after everything.

"Still. You may feel differently when you see it plastered in black-and-white. They will do their best to smear us and to smear you."

"I can handle it," she said.

"I hope that's true. Because we are going to have to ramp up our efforts. We will be attending a great many events leading up to Christmas. I'm going to get you a wedding planner, and we are going to plan a Christmas charity event."

"That's a lot," she said.

"I'm a lot. If you hadn't noticed."

"Yes," she said. She sounded sad.

Perhaps it was the reminder that all of this served a very specific purpose. He could admit, even if just to himself, that he was somewhat surprised by how jarring it was to have to contend with the fact that there was a scheme at play here. Especially when last night had felt… Like they were the only two people on earth.

"You forget," she said. "I have run a Christmas tree farm in a small town for years. I can handle intense. I can handle holly and jolly. We have nearly a month until the big day. We can accomplish a lot in that time."

"You are perfect for this," he said.

And only after he hung up the phone did he realize how true that was.

"You are perfect for this."

Noelle clung to that. Day in and day out over the next few weeks.

She started working on planning the charity event he wanted to throw. She talked about it endlessly when they would go out to different functions. And she ignored the venomous headlines that came out about them.

The tell-alls from women he had slept with before. Talking about his prowess and how cold he was.

It hurt her, to read those stories. She tried not to. Because there really was no point. It didn't benefit her in any way.

It didn't help her. It only hurt.

So she ignored them. Because he had warned her. And he had been very, very right.

Their outings together created their own fight against the narrative.

She stood by him.

She nearly had apoplexy, though, when a story came out about her mother.

The gold-digging mother-in-law who had been unfaithful to her husband before his death, and who wanted nothing more than to get a big payout. Had she in fact orchestrated this alliance between her daughter and Rocco?

The idea of her mother being that strategic was hilarious.

The revelations about the infidelity less so.

This just… It destroyed everything. Shattered her pretty childhood snow globe into thousands of pieces. Had she known anything about her own life?

She didn't know if the allegations were true or not. But Christopher Farmer, a man who lived down the road from them had given an interview in the paper about it. That they had been lovers. He had clearly gotten a payout of some kind.

Noelle called her mother. "Mom," she said. "Is this true?"

"Noelle, life is complicated," her mom said. "I regret it. And your dad forgave me. It happened a long time ago."

"You just never really loved us, did you?" Noelle asked.

"I do," her mom said. "I did."

"Well, you're partying in Boca with my fiancé's money, so I guess you love how useful I am to you."

Noelle hung the phone up.

She tried to forget that happened when Rocco came home and she lost herself in his touch.

That was the one place where everything felt like it made sense.

In bed with him.

At least there she had some sanity. Or rather, a really perfect brand of insanity. There was also Melody.

And Daniela, her wedding planner, who was lovely, and quickly becoming a friend.

"Weddings are stressful for anybody," she said. "But especially so when there's this big of a circus around it."

"The board is bound and determined to mess all of this up. I'm not going to let them," she said.

Because she thought of that little boy, whose mother had controlled everything, and hadn't taken care of him at all. And that helped. When nothing else did.

Of course, nothing helped the shambles she felt like her emotions were in, but it at least gave her the will to go on.

She found that she liked New York more than she would've imagined. Was happier there than she had thought possible. When she didn't wear makeup, and she put on a hat, nobody recognized her. Because she was only famous as Rocco Moretti's beautiful, made-up fiancée.

So when she was just Noelle, nobody looked at her. Nobody saw her. That was something that never happened at home. She couldn't be anonymous if she wanted to, and given the amount of phone calls she had gotten since the news about her mother's infidelity had been splashed all over the news, there would be no sanity to be had at home.

She understood that.

And she wanted nothing to do with that.

At Christmastime, the city was beautiful. And she found herself going to the tree at Rockefeller Center often, gazing up at it, thinking about home, and finding a way to feel nostalgic about it.

She was meeting Daniela for lunch, and to have a conversation about flowers. The Christmas event was looming, and she was feeling especially... Fraught.

It was just a lot. Everything.

She wasn't used to this. This feeling of being turned inside out, exposed. Yes, in a small town everybody knew her, which was its own issue, but there was also the issue of the way she lived her life. She didn't parade her business around. She never had. She went internal. She focused on her bed-and-breakfast. Her only sanity was him. That was her version of going internal now. Losing herself in his touch, in his arms.

She and Daniela passed by a storefront on Fifth Avenue that had exceedingly shocking lingerie outfits on the manikins in the window.

"I think I'd like to go in there," she said.

"Planning for the honeymoon?" Daniela asked.

"Or just Tuesday," she said brightly.

Because she really was this whole other person now. This woman who reveled in her sexuality.

She was cautiously amused by herself. By this change in her.

Even while there was a bit of foreboding lingering in the background. A small amount of fear that this could rebound on her. That she would be utterly entirely lost at sea if something happened to their relationship.

But it was no matter.

Because it was too late, that was the thing. She was out in the middle of the ocean, in a small inflatable raft, clinging to a rope that kept her tethered.

Rocco was the rope.

If she lost hold of him, she didn't know what would happen.

But she was already in the middle of the sea.

So she bought five different lace and transparent silk outfits, so little fabric for so much money, and she let herself enjoy it. Let herself get excited thinking about what he would do when he saw them.

What are you doing?

It was a text from Melody, right as she exited the store.

Just spent a ridiculous amount of Rocco's money on underwear.

I have to get an Italian boyfriend.

Fiancé.

And she added a smiley face for good measure.

Even with the heaviness of the media barrage, she felt buoyant.

And she followed that buoyancy down Fifth Avenue, and she and Daniela made an appointment with one another to do wedding dresses the next week.

Then she walked the rest of the way back to Rocco's

penthouse, enjoying the bustle. Now that she was getting used to the rhythm of the city, she did find beauty in it.

It was different than the beauty she was born into. Different than the life she had chosen for herself.

But it was beautiful all the same.

She didn't expect to find Rocco home in the middle of the day, and yet when she got to the penthouse, he was. Standing there with his back to her, facing the scene below. His posture looked especially straight, his figure imposing with his jet-black hair ruthlessly tamed into place, and his black suit so expertly cut to the lines of his body.

But there was an aura of something radiating from him that actually frightened her.

"Rocco?"

He turned toward her, a glass of scotch in his hand. He was home in the middle of the day, and he was drinking in the middle of the day. That was a bad sign.

"What…"

"Have you not seen?"

"No. I've been out shopping with Daniela."

"Well, it is only a matter of time. They've done it."

"They've done what?"

"The board has decided, in their infinite pettiness, to publish my mother's greatest secret."

"Oh…"

And admittedly, she didn't understand why that was a problem. She couldn't say that to him, not while he looked like the very angel of death, but Rocco was amazing for what he had been through. For coming out of the life that he had been brought up in as well as he had.

He shouldn't bear any embarrassment or shame because of it.

She could see, though, that he did not feel that way.

"Rocco..."

"They published pictures of the house. The inside of the house. Of all the things. All the horrible, disgusting things, piled up past the windows. You couldn't even see outside anymore. It blocked the daylight. My mother's staff... They betrayed her. They were complicit in it. They lived in it. They enabled her, and now they have gone and exposed her. Exposed me."

"Rocco, none of it had anything to do with you. You were just a child."

"I lived in it," he said. "And you scrub your skin, and try to clean yourself, but the smell will not come out. It still doesn't. I can still... Feel it, on me like a film. Don't you understand? Nobody that lived in that house was separate from it. I am not separate from it."

"But it isn't... None of it was your fault."

"She was my mother. And... There is nothing half so horrible as hating a person for what they do to you and loving them just as fiercely. Wanting to protect them. Because even if she didn't know the full scale of how ashamed she should be, I did. I did, and I took it all on myself, onto my own shoulders. I know how wrong it was. I know how... How sick she was. But it was never out. It was not her legacy. I took that all into myself, onto myself, to avoid ever having it be something that marred her name forever, and now they have just done it."

She took her phone out, and she googled it. And there it was. Pictures. This beautiful, stately manner home, with piles of garbage as if it were a bespoke landfill.

There were rooms that had semblances of order to the stacks. Books, magazines, newspapers. But others that were simply... Indistinct mounds of trash. The kitchen... There was food everywhere. On every surface. She could imagine the smell. Why it had been so difficult for him to eat, why he couldn't just trust anything.

He was so fastidious, so clean, so perfect.

It was an assault to think of him living this way. To think of how he'd had to bear that. And even though she didn't think he should carry any of the shame, she could see that he did.

Perhaps it was very like her own shame. This feeling of not being enough to make her mother happy. Maybe he felt that too.

Because for all that he was this creature of order and authority, he had been helpless then.

The kind of man he was... It no doubt aided him.

He likely thought the world saw this and saw his failure.

"I have lived with you for nearly a month," she said. "And you do not allow me total control of your space. It is yours. You have very clear boundaries."

"Yes," he said.

"In her way, so did your mother. You could no more sweep in and control everything than I can now."

"I'm not like my mother," he said.

Horror burst in her chest. "I didn't mean it that way. I only meant—"

"Do not seek to give advice on something you can't possibly understand. You are upset because your parents had the same sort of issues that everyone has the world over. A minor infidelity, the ache of suburban ennui.

Your childhood was happy. Your parents managed to hide it from you. You have any idea what I would give to have had my mother hide her psychosis from me? Rather than including me in the middle of it? Do not try to understand me. Do not seek to compare. It is an absolute injustice."

He stepped away, going into his room and closing the door firmly behind him.

And she knew there was no reaching him. Not now.

He didn't care about this…this thing that had hurt her so much and he'd used this to push her away rather than bringing them closer together.

Over the next few days it was a grim march to Christmas Eve. She didn't even try to ask him about having a Christmas tree in the penthouse. Of course he would never allow it.

It would be clutter.

And he didn't allow that, however mad he got when he felt like she was attempting to compare him to her mother.

But they had their charity event tonight, and the entire purpose of the barrage of attacks that they had been under was so that they couldn't show their faces. Was so they would decide to call off their marriage. This trial by media had one purpose. And even if Rocco couldn't do this now, she would.

He was her lifeline.

And he had denied her these past few days. He hadn't so much as spoken to her, much less touched or kissed her.

She felt alone. Adrift.

It was as awful as she had feared that it would be.

And yet she was still here, so she would still fight.

The night of the gala, she dressed up in a very fitted emerald green dress with a sweetheart neckline, one of the strapless, glorious concoctions she had bought the other day with Daniela, before everything had fallen apart, securely underneath.

If only she could feel as put together as she looked.

But not even very fancy underwear could save her from the havoc Rocco was wreaking on her heart.

CHAPTER TWELVE

HE EMERGED FROM his room, dressed meticulously, of course. But she could see the distance there. When he moved to her, he did not touch her.

She lifted her chin. "So this is how it's going to be?"

"What are you talking about?"

"You're going to let them win. This is what they wanted. They want to stop the two of us from getting married. So you're going to act in a way that's going to guarantee to drive me away, you're going to act in a way that will guarantee we appear compromised and defeated at our own charity event."

"I am not compromised or defeated," he said, a defiant light in his dark eyes.

"You won't even touch me. You don't think that people are going to notice that? You don't think that it is utterly, horribly apparent that whatever connection we have is not functioning right now?"

His lip curled. "I am in command of this."

"Then be in command of it. Don't just perform. Don't let somebody else decide how much shame you should carry." She lifted her chin. "And I don't need you to tell me what I understand and what I don't understand. I have lived with you for a month. I'm getting to know you.

Maybe I didn't go through all the same things that you did. But everybody… Everybody is a little bit messed up by something. We all are. That isn't a bad thing, it isn't necessarily anybody's fault. But it is the way that it is. So no, maybe I haven't experienced the trauma that you have, but I know what it's like to have something very personal put out there for the public to see. Maybe it doesn't seem like a big deal to you, but it does to me. And you don't need to protect the pain that you feel by trying to minimize mine. You also don't need to hide. I'm here. And I'm willing to talk, to listen, whatever you need."

His black eyes remained cold, but he looked her up and down. "I don't need anything."

"Of course not. You don't need people. You are Rocco Moretti. An island." She felt terrible, for saying that. After everything he had been through. She pinched the bridge of her nose. "You are not a small boy stuck in your bedroom anymore." She looked up at him. "I'm sorry. I'm sorry that they dragged all of that out. I'm sorry that they've dredged all of this up. It isn't fair."

He looked… Regretful then. "No," he said. "I'm the one that is sorry. I was completely unsympathetic when these things were dragged out about your family. I was entirely cold about it. I did compare it both to my own pain, and to my own goals. And your pain meant nothing in light of them. I didn't care if past lovers talked about our sexual encounters, because I don't feel… I chose that. At least. You have to stand by your choices. But now that something I have no control over has been brought out for public consumption, I get it. I feel it. And I also feel regret, for not understanding before. For giving you no sympathy. I at least chose this. I knew on some level that there could be consequences for it. But I dragged you into this, and this is not your life. I was born into a life where aspects of me will be a public consumption. You weren't."

"No," she said. "I have no experience with it. But as long as you… As long as I didn't feel completely cut off from you, it was bearable. The past few days haven't been."

He looked as if he didn't know how to respond to that. And so he didn't. That was the best that she could read of him.

If he didn't know, he simply wouldn't. And it was okay, because what she could see, what she understood was that her words had changed something inside of him. She would cling to that. So he moved near her, and he looped his arm through hers. And that was affirmation of something.

"Come along, *cara*. We will make it a night to remember."

Looking at the pain that he had caused Noelle created no small amount of shame inside of him. But he had work to do. He had to make sure that this charity event went off without a hitch. He had to prove that he was untouchable. He had to reclaim his control.

To prove that they would not have a win over him. It wasn't that he doubted that. It was only that he was not used to having another person present when he was contending with anything. Having her in his house, in his life, was unprecedented.

And it made him have to consider things in a way he had not before. He had hurt her feelings.

He held on to her the whole way down to the car, and

then into the car. He was aware that they were having their photograph taken, but that was not why he held her.

When they arrived at the venue, an outdoor garden, heated by a large rig set up all around, with lights strung above them, he was amazed.

"You planned this?"

"Yes," she said.

"How did you even know where to begin?"

"I might be a small-town girl, but there's nothing I know or love more than Christmas. Or a big Christmas event."

There was a large Christmas tree at the center, reaching up past the string lights, the angel on top glittering brightly.

For some reason, it hit him square in the chest. They'd had so many things in their house, but never a Christmas tree. Never anything that was there with purpose or beauty. It was all ugly, desperate consumption.

This was not clean or spare. It was resplendent. Glittering.

It did not disgust him.

It made him feel something.

And he had no idea where to put it or what to do with it.

There were so many people waiting to speak to her, to congratulate her.

When he had chosen her to be his wife he had not imagined that she would shine on this level. She had been dragged through the mud. The media had been merciless to her.

And yet, here she was, with the glow on her face that could not be contained.

How could he have shut down as he did? When she deserved his unending praise?

This was his pattern, he supposed. When he felt out of control. When life felt out of his control.

He could not lock himself in a bedroom anymore, because he was not alone.

You would be the one freezing her out. And in that way, you would be like your mother.

He tried to push that thought to the side. He had been angry when she had drawn parallels between himself and his mother. But he couldn't deny that they existed. It was becoming harder and harder to do so.

Control.

What a strange thing that control could take such different shapes, and essentially be from the same root.

The need to hoard, the need to consume, the need for space, the need for nothing.

It was only through her eyes that he could see the similarities. And clearly.

He pushed that thought to the side, because he didn't need to have it tonight. Tonight was about her triumph. Tonight was about showing the world what they really were.

No. It's not about showing the world what you really are. Your relationship is alive. It is for convenience...it is for business. You know that.

Except it didn't feel like it was only that. He had missed her these past days. He had denied himself her body.

Because he had been so disgusted with himself. Because those pictures, that story, had brought up the depths of his shame. Had left him feeling unclean. And then his own reaction to her had made him feel even worse.

Even more unworthy of her. And then she had appeared, in that dress, her determination a ring of light around her.

How could he be any less than she was?

How could he give less than she gave?

Nobody at the party brought up any of the news articles. Of course they wouldn't, not here. No one who had been given an invite to this was lying in wait. But that would not always be the case.

There would be times when they had to confront animosity, when they would have to confront the sneering delight of people who enjoyed their embarrassment. But thankfully it was not tonight.

She deserved this night. She deserved everything.

He did not dance. It wasn't in his nature. And yet when other couples went out to the dance floor he found himself compelled to do the same. With her.

He went to her, and reached out his hand. "Dance with me."

He let himself get drunk on her. The touch, the exhilaration of spinning with her on the dance floor. He let everyone around them fade away. He let himself feel the magic, the kind of joy he had never let himself feel around Christmas.

At the end of the evening, at the end of their last dance, she stretched up on her toes and kissed his lips, in front of everyone. "Merry Christmas."

CHAPTER THIRTEEN

SHE FELT THE intensity of what they had just experienced wrapping all the way around her skin. She didn't know what changes had been happening inside of him, but she could feel them. Like electricity crackling over his body. And when they got into the car to go back home, her breath exited her body as she caught his eyes across the seat. "A job well done," he said.

"Thank you."

"You were a triumph. In spite of everything. I was an ogre."

"Only a little bit."

"I'm sorry. I'm sorry that when you met me we were snowed in on a mountaintop, and it might have seemed like I was… Something that I'm not."

"How do you think you seemed?"

He laughed. Hard. "Normal?"

"You didn't know how to heat up a can of soup. You did not seem normal, Rocco." She closed the distance between them and put her hand on his thigh. "I came with you anyway."

He looked at her, his expression charged.

And yet again, she had the feeling that he didn't know quite what to say, so he wasn't going to say anything at all.

Instead, he claimed her mouth with his. Ruthless, hard. And it was a claiming. He pushed his fingers into her hair, knocking the pins out, and letting it fall loose.

She was breathless. Undone by it and him.

He kissed her until she couldn't breathe. Bit her bottom lip. Left her mouth swollen and aching with need.

When they arrived at the penthouse, it was all they could do to get out of the car. All they could do to make it up to the penthouse.

She had seduced him. Had teased him and tormented him before. But this was different. He was claiming her. Utterly and completely. His touch was rough, and exciting.

He tore her dress away from her body, and revealed the surprise she had on underneath. "What is this?" he growled.

"I got this for you. Days ago. But since you weren't touching me, you didn't know."

"I know now," he said, lowering his head and sucking at the tender flesh of her breast, hard. Then he bit her, leaving a mark behind. She loved it. She encouraged him. Because he was claiming her body for himself, and that was what she wanted. She didn't want to be adrift. She wanted him to hold on. She wanted everything.

He tore at the lace. She didn't tell him how expensive it all was. It thrilled her that he was destroying it. That it inflamed him enough that he couldn't be patient.

She responded in kind. She ripped at his white shirt, at his tie, she undressed him all backward, her hands growing desperate. Then she leaned in and bit the muscle on his chest. He gripped her chin, forcing her face up, claiming her in a hard kiss.

She loved it. It was everything. So was he.

This was no gentle coming together. No soft Merry Christmas. No snow falling outside on evergreens. It was a storm. The kind that left you isolated on a mountain. The only two people in the world. The kind that toppled trees and power lines, the kind that caused landslides.

That was what they were.

Even here in this land of glass and steel, they were elemental. He clung to her hips, kissing his way down her body, pushing her back against the wall as he parted her thighs and began to lick her deep. He gave no quarter. He took her to the heights again and again, made her cry out her need.

"Again," he growled, pushing two fingers within her and thrusting.

She came again, holding on to his shoulders, leaving blood behind where her fingernails dug in deep.

He pulled her down, wrapping her legs around his torso as he stood them both up, pressing her down onto the sofa and entering her in one swift stroke. It was brutal. It was magic.

It was the damn season of cheer and happiness and joy, and she cried out a hosanna at the top of her lungs.

When it was over, she was spent and breathless. She kissed him on the chest, and looked at his profile, hard cut and glorious in the darkness of the penthouse.

"I used to be a nice girl," she whispered.

"And now you're not?"

She leaned in and kissed his chest. "No. I am obsessed with sex. And you."

"You could pick a better obsession."

"Do you think so?"

"Yes," he said. "I do."

"Too bad. Obsession works in mysterious ways."

"Good for me, I suppose."

He rolled so that he was over the top of her, looking down at her, his dark eyes burning with intensity. And that was when she realized, it wasn't simply another half of herself that had come to the fore. It wasn't simply that she had found a part of herself that she had never known before.

Being with him had changed her. Fundamentally.

It made her more assertive. It made her more sexual. It made her want things that she had never wanted before. It made what had been so important only a couple of months ago feel like a distant memory.

Being with him had changed her. It changed what she thought about. It changed what she ate, and where she was willing to live.

It upended every plan that she had ever had about herself. It was incredible.

She reached up and touched his face. And right then she knew. With a certainty. With a spark.

It was love.

She had fallen in love with him.

By inches. In hours and minutes and days. In his eccentricities, in his revelations. In the things that she learned about herself when she was with him.

The way that he made her feel. The way that he made her want to. The way that he was.

She loved him, and it was a stunning, stirring realization.

And it was a terrifying one. Something she didn't

know what to do with right then. Something so deep that she knew she couldn't simply say it.

Because the problem with love was that it could be very real, and still not be enough.

At one time her mother had loved her father, that much she was certain of.

But she had folded herself into a life that she apparently hadn't wanted.

And slowly, very slowly, everything had degraded over time.

She had betrayed the man that she once loved, because she was still searching for something else. It scared her. That realization.

That you could think you wanted something, and be so very, very wrong.

And it reminded her again of that feeling of being adrift. That feeling of being evolved. Like a creature who used to be at home entirely in the water, and had learned to walk on land, but still craved the sea. An amphibian. Not really one or the other. She wondered if that was love. Finding yourself trapped in the middle of two worlds, never being able to fully inhabit either anymore. That was the scary thing. That the change was the sort that left her destined to be unsatisfied.

He wanted to live with her half the time. He wanted to allow her a chance to go back home. To raise their child in a small town.

Being away from him she would never feel whole.

Being entirely away from Holiday House, she would never be whole.

That was the bargain that she had made.

It was the impossibility of loving him. Or maybe of

loving altogether. A series of compromises that left you only ever half alive.

"You are thinking," he said.

"I'm sorry. I'll stop."

"You don't need to stop."

"I probably should."

She kissed his neck, and scooted to the side just a bit. He lay down next to her. "Maybe we should get a Christmas tree," he said.

"It is eleven thirty on Christmas Eve."

"I'm a billionaire."

No sooner had he said that than he was on his phone. And a record thirty minutes later, a Christmas tree was being placed in the center of the penthouse.

Pre-lit and glowing.

The delivery crew had left behind a box of ornaments.

"We should decorate it," he said.

Oh, yes. She loved him. Looking at him as he said that, with absolute earnestness, she was certain.

You can find a way. Just maybe. But still, she didn't speak of love out loud. Instead, she looked at him, at the Christmas lights reflected in his eyes as he hung the ornaments up on the tree, and she hoped.

As a child, she had a life that had seemed perfect.

But it hadn't been real.

It hadn't been real.

But this was. That much she knew. If she never knew anything else, then she knew that.

And she would just have to hope that the sort of magic that had enticed him to get a Christmas tree would bloom into the sort of magic that would keep them happy forever.

CHAPTER FOURTEEN

SLOWLY, SIGNS THAT another person lived in his home began to creep in. It wasn't only the Christmas tree. That was gone by the day after Christmas. He had to have some respects for his own rules. But she began to cook for him, which meant keeping food in the house, rather than simply ordering up every time he wanted something.

She collected pots and pans and other gadgets.

There were places for everything. It was clean.

And yet, sometimes something would be left in a place that he didn't leave it, and it was a bit jarring.

He wasn't accustomed to it.

He didn't hate it.

She was… Changing things inside of him fundamentally. Making him want to change, to compromise, even. To find a way to be close to her, and not simply shut away in a fortress.

And he didn't know what to do with that.

She had a binder with all of her wedding plans in it, and he came home one day to find it all spread out on a new coffee table in the living room.

She was sitting there, chewing on a pen and looking at things. "I don't think there are enough flowers."

He lifted his brow. "Have you met me?"

"My wedding isn't going to be minimalist." She sighed. "I do wish we could have it at the Christmas tree farm."

She sounded wistful. And the truth was, he was in this moment the same man who had demanded that a Christmas tree be delivered at eleven thirty at night on Christmas Eve, and they could easily have their wedding at the Christmas tree farm. But for some reason, he didn't want to allow it. For some reason, it felt like too much of a shift. Too much of a compromise.

"If only," he said. "But the venue is booked."

She looked up at him and squinted. "Of course. I mean, I would think that with money like yours the real barrier is that you want to impress the people who are coming with a city venue?"

"You are quite comfortable spending my money," he said.

She drew back as if wounded. He hadn't meant to hurt her. He did that sometimes.

He was… He only knew how to be alone, he supposed. But she was here now, and he had to learn to be with her. He wanted to learn.

"Sorry," she said. "I didn't mean to imply that the cost didn't matter."

"No," he said. "I'm the one who was mistaken. I shouldn't have said it like that. I did not mean it."

"Oh."

She looked around. "I made a little bit of a mess."

"You live here," he said, though he said the words with some difficulty.

"You almost mean that!" she said, laughing just slightly and he felt some of the tension in him ease.

The problem was, he often felt caught between his desire to maintain his boundaries, and his desire to give her whatever she wanted. Whatever would keep her with him.

He suddenly felt an overwhelming sense of urgency. To keep her with him. To do the right thing. If he didn't, he would be left alone again, and now he had changed so much he did not think he could face it.

What an uncomfortable thing.

To have changed so much he could no longer find solace in solitude.

To not have yet changed enough to be all that she needed.

He felt very resentful, then, of the childhood he had spent in isolation. Because he blamed that, more than anything, for his inability to figure out what to do with her now.

And it hadn't mattered. Until he had wanted to keep somebody with him, it hadn't mattered. She was right, he had gone around wielding power, money and influence, and that had compensated for his lack of people skills. For his inability to compromise. For the mountain of trauma that existed inside of him that he had to scale every single day.

He didn't know how to cross that threshold with her. He didn't know how to fix it.

There were moments when everything was perfect. Then there were moments like this, where it felt like there was something missing between them. Where it felt like there was a gap that he could not close.

"It is not a money issue," he said. "But I wish to be married in the city. However, everything else regarding the wedding planning is up to you. If you wish to go maximalist, then I will give you my blessing."

She looked up at him, her eyes glittering with a kind of joy that he wasn't certain he had ever seen on another person's face. There was something so genuine about her. She seemed to feel everything. It was intoxicating. Astonishing.

He wanted to capture that. Keep it with him always. Because sometimes he disappointed her, and he was so keenly aware of that. And then moments later, this.

"We should go away," he said.

"Where?"

"Italy," he said. "I have seen where you grew up."

"You really want to go back…"

He lifted a shoulder. "I love Italy." Though the truth was a little bit more complicated. He tried to find a way to untangle it inside of him, to untangle it in his mouth so that he could explain it. "Parts of it are entirely divorced from the harder parts of my childhood. I would not go back to that house. But… Lake Como is beautiful. Milan."

"I don't have a passport," she said.

"You don't need one. Or rather, I will arrange everything. And you needn't concern yourself. You are traveling with me, and you will be taken care of."

That was a promise. One that extended well beyond just this trip. He would take care of her. She had entered into this agreement without full understanding of who he was or what it could cost to be with him. He owed her that much. She was going to be the mother of his child, after all. And more than that… There was something indescribably pure about her. Something that he had never experienced growing up. An optimism, a capacity for hope, that he simply did not possess.

He did not want to be the reason the light left her eyes. He did not want to be the thing that extinguished her hope.

He wanted to protect her. He could imagine himself easily as a knight in shining armor, wielding a sword and stepping between her and any imagined enemies.

Though the odd and instant picture that came to mind was himself, pressing the tip of the sword against his own throat. As if he was potentially the biggest threat.

She was everything he was not, and he had identified that from the first moment of illicit attraction.

Did that mean he would be the one to crush her?

No. Not if he decided he would not.

"When?"

"Now," he said.

"I have… Some appointments with Daniela."

"They can be rearranged. If you don't mind, of course." Compromise. He had done it. He was quite proud of himself.

"All right. If you're sure it's okay."

"It's more than okay. It is good. You deserve…" Everything. She deserved everything.

"What?" she asked, her eyes filled with humor.

"You deserve a break," he said. "Because being here, being in the media, I know it has been difficult for you." He hesitated. "You didn't know that your mother had an affair, did you?"

She shook her head. "No. I was convinced that she loved my father. I thought he was the one keeping her at home, and that I was the reason she left. But more and more, I realize that everything around me just wasn't true."

"I am sorry that I said what you went through wasn't difficult. I know that it was. I know that it is. I cannot imagine what it's like to have a happy childhood. But to have a happy childhood and have it proved to be an allusion…"

"It wasn't," she said softly. "In some ways. The truth is, they worked to make it a happy childhood for me. It's just that they weren't happy, I don't think. I'll never know my dad's side of things. That makes me sad. The realization that I will never really know him. My mother claimed that he knew about the affair. But how? How could he let that go? And why? Was it only for me? Did he love her that much. Did he love the facade of our family that much? I can never ask him. I feel like I'm just now realizing my parents were whole people, and it is too late for me to treat my dad like that. It is too late for me to really understand. It's a terrible thing to regret."

He felt that lodge somewhere at the center of his chest. The concept that his mother had been a whole person. Tormented, obviously, by tricks in her mind. By mental illness that had held her in such a tight grip that she had not been able to live better, not for herself or for him.

He cleared his throat. "I can imagine."

"But yes, I would like a break. This has been the most eventful couple months of my life. And I run a Christmas tree farm. So when I tell you that December can be pretty eventful…"

"I am quite certain," he said.

"You don't esteem my Wyoming wisdom."

He shook his head. "On the contrary. I do very much.

Your perspective is so different than mine, and yet somehow, it brings me back around to interesting conclusions."

"Well. I'm glad to be interesting."

"Always."

He had a home in the mountains outside of Milan, and they flew there directly, with Noelle exclaiming about the private jet the whole time. And he wanted to hang on to that infectious excitement.

He wanted to hang on to her.

To give her whatever was required. He watched her face avidly when they landed and drove through the city. As she looked at all the sites. He wanted her to be pleased. To be invested in this place that he had come from.

And even more so, he wanted her to find his house beautiful. Because it was hers now too.

He reminded her of that when they went through the wrought iron gates and up to the elaborate stone facade. He never went here.

He had bought it as part of his expansion efforts. A property to add to his portfolio, and nothing more.

It was furnished in far too classical a fashion for his tastes. It bordered on cluttered, in his opinion. But because of the nature of the historic origins of the home, he had not changed anything in it. The designer of the place would have keeled over in horror had he done so. And it was more an investment, than a place for him to actually visit. An effort at keeping a hand in his homeland, rather than something that existed for him. But she would like it. It was the closest thing to Holiday House that he possessed. Because it was a time capsule of his family. Of their legacy.

A replica of what the house he grew up in could have been had his mother not let it decay under the weight of her illness.

He knew another nudge of discomfort.

Like he was on the verge of truths clicking into place, but he didn't quite want them to.

He ground his teeth together.

And then he turned his focus to Noelle.

"This is extraordinary," she breathed.

"I hear they decorated quite magnificently at Christmas."

"You haven't seen it decorated?"

He shook his head. "No. I don't often come here."

"I would love to see it at Christmas. But why decorate it if you're not even here?"

"There is a full staff. And I believe people rent it out for parties and the like."

"Oh," she said. "I suppose as a property developer you own all kinds of places that you never really go to."

"Yes. Though… Come inside."

They approached the ornate double doors, a dark walnut with brass handles, and they opened for them. Two staff members one on either side, holding them in place. "This is meant to replicate my family home."

A glint of pleasure lit her eyes. "Oh. Thank you for showing me this."

He looked at it through her eyes. He did not see dust and clutter. Rather the velvet furniture with its ornate wooden scrollwork suddenly became beautiful to him. The large, heavily framed paintings on the wall took on new life. Became a window into another time. Into the vision of the artist. Not simply a relic that would be better off in a bin than taking up space.

What was it that she did to him? It was untold.

It was completely unfathomable.

"It's incredible," she said. "I love it."

"I'm glad that you do. We will stay here for a time. There is… A beautiful train ride through the Alps, I can take you there."

He hadn't realized until this moment that his desire to keep his life so spare, so filled with space, kept him isolated. Had kept him closed off from beauty, from joy. Being with her…he felt so close to something new that he could just about feel it. Not quite.

He wanted to feel it.

He wanted to have something now, so that he could give it to her. It suddenly felt essential.

That if perhaps he could find a way to make her happy enough, it might spill over into himself.

They rested well that night in a bed he would've normally been scathing of. For all its extra pillows, and drapery around it. He had nothing scathing to say about it, especially not given what had happened between the two of them in that bed.

She was a vixen and a sex goddess, and at the same time, irrevocably his. It filled him with wonder.

He had arranged for them to have their own glass railcar attached to one of the luxury liners that traveled between Italy and Switzerland through the mountains. It also had their own luxury sleeping accommodation. The train was not a high-speed train, rather it was designed to move slowly and allow the rider to take in the majestic view of the Alps all around them.

Their car had glass walls and a glass ceiling, and was outfitted with blankets, a table, and several places for them to sit and enjoy the view.

When they boarded, they were served hot chocolate with marshmallows, and Noelle immediately curled up in a large reclining seat, a blanket over her knees. She clutched the hot chocolate mug and looked up at him. And he felt not alone in a way that was profound.

He sat beside her. He had no interest in hot chocolate or blankets. Both were sweet and soft in ways that he could never be. But she wanted them. So he embraced them.

She looked at the mountains as they crept slowly down the track, and he looked at her. At the way the sun shone on her hair. The way her skin was illuminated by the fresh white snow.

"This is incredible," she said, snuggling against him.

"Yes," he agreed. "It is."

"I love mountains," she said. "This reminds me of Wyoming. Of the Grand Tetons. And yet I don't and I can never tire of mountains. It doesn't make them commonplace. It's stunning."

"I cannot remember what it feels like to love things. I… Have never been fascinated by nature because I cannot control it. And as far as what I bring into my home…"

"I know."

"You make me wish that I did," he said, an ache suddenly expanding in his chest. "You make me wish… I wish I could feel the things that you do. But I can watch you feel them, and that is nearly as good."

She looked at him, a smile curving her lips. "Why don't you feel them?"

"It's not that simple. It's not I…" He had the realization that in order to fix some of the issues with where he was now he would probably have to go back to when they started. And the idea of that was… Unbearable.

So he would watch her. He would feel it through her. Because that felt manageable, at least. Because it felt good.

They took their luxury dinner in the car with the lights dimmed, so that they could see the stars up above them.

And when they retired to bed, they found it plush and lovely, walls closed in to offer privacy, but the ceiling glass so that they had the view.

He stripped her slowly, kissing her neck, the lovely curve of her shoulder, her breast.

If he was to have one possession in all of his life, he decided it needed to be her.

He could say whatever he needed to to keep her with him. He could give her pleasure in all the ways he desired most.

She would not live in her little town for half the year, though. That would not work. Not before they had a child, and not after.

She had to stay with him.

But he would make her happy. He could show her all these things. He could spend a lifetime capturing her wonder like fireflies in a jar, enough for her, and enough for him.

He could.

He kissed his way down her body, down to her hip bone. To that glorious tangle of curls between her legs. He loved the taste of her.

He loved the way she cried out when he licked her.

It was carnal, and yet it felt holy in a way that he would never be able to explain. He didn't have to. Because he was Rocco Moretti, above all else. And she might have bewitched him in more ways than one, but it didn't change the foundation.

He could have it all ways.

He could be this with her, and the ruthless businessman he had become.

The one that kept that lonely little boy locked in a bedroom light-years behind him.

And he would think of none of it now, because her sighs filled the room, and her flavor coated his tongue. And that was enough.

More than enough. Any more would simply be hoarding.

One did not need everything. That, he supposed, was the root of that illness. The need to have it all.

He would have bits and pieces. Here and there. It would be enough.

He laid her down on the bed, and thrust inside of her, watched as her expression contorted to one of wonder. Felt it echo inside of him.

With nothing but moonlight pouring down over them, he claimed her. Over and over again. He made a promise. To make her happy.

He kissed her, with everything inside of him, and he thought that maybe it would do something to ease the ache in his chest. It didn't. It only got worse. But she was with him. She was with him still.

He thrust hard, fast, taking them both to the peak. And he swallowed her cry of need, so that it met his growl of completion.

He gathered her against his body, after they had found their release, and held her there. Their hearts beat in tandem, and he closed his eyes.

He was on the edge of something.

Something.

As he drifted off to sleep, the last image that filtered through his mind was of him, locking her in a room with him. So that she could never leave.

So that he would always have her.

Always.

CHAPTER FIFTEEN

NOELLE HAD NEVER been so happy.

Italy was beautiful. They had stayed in his house in Milan for a while after the train trip, and then they had gone on to Lake Como, then to Florence. Then on to Rome. It wasn't anything like the quiet life she had imagined for herself, but it was magical.

It was because of him.

She realized that her concept of home had shifted.

Rocco Moretti now felt like home. More than Wyoming ever had.

Even more than Holiday House. It was terrifying how quickly something like that could shift. Terrifying just how glorious a shift like that could be. If she had been told a few months ago that her whole life would change, she would have been sad about it. But now she realized that change wasn't always bad. Sometimes it was simply the right time.

Sometimes, you were ready for it.

That was astonishing.

After a month overseas, though, she was beginning to feel like she wanted to visit home. It had been three months.

Three months in total since she had seen Melody, since she had been back in her familiar territory.

Just a small visit would be nice.

It was the strangest thing, because she had a deep level of intimacy with him, and yet there were some things she still felt afraid to approach him about at times. The way he handled his issues around his childhood being the biggest, because last time it had been such a disaster. He talked about things, but she always felt reluctant to push when he wasn't the one leading.

It was because there was something under the surface, and she couldn't quite put her finger on it, but it was beginning to fill her with a sense of disquiet that she didn't quite know how to manage.

She could tell him that she loved him, of course. Take the pane of glass she felt like was between them sometimes and shatter it. Test to see if it was her fault. If her not being able to tell him the truth of her feelings was why sometimes she felt distant from him.

It was a beautiful day, and the apartment they occupied in Rome had the most stunning view. In the evenings, they sat out on the balcony, and looked at the city below.

She had a new appreciation for cities. She didn't think they would ever feel like home, but now that she had been to a few, she could appreciate that they were all different. That they had different rhythms, different personalities.

She really did love Rome.

The history, the iconic sites, the food.

She loved listening to Rocco speak Italian. She tried to learn a little bit herself. It had turned into an extremely dirty lesson. He had taught her words that she didn't think she could ever repeat in polite company. But that she used on him with impunity, whispering in his ear when they were at restaurants, or galleries. So why couldn't she say the one thing she probably needed to say most?

Because of the illusion.

That realization stunned her. Astonished her. She stood there, on their balcony, looking out at the city, realizing that she was afraid.

That it was terribly, terribly worrying that someday, she would say the wrong thing to him. That she would uncover the fact that this happiness wasn't real. Just like her childhood. Because you could be blissful, and not realize the people around you weren't.

That filled her with panic. It made her feel like her little boat was adrift, not connected to the shore.

No. She was fine. And Rocco wasn't her only anchor. She had Snowflake Falls. She had Wyoming and Holiday House, and friends. She just had to remember that. She had been lost in a haze, and it had been lovely. But she had perhaps let herself become too comfortable with this part of her life.

Maybe she needed to remember to anchor herself.

So she went and found him, lounging on the couch in the living room, and she decided to crawl on top of him, folding her hands and resting them palms down on his chest as she looked up at him. "Hi," she said.

She could feel his body hardening. And she smiled.

"Hello," he said, wrapping his arm around her waist.

"I wanted to talk to you," she said.

"This does not feel like a prelude to talking," he said.

"How very rude," she said. "As if me pressing my

body against you could only be an invitation for one thing, and not conversation?"

"You know how it is between us," he said. He held her chin, and she looked at him. She wanted to freeze time. She wanted to make it so that this moment was the only moment. Nothing after it, nothing before. Nothing to worry about.

"What?" he asked.

"Nothing I… Except something. I need to go home for a while."

He frowned. "Why?"

"I just… I miss everybody. I miss home. I'd like to actually invite people to the wedding in person. Just maybe spend a little time getting back to myself…"

"You don't need to leave," he said.

"Rocco, I have other parts to my life. I still own a bed-and-breakfast. I need to go and check on things."

And she needed to reclaim old parts of herself, but she wasn't going to say that. Especially not when the expression he was treating her to was so stormy.

"You can come with me," she said.

Though she did think that might be defeating the purpose.

"You don't need to leave," he said. "And in fact, now that we are on the subject, I no longer think it is a feasible idea for you to live away from me for half the year."

She agreed, actually, but she wanted to know why he thought that.

"Why is that?"

She was so close to him, she could feel his heart beating beneath her hands, she could see his chest rise and fall with each breath. And she could see the tangle of emotion in his eyes. The confusion there. He didn't know the answer. And she already knew that when Rocco didn't know, he simply didn't speak.

He didn't share, he shut down. Shut parts of himself away.

"Rocco," she said. "Please... Just tell me. Tell me what the problem is?"

"There is no problem," he said. "It is only that I need you in my bed, so I cannot have you away."

She stepped closer to that glass pane that existed between them, and she pressed against it, taking the chance that it might crack.

"Is that all I am? Am I simply sex to you?"

"Of course not," he said.

"Then what else am I?"

"It isn't that simple. I cannot simply... Name all of these things. But you know that you are an important part of my life."

"You're an important part of mine. I don't want to be away from you half the year either, but we are going to have to work some things out. Because me keeping the bed-and-breakfast was part of our marriage arrangement."

It was the wrong thing to say. He growled, and rolled her off him, safely onto the cushion of the couch, as he stood, pushing his fingers through his hair. "I see. And you remind me of our agreement now, is that it? Because that is why you're here, isn't it? You are here because you want me to let you keep your bed-and-breakfast."

"I'm here because you have to get married to appease the terms of your mother's will. Has that changed?"

He looked at her again, with that same conflicted look.

Why wouldn't he just say it. Why wouldn't he tell her what he was feeling. It didn't make any sense.

"I… I have no words for you, Noelle. You are being impossible."

"I'm not being impossible. And here's an idea, you can say some words, and if they are the wrong ones, you can try to find some right ones. It's all right."

"What's the point?"

"I need to… I need to understand you. Because I can't… I can't live life thinking that everything is okay between us and then randomly finding out that it isn't."

"I see. So when I am not my mother, I am your mother."

"That's not fair," she said.

"I think it is."

Maybe this was what she had sensed, this fight. This unrest between them. Maybe this was the disquiet that she felt.

She hated it. And yet, she didn't quite know what to do about it.

She wondered if it had to happen. If they had to have this discussion.

What about you? Are you ever going to tell him? You're demanding information from him, and yet you're keeping plenty to yourself.

But he was so important. She couldn't mess it up.

He was integral. If she took a risk, then she might lose everything. She had accepted this change, and she couldn't endure another one. She couldn't lose him.

Because she had chosen him. And chosen this life with him.

And what if all it ever is to him is an arrangement.

What if it's only sex? And you fall deeper and deeper into love with him, and you have a child, and then that child leaves, and then he leaves you. What if he has affairs?

She had to know.

She had to know.

Her heart was thundering so hard it made her sick.

"I do not wish for you to be away from me," he said. "I want to keep you." His words were feral and fierce, and they tugged at her soul.

It felt so big. So impossibly big.

And she had just wanted to be a simple girl who lived on top of the mountain. She hadn't asked to fall in love with a man that was bigger than any mountain she had ever seen.

She hadn't asked to live an extraordinary life. She had wanted safe. She had wanted ordinary.

No, you didn't. You never did. Or you would've never left. You would never have touched him. He was an invitation to risk the entire time. Because you're not going to live like your mother.

No. She wasn't. She had been worried that love would be an endless series of compromises, but she had a feeling it was only if you didn't speak the truth to the one that you loved.

That meant she had to.

She had to.

"I love you, Rocco."

He looked at her, something like granite in his dark gaze.

"You…?"

"I love you. I realized it a while ago. But I didn't know

how to tell you. I didn't want to disrupt what we have. But I… I love you."

"I don't know how to give you that," he said.

"I don't think that's true. I think you do. I think you can, I think…"

"You don't know," he said. "You don't know… I don't love you, Noelle. I fantasize about putting you in a room and locking you in there. Keeping you. Because I am like my mother, I suppose. In all the ways that matter.

"I need to control everything and everyone around me. I need… That's why I can't let you out of my sight. I can't bear it. I brought you to Italy to make you happy. Because I want you to stay with me."

"I'm happy with you," she said slowly. "I promise you that I am. I am happy with you, Rocco, but I also need to have other things in my life. You cannot be everything to me. That is far too dangerous of a proposition for me."

"You are the only thing that I have," he said.

"One billion dollars, and you. A thousand properties, and you. And if I had to choose to keep one, it would be you. But that isn't love. It's like a sickness inside of me. And it grows, more and more by the day. I don't want you to leave. I don't want you to have a bed-and-breakfast. I want to keep you so happy that you forget that you ever had a life with anyone else."

"Rocco…"

His eyes were wild, and she knew that what he was saying was true, but there was a fury in it. One that she couldn't even see the bottom of. He was angry. With himself, possibly. With her.

With everything.

"We can talk about this…"

"No. It's unbearable. You… You need to go home." He forked his fingers through his hair. "I need you gone."

"What?"

"I need you to go. Because this growing thing inside of me is… It's the thing that I'm most afraid of. And I will trap you with me. In my room. There will be no boundaries, there will be no escape. I won't do it to you."

"You can't make my choices for me."

"The hell I can't. Because I'm making them for me too. I need things to go back to the way they were. There is… There is something… I can't put my finger on it, I can't name it, but ever since you came into my life something inside of me has shifted, and I can't figure out how to put it back."

"It's the same for me. It's love. It changed me. It made me want different things."

"If you wanted different things you would never have asked to leave."

"No, I would have. Because it is still part of me. But so are you. Love doesn't have to destroy everything that you are. It just makes you more."

"Not me. It is destroying me."

Love. He said it was destroying him. Which meant that he must feel it. But he wouldn't admit it. He was absolutely terrified, and she could see it. This brave, mountain of a man.

Was afraid of her. Afraid of what she made him feel.

"You said you wanted to feel the happiness that I felt. The wonder that I felt, can't you try to feel the love that I feel."

"No," he said. "Please… Do not ask me to."

"Rocco… Don't ask me to go."

"The damage is done," he said. "I have ruined us both. The papers have already run all the stories and…"

"So don't send me away."

"It is one or the other," he said. "Either I want to hoard, or I want nothing. And I need to go back to wanting nothing. I need to go back to when it all felt simple. When I figured out how to need no one."

"This isn't about you wanting to lock me away. This is about you being afraid of needing me. Because your mother left you alone, and you couldn't count on her and…"

"You are not my psychiatrist. Do not seek to tell me what is in my heart or in my mind. Just go."

It was shattered. The glass. The illusions.

But perhaps it was for the best.

Because it would have ended. She had been right. All those years later, it would've ended. There would've been infidelity. There would've been messes and weeping and their children would've gone, and it would've been the two of them, not knowing how to be.

But even as she obeyed him, as she allowed herself to be driven to the private plane with her heart shattered into pieces, and her very breath painful, she foolishly wished that they'd had that life. All those years between now and heartbreak. Because at least they would've had that life.

And now, she had nothing. Nothing at all.

She knew the plane would have to stop for fuel on the East Coast, and she asked that they go through Florida.

When she ended up at her mother's new home, furnished by Rocco, her palms felt slick and sweaty.

"I need to talk to you," she said.

"What about?" her mom asked.

"Everything. I just want to know… Was everything in my childhood a lie? Did you not love dad? Did you not love me? What did you want instead? Were you so unhappy that you were just dying to get out?"

Her mom's face softened. "Come in, Noelle."

Noelle did. The house itself was an explosion of color. Rocco would hate it, and that kind of amused her.

"Do you want a margarita?"

"No," Noelle said, feeling somewhat taken aback by the question.

"Well, I might have one. I'm surprised you're finally asking these questions."

"Well. I don't think I wanted the answers to them before."

"I think that's kind of the moral of the story, honey. It's really easy to not ask questions when you're afraid of what the answers might be."

Noelle frowned. "Do you mean you?"

Her mother got out margarita mix, tequila and ice, and poured it all into the blender. She pushed the button, and it twirled around while Noelle stood there, trying to find her equilibrium.

"That was my whole marriage to your father. Being afraid of asking questions. Afraid of what the answers would be. But no, I wasn't unhappy the whole time. And of course I loved him. I love you."

"Then why did you have an affair?"

"Because things are complicated sometimes. And I'm not perfect. Because instead of talking to your father when I felt like he was distant from me, I thought it was easier to pour my heart out to a man who didn't actually know me. A man who wouldn't bring my own frailties into the conversation. What a neat trick that is. If you bring up the problems that you're having to your husband he might tell you things you don't want to hear. I didn't want that. No, I wanted easy. So I took easy. Except, in the end of course it wasn't. Because I hurt your dad, and I didn't actually want to do that. Whether you believe me or not. But it's easy to get caught in your own made-up stories. Way too easy. Our life wasn't a lie. It wasn't nothing. It was everything to me. And within that there were failures. On both our parts. It was imperfect, and it was hard, but it was good. You were always the best part of it. So sunny and warm and you loved everything about Holiday House. I would never have asked you to leave it."

"But you did. You wanted to sell it."

She sighed and pinched the bridge of her nose. "You were an adult, and I thought maybe it would even do you some good to have some other experiences."

"Well. Now I have had them. And honestly, they just kind of hurt."

"Being an adult hurts sometimes," her mom said. "There was no way to spare you from that forever. I... Maybe it was selfish of me. I wanted to leave some of the harder parts of that life behind. And get something out of it. I've been living a different life, and it makes me feel new. I can finally escape the ways in which I disappointed your dad. The ways I disappointed myself. It isn't that it was all bad. And in the last few years, it was really good. But it's my mistakes that haunt me now that he's gone."

"Oh," Noelle said.

She didn't know what to do with all this information. It didn't solve anything, not really. It didn't magically fix what had happened between her and Rocco. But it definitely showed her childhood through a prism of fractured glass, rather than an illusory windowpane. It wasn't half so simple as perfect or not perfect. A life her mother loved, or a life she hated. It was just human frailty. It was a difficult thing to accept. But her father was gone, and she could never really have that revelation with him. That whole realization that he was just a person like she was. Trying his best, or not on a given day.

She could still have that with her mother.

"I keep wanting things to be simple," Noelle said. "Right or wrong, happy and unhappy. Perfect."

"But it isn't."

"Rocco sent me away. Because I asked him the hard question. I told him the hard thing."

Her mom closed the distance between them and put her hand on Noelle's shoulder. "Noelle, you will always be glad you did that. Because eventually, secrets come to collect. And the unspoken things come out in ways that are far more painful than if you had just talked about them."

"But I don't have him anymore."

"I'm sorry, honey. You're welcome to live a single life with me here."

"I think I'm going to go back home. Try to get back to who I was."

"Don't do that," her mother said. "That's actually what keeps you in regret. When something changes you, you have to follow that change all the way through to the end. There's no point resisting it. That's how I ended up here." She gestured around her pink and aqua kitchen.

And Noelle realized that what her mom said was true. She couldn't go back to how she was. To how things had been.

She was going to have to persist with what was new. Figure out what living with heartbreak looked like.

"I'm still going to go back," she said. "But I'll remember what you said."

"I'm sorry I didn't have some magic words for you."

"I think you gave me better than that. You gave me the truth. And I'm thankful that you're still here to give it to me."

CHAPTER SIXTEEN

EVERYTHING WAS TERRIBLE. The worst that it had ever been. He was alone. Alone, alone, and the space closed in around him like an oppressive fog. It was unbearable. Unmanageable.

He missed her. He needed her. He had failed her.

You have to get back.

No. He didn't want that. He didn't want to go back to that dark place. *But you're already there.*

That was how he found himself going out to the old house. Going through those old gates. The property was overgrown. It was awful. It was untouched, he knew. A monument to his mother's insanity. *Why did you keep it?*

That question echoed inside of him, as he took a key and turned it in the lock, opened the door for the first time in so many years. His palms were sweating, his heart beating far too fast. Why did you keep it?

If you're so ashamed of it, why did you keep this monument to it?

Because he hadn't figured out how to let it go yet. And so it stood. A monument to all they were. To his loneliness. The smell was terrible. It was also home. He hated that truth.

He walked through the dark rooms, filled with piles, filled with shame.

His heart rate quickened, and his own fear started to mount. And suddenly, he saw each and every object in the house for what it was. Fear.

It was her grasping at anything, everything.

Fear that blocked her from giving him the love that he needed. Fear that left him alone, locked in his room.

Because that was what a need for this level of control was. And for her, as chaotic as it looked, it was control.

Just like for him... For him pushing her away had been control.

Fear directly blocked love. And as he stood there, looking at all of it, at his mother's humanity, he felt something shift within him.

He saw his mother differently.

Not her failure, but simply struggles in herself that she could not figure out how to overcome, he wanted to overcome his.

A lump was in his throat, and he walked up the stairs, to his bedroom.

He reached out and turned the doorknob. It was locked.

Locked because he had locked himself in it. Locked because he never left through that door. Because he had been afraid. Afraid, afraid, afraid.

His whole life was marked by fear.

"Enough," he said to the closed door. To the little boy that, in his mind, was still behind it. "Enough." He turned and slammed his shoulder violently against the door.

"Unlock the door," he said. "Open this door right now." He threw his body against it again, and again. And then, with one final, brutal blow, he kicked it open. And inside was nothing.

That boy wasn't there.

He was just inside of him.

It was clean. So much space around that bed.

Empty.

He was just so tired of empty space.

He kept it empty because he was scared.

He didn't want to be afraid anymore.

He wanted Noelle. He wanted the chaotic, intense feelings that she created inside of him. The feelings that he couldn't control.

But he would learn to make them better. He wouldn't lock her away.

Because he didn't want to be ruled by fear anymore. He just wanted her love.

"I love you," he said to the room.

Maybe to Noelle. Maybe to his mother.

Perhaps to the boy that had once sat in here alone. Who had wanted to be cared for more than anything in the world, but hadn't been.

But she does.

He wanted her to. He wanted her to care for him. And he didn't want to be afraid of how much he wanted it. Not anymore. He was ready to let all this go.

So that he could embrace her.

Noelle loved Christmas in Snowflake Falls. It was always hard after Christmas. When the lights were gone, and you were left with nothing but the gray persistence of January, February, March. As winter dragged on in Wyoming, far longer than in many other states.

She felt caught in that gray haze now.

She had been right about this. That home wouldn't

quite feel like home, because part of her heart was somewhere else.

Part of her heart was with him.

So when she looked up, on the much less crowded
streets of Snowflake Falls, and saw him standing there,
in black, severe clothes, she thought she might've hallucinated him.

"Rocco?" She said his name, as if to test her own sanity, as much as anything else.

"Yes," he said.

"What are you doing here?"

"I am here because… Because I've changed. You told
me that people changed when they were in love."

Her throat went tight, tears immediately stinging her
eyes. "I did tell you that."

"Well, I have changed. Because I love you. But I had…
Work to do. Before I could understand it. I do now. I
went back to my home. And I saw it all. All of it for
what it was. My mother seeking to control everything in
the house, me seeking to control everything behind that
door. Both of us held captive by fear. I saw that I am like
her. I am. And… I am sorry. That I'm… Like that. That
I have such a strong need to control everything that… I
created so much space around me I didn't have room for
you. And you were all I wanted. But that space was made
out of fear. I just wanted to not be so afraid. But the fear
was what was holding me back from love, all this time.
And I don't want to be afraid anymore."

"Oh, Rocco." She wrapped her arms around his neck,
not caring who saw them. She kissed him, right there in
the middle of town, and she knew that there would be
talk. But that was fine.

"I wanted easy. I thought my childhood was easy and perfect, and that recreating it would… Give me that same peace that I had. I talked with my mom. She made me realize we do hurt people we love sometimes, and it doesn't mean we don't love them. And… I don't need simple. But I do need you. That is what I need to be happy. It could be here…it could be in New York…"

"It will be in both places. Because this place is you."

"But you hate it," she said.

He laughed, and the sound filled her with glory.

"I do. But I love you. And so it is an easy answer to a very easy question. I don't need control over my surroundings. I need you."

"Let's go up to Holiday House," he said.

"Okay," she said.

"You think we'll get snowed in?"

"I don't think so."

"That is a shame. Because I love being snowed in with you."

EPILOGUE

ROCCO GREW TO love Christmas at Holiday House. It was cluttered and often noisy. Noelle's mother always came to visit. Oftentimes there were guests. The rooms were small, and their children invaded their space frequently. But he had learned to love the chaos of it all. When Noelle had had their first child, he had realized he would never truly be in control of anything ever again.

To say that he had let it go graciously would be an overstatement. But he had love. So what else mattered?

Christmas Eve, ten years after their first Christmas, they walked through the snowy streets of Snowflake Falls, holding hot chocolate, their four children racing about in front of them and causing mayhem.

He stopped, and looked at the Christmas tree, at all the quaint buildings.

"You know what," he said.

"What?"

"I love it here."

Noelle's eyes went wide with shock. "You do?"

"Yes. Because my family is here. And that means it is the most wonderful place on earth."

* * * * *

COMING SOON!

We really hope you enjoyed reading this book.
If you're looking for more romance
be sure to head to the shops when
new books are available on

Thursday 21st November

To see which titles are coming soon, please visit
millsandboon.co.uk/nextmonth

MILLS & BOON

MILLS & BOON®

Coming next month

RESISTING THE BOSSY BILLIONAIRE
Michelle Smart

She stepped through the door. 'I am your employee. I have a contract that affords me rights.'

The door almost closed in his face. Almost as put-out at her failure to hold it open for him as he was by this bolshy attitude which, even by Victoria's standards, went beyond minor insubordination, Marcello decided it was time to remind her who the actual boss was and of her obligations to him.

'You cannot say you were not warned of what the job entailed when you agree to take it,' he said when he caught up with her in the living room. She was already at the door that would take her through to the reception room. 'It is why you are given such a handsome salary and generous perks.'

Instead of going through the door, she came to a stop and turned back round, folding her arms across her breasts. 'Quite honestly, Marcello, the way I'm feeling right now, I'd give the whole lot up for one lie-in. One lousy lie-in. That's all I wanted but you couldn't even afford me that, could you? I tell you what, stuff your handsome salary and generous perks – I quit.'

Continue reading
RESISTING THE BOSSY BILLIONAIRE
Michelle Smart

Available next month
millsandboon.co.uk

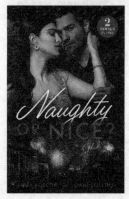

LET'S TALK

Romance

For exclusive extracts, competitions and special offers, find us online:

f MillsandBoon

X @MillsandBoon

◎ @MillsandBoonUK

♪ @MillsandBoonUK

Get in touch on 01413 063 232

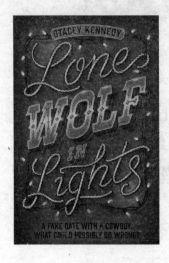